SAINTS

like

HIM

AIMEE NICOLE WALKER

SAINTS
like
HIM

chapter
ONE

CASH PURSED HIS LIPS WHILE STUDYING THE CHIP SELECTION at the grocery store in Last Chance Creek. What snack was most suitable for a forty-nine-year-old man while bingeing the newest season of *Heartstopper*? Cash wasn't one to use his age as a reason to avoid many things, but he wasn't proud of his obsession with the series about queer teenagers and their first loves. Their vitality and innocence sometimes made him feel older than dirt, but mostly it made him grateful that a new generation could see themselves in the characters.

It was unlikely Cash's life would've turned out differently if he'd had positive representation as a teen. He'd lost his mom to poverty and drugs and had gone to live with strangers at a time when he was figuring things out about himself. Cash hadn't felt comfortable coming out, or letting others in, until he was thirty. He'd rebuilt his life from the ashes of his past and had been tired of living a lie. The penniless dirt track racer had to pretend, but the successful technology inventor did not. Cash had thought his newly gained wealth would insulate him from scrutiny and scorn, but it only perpetuated the narrative that he was an outsider who didn't belong. But those closed doors and snubs didn't deter him; they fueled the perpetual fire in his soul and made him richer.

He couldn't think of a single hard knock he'd change because they'd all led him to this point. Well, maybe not to standing in a grocery store staring at the same bag of Fritos for a solid ten minutes. He meant his ranch, his people, and the journey he'd taken to have them in his life. Contentment didn't negate his few regrets or warm his bed, but the one man who could fix both problems was across the country. Who the hell was he kidding? It wouldn't have mattered if Nick was at Quantico, on Mars, or standing beside Cash. He was off-limits. Cash just needed to convince his foolish heart of that fact—a feat he hadn't accomplished in twelve years. But had he really tried that hard?

A warm, masculine chuckle invaded his thoughts, and Cash jerked his head to find Seth Burke approaching him. He bit back a snort. Burke didn't approach; he swaggered with big dick energy. The sheriff was a good five inches taller, a few years younger, and had the persistence of a bloodhound when it came to Cash. Burke's uniform consisted of a pressed khaki shirt, dark denim jeans, boots, and a white Stetson hat. Cash wasn't sure what shone brighter in the store's overhead lights— the shiny sheriff star pinned to Burke's shirt or his white, toothy grin. Damn, but the man was fine as hell with jet-black hair, gray eyes, and sun-kissed skin. No matter the time of day, that superhero square jaw was clean-shaven to show off his magnificent bone structure. Why the hell couldn't Cash return the man's interest? He could trade heartache for the kind of twinges and stings that left a man smiling instead of moping.

"What'd that bag of chips do to you?" Burke asked when he reached Cash. His voice was jovial, pure good ole boy, but the tension around Burke's mouth betrayed him.

Cash snorted and faced his friend. "I was just lost in thought." He glanced down and saw Burke had already placed several items in his basket. "I didn't see your truck in the parking lot."

A dark brow arched. "Or you would've kept driving?"

Cash sighed. "Of course not. I was just making conversation."

"The inane kind you make when you've been avoiding your friend?" Burke pressed.

Were they friends? They met for lunch regularly at the diner and texted often, so definitely more friendly than acquaintances.

It was Burke's turn to sigh but his was deep enough to pull his shirt taut across his chest. "Okay," he said, "maybe our friendship is more of a one-way street, but I thought we were at least *friendly*. You've blown me off for lunch the past few weeks and only text after I initiate the conversation. What's going on?"

"We are friends," Cash said and realized he meant it. He enjoyed having Burke in his life, but that would change if he spoke honestly. Cash wasn't one to back down from a confrontation, but he didn't initiate them either. He chose avoidance until the showdown was inevitable, which he guessed was now. If their friendship was genuine, it would survive the conversation they needed to have. "Look, Burke—"

"Seth," he said. "How many times do I have to tell you to use my first name?"

The sheriff's authoritative tone took Cash by surprise. Burke sounded more like he was interviewing a cagey perp than talking to a friend. And Cash wasn't used to having his decisions questioned, let alone getting grilled by someone else. Still, he was responsible for the frustration rolling off the broad-shouldered sheriff, so he forced back his irritation, cleared his throat, and said, "It's meant as a sign of respect. Besides, lots of friends refer to each other by their last names."

Burke snorted. "It's another way you keep me at arm's length."

He stepped closer until only their red shopping baskets separated their bodies. The proximity was unnerving, but Cash lowered his gaze instead of backing away. Burke's smoky aftershave conjured images of bonfires and shared blankets, but when Cash allowed his mind to go there, it wasn't the sexy sheriff's body pressed to his. A pang of longing swept through him, forcing Cash to close his eyes. He might've even swayed a little closer to the brawny body that promised a physical release from the loneliness that rattled his bones.

"Why won't I stop pursuing you when a smarter man would?" Burke asked, his voice low and husky.

That caught Cash's attention, and he jerked his head up. He almost regretted it when he met Burke's hungry gaze. Cash wouldn't pretend the heat and intensity didn't affect him, but the reaction was purely physical. Seth Burke, as sexy and virile as he was, didn't stir Cash's soul. If Seth was a stranger he'd met far enough away from the ranch to maintain his privacy, Cash would have given in to the physical attraction. But Burke was his friend, and he wanted to keep it that way.

"Have dinner with me at the Feisty Bull." Burke held up his hand to block the decline forming on the back of Cash's tongue. "This isn't a date. I just want to talk and eat a good steak. It's no different from us catching up over lunch at the diner."

Cash studied Burke's mercurial gaze, looking for any hints of insincerity but came up short. The hunger and yearning he'd witnessed earlier was gone. "Name the time."

Burke's full lips curved into a devastating smile that made Cash question his sanity. "Seven."

"I'll meet you there."

Burke leaned into Cash's personal space, so Cash stepped back. The taller man just rolled his eyes and reached for the bag of corn chips Cash had been staring at while lost in thought. Burke dropped the bag into his own cart, winked, and continued down the aisle. "See you tonight."

Cash blew out a breath once his friend turned out of sight. What the hell had he just agreed to and why? He knew why. Nearly everyone on the ranch had found their happily ever after, even if two of them were too dense to realize it yet. While it warmed his heart to see his little family flourish and grow, it fed his loneliness until it had become a ravenous monster. Cash knew he was due for some serious soul searching. He'd allowed his pining over Nick Scott to sabotage any potential relationship before it could flourish. What opportunities had he overlooked while obsessively watching Nick for the tiniest clue he might return Cash's feelings? He wanted better for himself. No, he deserved better. Cash just didn't know how to get over his feelings for Nick. *Because you don't want to get over him.* Hence, the required soul searching.

Cash snagged a bag of Fritos and a can of bean dip off the shelf and placed them in his cart. Now he just needed something sweet for his *Heartstopper* marathon, which he'd postponed until everyone was gone. Ice cream was his real weakness, but Burke had headed in that direction. Wanting to avoid another run-in, Cash headed toward the bakery instead. He perused the cookies, pies, and pastries, but nothing grabbed him. When he was sure enough time had passed, he headed toward the freezers. Cash expected to take twice as long to choose his ice cream, but his gaze immediately landed on a pint of Twix. He pulled two out of the freezer and placed them in the cart. A guy never knew when he'd have an emergency and need a fix. Like maybe ruining a friendship with honesty? For good measure, he grabbed a bottle of wine on his way to the checkout lanes.

Cash patted aftershave on his smooth neck and studied his trimmed beard with a critical eye. He'd cut the salt-and-pepper bristles with great care. Nick once said the sharp symmetrical lines drew the eye to Cash's lips. Had that been a compliment or one of the signs Cash longed for? Just thinking his best friend's name triggered a cocktail of emotions that made Cash want to reach for his phone and cancel his date. *Not a date.* It was just a steak dinner and a conversation with Burke. Guilt tied his gut in knots, though he didn't understand why.

Cash hadn't been exactly celibate during his twelve years of pining for Nick Scott, but the men he'd taken to bed were hookups who didn't have feelings for him. Burke was different and deserved better. The chemistry just wasn't there to build a relationship on, even though Cash found the man attractive.

With a heavy sigh, Cash ended his critical assessment and headed into his walk-in closet to pick something to wear. He didn't want to dress up too much and give the wrong impression, but he wasn't about to insult Burke or himself by showing up in joggers and a hoodie. He settled for a pressed black dress shirt, dark denim jeans, and his black Stetson. Cash carried the outfit into his room and laid it on his bed next to his sleeping border collie. Patsy raised her head and wagged her tail.

"It's not a date," Cash told her. She released a series of sharp barks. "I'll be home long before eleven, girl."

Patsy released a soft growl, laid her head on the bed, and covered her nose with a paw. Even she knew his pining over Nick was pathetic. Cash left her to remove a pair of boxer briefs from his dresser drawer and pull them on. He'd just snapped the waistband into place when his phone pinged with an alert from the security camera at the gate. It had a motion sensor that triggered a notification. People with the gate code would enter on their own, and he would receive a second alert whenever that happened. Visitors would hit the intercom button, and Cash could communicate and open the gates from the app. When he didn't receive an opened-gate notification or intercom call, Cash thought maybe wildlife had triggered the motion sensor. Or perhaps someone turned around in the driveway.

Cash pulled on his jeans but didn't zip or button them since he'd need to tuck in his shirt. His phone alerted him that someone had entered a valid gate code. Everyone had left an hour ago to attend poker night at Harry and Dylan's house since Ivan and Rory were still traveling back from Kansas. The delay between notifications made him curious, so he retrieved his phone from the nightstand and accessed the security camera through the app. He rewound the feed a little, and his heartbeat kicked into a gallop as he watched Nick's sleek, black BMW pull up to the gate. The last he'd heard, Nick was still at Quantico, filling in for an instructor out on paternity leave. They'd only chatted and texted a few times since Nick had dropped Rory off at the end of March. Nick had warned him that communication would be limited while he attended meetings, took specialized training, and assumed instructing. He'd expected Nick to let him know when he returned out West, and maybe that's what he was doing.

Instead of rolling down the window and entering a code, Nick had opened his door and clambered out. That's when Cash noticed Nick's left arm was in a sling. Snatching his shirt from the bed, Cash shoved his arms into the sleeves as he exited his bedroom. Patsy must've sensed his distress because she jumped down off the bed and followed him. Nick showing up unannounced and injured wasn't good. Cash didn't bother buttoning his shirt as he hurried through the house. The driveway to the ranch was long and winding, so Nick's car still hadn't driven into view by the time Cash and Patsy exited the front door and stepped onto the porch. It wasn't long before the sleek sedan eased from the dense trees and made the last turn toward his home, toward him. Patsy released a series of excited barks, but Cash bade her to stay put.

He tried not to read too much into Nick's presence, especially with an injury, but his heart wouldn't listen. The stubborn organ always had a mind of its own whenever Nick was near. From the first moment their eyes had locked at a charity event twelve years prior, Nick had owned a piece of Cash's soul. Their chemistry had been undeniable, but neither man had room for a relationship. Cash had targeted flailing companies that were ripe for raiding. Nick had been about to start his FBI training at Quantico for twenty weeks. Neither of them wanted to ignore the energy crackling between them, so they gave themselves one weekend to fuck it out of their systems. Three days of endless pleasure, passion, and laughter. The experiment had failed miserably because the attraction was even stronger when their paths crossed a year later at the same annual charity event.

They hadn't gone back to Cash's penthouse apartment in Denver that time. Maybe they feared they couldn't replicate the intensity of their first encounter, or perhaps they feared a second round would melt the skin off their bones. If the latter were true, then what? Both of them had been madly in love with their careers, and a repeat of the passionate weekend seemed like an unwise risk. Over time, their run-ins became more frequent and intentional. Quick cups of coffee turned into long lunches, intimate dinners, and platonic weekend getaways. Nick became the most important person in Cash's life. Which was why he tapped out a quick text to let Burke know something had come up and he needed to reschedule their dinner. Nick had sought him out, and that was the only thing that mattered.

THE EXHAUSTION WEIGHING DOWN NICK'S BONES EASED UP when Cash's sprawling home came into view after hours of uncomfortable driving. The mammoth wood, stone, glass, and iron structure was exactly the place he wanted—needed—to be after five months on the East Coast and five hours in the ER almost immediately upon his return. The man leaning against the stone porch pillar was the balm Nick's soul needed—more home to him than any building would ever be. Cash emerged from the shadows on the front porch, leaned against a tall stone pillar, and crossed his arms over his chest. His unfastened dress shirt and jeans gave Nick a peek at toned abs and black underwear beneath the denim.

"Well, hello to you too," Nick said to himself as he pulled up to the house and parked.

A subtle quivering started in places that had gone dormant during his battle with burnout over the past year. He'd hit professional highs that couldn't compensate for the personal lows, and Nick only wanted to feel whole again. Heat spread low in his belly as he imagined nuzzling his face against Cash's happy trail, just as he'd done during their three days of debauchery. Damn, that weekend felt like a million years ago instead of a dozen. And yet, it also seemed like just yesterday. Nick didn't need to close his eyes and strain to recall the way Cash's body had felt against his, the sounds he made when aroused, or Cash's expression when he came apart in Nick's arms. It was all there in the forefront of his mind—the marks he judged all others by and ultimately found them lacking. Even those memories hadn't been enough to stir his libido back to life…until maybe now. There in his car, Nick could almost feel the heat rolling off Cash's skin and smell his desire. For the first time in eight months, he felt the promise of something more than a dark void.

Cash straightened to his full height and trotted down the stone steps in bare feet. His faithful sidekick, Patsy, was quick on his heels. All Nick could do was stare at the gorgeous man smiling at him through the windshield. For far too long, Nick had had a gnawing emptiness riding shotgun in his soul. There was no doubt his best friend was happy to see him, but it suddenly wasn't enough. The five-month stint was the longest they'd been apart since the first time Nick had gone to Quantico, and it brought many things into sharper focus. He didn't just love Cash; he was *in love* with him.

But seeing Cash's partial state of undress made him question his decision. Was he getting ready to go out, or was he preparing to stay in? Was he alone? Cash didn't bring men back to the ranch, but Harry no longer lived in the house with him, and the crew was usually busy with poker or other things on Saturday evenings. Had he fucked up by showing up unannounced? *Am I too late?*

Cash reached the car before Nick thought to shut off the engine. He killed the sleek beast and reached across his body for the handle. Cash opened the door as soon as the locks disengaged. "This is a surprise." The deep, gruff voice sent a shiver of excitement down his spine.

"A pleasant one I hope." Nick plastered a smile on his face, but his voice betrayed his exhaustion. His words sounded thick like the molasses his mother had put in her gingerbread cookies, reminding him of why he'd made the trek. He'd needed the comfort of home to heal and recharge. His professionally decorated but impersonal condo just wouldn't do. There was no warmth or Cash to be found there.

Cash's beautiful smile faltered with concern, and Nick knew he'd heard the weariness too. "Of course I'm pleased to see you." His gaze fell to the sling, and Nick knew Cash was seconds away from pulling him from the car and making a fuss.

Nick hadn't latched his seat belt after opening the gate, so he swung his legs around and placed his feet on the graveled driveway. Bracing the hand of his good arm on the dashboard, Nick levered himself out of the car. Cash hadn't stepped back, so they were nearly touching when Nick stood up. The scent of Cash's aftershave tickled his nose, and his body heat drew Nick even closer as if an invisible rope pulled them together. The urge to hug Cash was too intense to ignore, but he needed closer contact than his sling would permit. Nick slid a hand inside Cash's open shirt and settled his hand on the bare skin above the waistband of his jeans. Intelligent, sky-blue eyes widened, and Cash's mouth parted in surprise. Before Nick's brain could even process his next move, he leaned in and kissed Cash. It was just a mere brush of flesh, but it felt like someone had hooked Nick's heart to a set of jumper cables. His chin tingled from the brief rasp of beard bristles, and the sharp lines drew Nick's gaze to the mouth he longed to kiss again.

"Oh." Cash's eyelashes fluttered before he lowered his eyelids to half-mast, making it impossible to tell if he felt the spark too or if Nick's gesture had just caught him off guard. Cash was a pro at shuttering his thoughts from others. *Except for the weekend when I'd kept him naked and sated.* The pink tip of Cash's tongue appeared and made a quick swipe over his lips. An act of nervousness, or was he seeking Nick's taste? The urge to push his luck and swoop in for another kiss was strong, but he suppressed it.

"Sorry," Nick said. "I wanted to hug you, but my stupid banged-up shoulder is in the way."

He withdrew his hand and practically heard electricity crackling in the air from the rasp of his fingertips against Cash's skin. It reminded him of the cute special effects in the series Cash watched. Nick never let on that he'd seen *Heartstopper* in Cash's Netflix "Watch Again" queue the last time they'd watched a movie at Nick's place. They'd always talked about shows and movies, so Nick had been extremely curious why Cash hadn't mentioned that one. Nick checked it out for himself a week later and was completely charmed by it. Had he ever been that young or innocent? Nick had thought of Cash when he saw a new season was out.

"Don't apologize," Cash said, capturing his hand before he got too far. His brow furrowed as he studied Nick's face. "Unless you've put yourself and others at risk by driving with one arm in a sling or under the influence of medication."

Grateful for the connection, Nick just shook his head. His brain felt as fuzzy as if he'd taken the muscle relaxers the ER doc had prescribed. "I refused pain meds, and I waited to get here before taking the muscle relaxers."

"What happened, Nicky? You look like you're about to collapse."

"Feed me first?" Nick asked. As if on cue, his stomach growled in protest at its abuse. The last thing he'd eaten was a pack of cookies on his first flight of the day. Weather delays on the first leg had jeopardized making his connecting flight. The quick trip to Denver was fraught with turbulence, so the flight crew didn't get out the drink cart, and Nick had passed on the snacks they'd offered. If he'd known an accident involving his Uber would land him in the ER for five hours, he'd have devoured the chips and cookies.

"Of course." Cash took a step back so Nick could clear the car. "Is there anything you want to take inside?"

Nick reached down and pushed the button to pop the trunk before he cleared the door and closed it. Cash walked around to the back of the car, then peered around the corner at him. "Moving in?"

"I came straight from the airport." It was mostly true. Nick had taken his luggage with him on the ambulance. He'd hired a second Uber to take him from the hospital to his condo. The driver had been kind enough to transfer the luggage from his trunk to Nick's. "I can make do with the smaller bag for now."

Cash ducked out of sight long enough to remove the small suitcase before closing the door. When their gazes collided, Cash didn't bother to hide his curiosity or concern. "Did you get injured during drills?" Cash asked when he rejoined Nick. "Did a trainee take you down too hard?"

Nick's stomach howled in protest again.

Cash threw up his free hand and dropped his gaze to Nick's belly. "Okay. Feed you first." He met Nick's gaze. "Your stomach has always had a mind of its own. We have all kinds of leftovers in the refrigerator." He placed his hand on Nick's lower back and led him toward the porch steps. "We can start there just to shut that thing up, and I can make you something else if your beast still needs appeasing."

Nick couldn't help but think of a distinct moment when Cash had exerted all his energy to appease a different monster. They'd had most of their meals delivered that weekend, but Nick's mouth watered at the memory of the breakfast Cash had made for him on their last day together. "I would love one of your omelets."

Cash's fingers flexed against his lower back. Had it been wise to bring up their weekend together? Cash never mentioned it and danced around the subject on the rare occasions Nick brought it up. Why did Cash treat their horny beginning like a taboo subject? They had nothing to be ashamed about, and acknowledging those debauched days wouldn't hurt either of them. Would it? Did the memories bother Cash? Nick turned his head to study Cash's expression and missed the first step. He stumbled forward and reached out his uninjured arm to brace himself, but Cash slid his arm around Nick's waist to steady him. Adrenaline flooded his system, and Nick shook.

"Easy there," Cash whispered. "I'll always have you."

Nick angled his body so he could lean his head on Cash's shoulder. He closed his eyes and breathed in Cash's woodsy scent. Christ. He smelled like a pine forest, a glass of really expensive bourbon, and a bonfire. The urge to nuzzle against the man returned with a vengeance.

Nick's heart rate returned to normal after a few deep breaths, but he didn't budge from the comfort of Cash's embrace. "God, I've missed you, Saint." Nick was one of only a few people who knew Cash's middle name and the only one brave enough to use it. In that moment, Nick truly understood that Cash was his savior. Perhaps he had been all along.

"You look like you've been through it," Cash said tenderly. His lips brushed against Nick's temple—there and gone—and he pressed his fingers into Nick's lower back. "Let's get you inside before you fall down."

Nick wanted to protest that no such thing would happen, but he needed to allocate his energy to putting one foot in front of the other. His nearly feral determination to see Cash had acted like a nerve block, making his shoulder nothing more than a mere discomfort. He'd had toothaches that hurt much worse for crying out loud. But now that he was at the ranch and quasi-cuddling in Cash's arms, the pain reemerged from its nap to make its presence known. The vibration from each step went straight to his aching joint, and Nick bit his bottom lip to keep from crying out. Maybe he'd been foolish to refuse the pain meds, but he hated feeling out of control. He desperately needed to take his mind off his discomfort and think of something more pleasant. And so his brain chose that exact moment to replay the time he'd sunk to his knees behind Cash and rimmed him to orgasm in front of the wall of windows at his penthouse. It wasn't something Nick had planned. He'd woken in the middle of the night to discover Cash looking out over the city he was taking by storm. The bedroom was dark as pitch, and the city lights turned Cash's gorgeous body into a work of art. He'd had one forearm braced against the glass and a pensive expression on his face. Nick had risen silently from the bed and padded naked to where Cash stood. Pressing his chest to Cash's back, Nick noticed how cool Cash's skin was. How long had he stood there? Cash moaned with the contact and leaned his head on Nick's shoulder, exposing his neck to eager lips. The hand he'd braced on the window moved to Nick's hair, holding him in place. Cash gave Nick his full weight, leaning into him—a virtual stranger—without concern Nick would let him fall. They'd stayed that way for several moments, Cash yielding to his touch. It wasn't long before Nick craved more submission from Cash—permission to do whatever he wanted to and with his body. He'd placed Cash's hands against the windows and spoke against his ear, "Brace yourself."

Nick had been a novice at rimming, an act more intimate than he'd been willing to attempt until that moment. He'd used Cash's moans and whispered supplication to guide him. Nick was never sure if it was his skillful tongue or the act of submission that had driven Cash to orgasm, but it was one of his fondest memories…ever. Right below it was seeing Cash's palm prints on the glass and the smeared cum from their failed attempt to clean it. His favorite memory was Cash's pink-cheeked embarrassment as he made Nick an omelet for the first time. He'd chopped, diced, and cooked while Nick debated the methods to get cum off glass. Cash had finally shut him up with a kiss and a down and dirty blow job on the stool. Nick had been half-cocked and ready to fire the entire time, so his omelet was still piping hot after their shared orgasm. Cash wore Nick's spunk on his face and chest while wiping his own off the floor.

"Did you remember to clean your cum off the penthouse glass before your cleaner showed up on Monday morning?" Nick asked.

It was Cash's turn to stumble a little, and he tightened his hold on Nick. "What in the world brought that up?"

"I think it was the omelet," Nick said. "And I was trying to distract myself from thinking about how bad my shoulder aches. My brain latched onto that night and the following morning in your penthouse. So did you get it clean?"

"Of course." Cash's voice sounded tight and pained. Did those memories hurt him? That was the last thing Nick wanted to do. "Here we are."

It took Nick a moment to realize they'd arrived in the kitchen without further incident. Cash had guided him to the massive island and stopped by a stool just like the infamous one in the old kitchen. Nick studied it closer. Nah. Cash still owned the penthouse in Denver and used it whenever he went there on business. Surely he'd purchased a similar design when he built the ranch house.

"Would you prefer a traditional omelet or egg whites?" Cash inquired before Nick worked up the courage to ask if this was the blow-job stool.

"Regular," Nick replied. "You still haven't converted me."

Cash snorted. "It's not a religion. Just a healthier way to eat the things you love."

"And I love egg yolks."

"Traditional omelet it is," Cash said with a nod. The bright kitchen light revealed that Cash's hair was more salt than pepper now, but it only made his eyes look bluer. Silence washed over the open and airy kitchen as Cash pulled ingredients from the refrigerator and set them on the island. The only noise that followed was Cash's knife cutting through peppers, onions, and mushrooms on a cutting board. His movements were quick and precise, unlike the time Nick had spent in the man's bed. Then, Cash had been slow, deliberate, and very thorough.

"Careful, you're listing to the left," Cash said.

Nick looked down at his crotch, where his dick slumbered, before meeting Cash's gaze. "I always have." That earned a snort and a slight blush from Cash before he returned to assembling the omelet on the stove. Nick raked hungry eyes over Cash's untucked shirt, long legs, and bare feet. "I got lost in thought."

Cash glanced at him over his shoulder, and a cute smirk tilted the corner of his mouth. Nick knew how to coax a genuine smile out of him. "Do I even want to know?"

"Where had you planned to go tonight?" Nick asked.

Cash's shoulders stiffened ever so slightly, but Nick caught the subtlest change in body language. "Dinner with a friend."

"A guy friend?"

Cash's posture didn't change, but Nick heard the catch in his breath. "Yes, a man."

"A date, then." *I am too late.* It was the second time since he'd arrived that a variation of the thought had echoed through his mind.

"Not a date," Cash replied too quickly, and Nick narrowed his eyes. Cash's shoulders heaved with an enormous sigh, and he added, "Not to me, anyway. I think Burke has other ideas."

Seth Burke, the county sheriff. Nick had checked him out when Cash had brought up his name in consecutive conversations. Hadn't a part of Nick braced himself for losing his best friend then? How much time could Cash possibly make for Nick while juggling the ranch and a new love interest? Cash had stopped mentioning the guy, so he figured nothing had come of the relationship. Maybe the silence meant they'd grown closer, and their bond was precious and worth protecting.

"Think or know?" Nick pressed, sounding more like an investigator than a friend.

The stiffness returned to Cash's shoulders, making Nick even more suspicious. Why wouldn't Cash look at him? He scooted off the stool to cross the room, but Cash turned from the stove with a skillet in hand. He set it down on a trivet and removed a plate from the cabinet. Nick eased back onto the stool without tipping over.

"Fine," Cash replied stiffly. "I know Burke has other ideas. I was going to use dinner tonight to let him know there could never be more than friendship between us."

"Why?" Nick nearly slipped and mentioned how smoking hot the man was. But then he'd need to explain why he knew what the sheriff looked like.

A pained expression flashed across Cash's face before he could lower the veil on his emotions. "We don't have... There's just no..."

"Spark?" Nick offered.

"Yes. I'm to the point in my life where I want something deeper and more meaningful than I've settled for in the past." Cash sighed. "But that doesn't mean I don't crave crackling chemistry."

"Like we had?" Nick asked before he could stop himself. *Have.* That invisible pull had never gone away, never frayed. If anything, it had grown stronger with time. The timing was never right. The closer they became the more they had to lose if they tried something that didn't work. So they pretended the sizzling chemistry wasn't there.

Cash's nostrils flared, and Nick thought he was going to dance around the question as he'd done in the past. "Yes, Nicky. If I'm going to settle down, I want the kind of chemistry we shared."

"Maybe we imagined the whole thing," Nick said. "I've never…" *Found it with anyone else.* Nick tried to think of a different way to finish the sentence without making things weird between them.

"Me either," Cash said before he could find one. He plated the omelet, retrieved a fork, and set it in front of Nick. "Would you like toast, a bagel, or an English muffin?"

"No, but thank you. This looks perfect."

"How about something to drink?" Cash asked. "I have fresh-squeezed orange juice." He almost sounded desperate to steer the conversation away, but suddenly Nick was just as eager to stay on topic.

"OJ sounds great," Nick replied, letting his friend think he'd won. Once Cash headed to the refrigerator, he struck again. "I think you've ruined me for other men."

chapter THREE

Cash's breath caught in his throat, and the juice carafe nearly slipped through his fingers. Nick had said he'd refused pain meds and hadn't taken his muscle relaxers yet, but had he ingested something else to loosen his lips? First there was the hello kiss, the surrender of…something when Nick rested his head against Cash's shoulder, and then the references to their weekend of sex. Cash's heart leaped to a faster tempo and wild assumptions while his brain applied the brakes. Nick was clearly going through it—whatever *it* may be. His injury was obvious, though he didn't yet know the source, but Cash sensed a stronger disturbance beneath the surface. Nick hadn't looked so good when he'd dropped Rory off at the ranch at the end of March. He'd been thinner than Cash had seen him and tense enough to snap in half if pressed too hard. His color had been off and his hair had looked unkempt. The Nick in his kitchen looked a far cry better, even with an injury. He'd gained most of his weight back, his color was back to normal, and he'd reverted to a typical tidy haircut. The sandy brown strands had picked up some golden highlights over the summer months.

Nick was at least partially on the mend, but his dark-wash-denim eyes still looked haunted. Cash knew from experience that deeper wounds took much longer to heal. His chest swelled with pride that Nick had chosen him to be his safe landing.

"You have nothing to say to that?" Nick asked.

Cash realized he'd been staring mutely into the refrigerator for too long. His discomfort couldn't be more obvious but not for the reasons Nick probably thought. Cash needed the chilled air to cool his blood after the rimming references. And yeah, talking about the weekend probably took on a different meaning for Cash than it did Nick, so he tried to avoid the topic. What good would come from constantly reminding himself of the one time in his life he'd truly let himself belong to another person? And not just any person. His best friend, who'd made it clear he wasn't interested in settling down anytime soon. If ever. But Cash wasn't normally one to back away from a challenge, so he stepped back from the refrigerator with the OJ carafe in hand and turned to face Nick with a smile on his face.

"I'm flattered you could think so," Cash said.

Nick snapped his head up and narrowed his eyes. Cash was surprised to see Nick had devoured three-fourths of the omelet already. Just how long had he hidden in the refrigerator?

Cash poured him a glass of juice. "You said 'you think.'"

Nick set his fork down and reached for his drink. Their fingers brushed during the pass off, and Cash's skin tingled from the brief contact. Nick's nostrils flared, and the hand holding the glass shook as he lifted it to his mouth. So he'd felt it too. Those tiny reactions emboldened Cash even more than the kiss had. He promised he'd act on the tiniest hint that Nick returned his attraction.

"My reaction would've been different if you'd said you *know* I've ruined you for other men." Because Nick had done the same for him.

Nick set his glass on the island, and his gorgeous lips glistened. Cash remembered a time where he'd licked the juice off them. Same stool but different location. Cash would unfortunately not be dropping to his knees to blow Nick's dick and mind. They had a lot to discuss if they—

Cash stopped himself right there. No good would come from getting his hopes up with Nick when his friend was obviously injured and wrestling with something. "Eat," he said, nudging Nick's plate closer. "Do you want something else? Harry made some banana bread. She tucked an extra loaf away for me."

Nick picked up his fork and lifted his gaze. "You'd share your banana bread with me?"

"I'd share everything I have with you, and I think you know it."

Nick arched a brow, and a wry smile tugged at his lips before he said, "I'm flattered you could think so."

Cash covered his heart with both hands. "You mock me after I offer you some of my banana bread?"

"Well," Nick said as he lifted his fork to his mouth, "you only *think* I know of your devotion and generosity. My reaction would've been different if you said I was certain of it."

Cash snorted and shook his head. They were either on the cusp of flirting or up to their ankles in it. It had been so long for Cash that he wasn't quite sure. Needing a moment to gather himself before he made a mistake, Cash headed over to the pantry to retrieve his jar of Nutella and his stashed banana bread. Nick had polished off his omelet and the glass of orange juice by the time he returned. Next to his empty plate sat a bottle of prescription pills. "Need more orange juice for those?"

"Nah. Already took a dose." Spying the bread and Nutella, Nick added. "Maybe a glass of milk with dessert."

"You got it."

Cash sliced two thick slabs of bread from the loaf and popped them in the microwave for thirty seconds to warm up. He poured two glasses of milk and placed them on the counter before spreading a thick layer of Nutella on top of the warm bread.

"That smells almost good enough to make me forget what we were talking about," Nick said. He tilted his head to the side, squinted, and pursed his lips theatrically. "Oh yeah. You dodged my remark about how you single-handedly ruined other men for me."

If Nick didn't let it go, Cash would need to keep the kitchen island between them to hide his erection. "I'll make you a deal."

"You have my full attention." Nick bit into the bread and let out the sluttiest moan Cash had ever heard. *Son of a bitch.* Nick sure had his dick's attention. Maybe Cash's mask slipped a little because Nick grinned wickedly. "Sound familiar?"

Cash would've recognized that moan anywhere. He'd heard it in his dreams and fantasies enough to have it permanently etched into his brain. "Yeah, I heard something similar coming through Ivan's closed office door when I swung by to discuss ranch plans. He wasn't alone." Cash added a wink to emphasize his meaning.

Nick scrunched up his face and looked like he might gag on the bread for a second. He inhaled deeply through his nose, resumed chewing, and swallowed. He chased it with a long drink of milk that left the cutest mustache over his lip. "Dick."

Cash smirked as he handed Nick a paper towel. "About that deal…" he said. "I'll give you a proper response to your accusation that I spoiled you for other men, though single-handedly is a stretch since both my hands got in on that action." Nick's eyes glistened with mirth, making it nearly impossible to resist teasing him more. But Cash wasn't the only one with some explaining to do. "You need to tell me about your injury first. You said you'd tell me what happened once I fed you. I made good on my end of the bargain."

Nick's shoulders rose and fell on a deep sigh, then he grimaced. "Let's eat the bread, then move someplace more comfortable for the rest of this discussion."

Cash recognized a delay tactic when confronted with one, but what could he do? Besides, he really wanted to eat the banana bread when it was still warm with the chocolate-hazelnut spread melting into the top, so he lifted his slice and took a bite. His moans were every bit as slutty as Nick's. Cash was grateful there was no one there to witness their shame except Patsy, and she wouldn't tell. The black-and-white dog lay down on the floor and covered her eyes dramatically with her paws. Though it seemed she would judge them harshly.

It didn't take them long to devour the bread and down the milk. Cash offered to share another piece, but Nick refused. He'd looked a little livelier once he ate, but that initial exhaustion was returning. Cash was sure the muscle relaxers would only exacerbate the fatigue. He decided to get Nick settled before his legs turned into limp noodles. Cleanup could wait until Nick was asleep.

Cash rounded the island and looped an arm around Nick's waist to assist him off the stool. *See? Not dropping to my knees and blowing him. Not even letting my mind go—*

Nick nuzzled his nose into Cash's neck and inhaled deeply. "Fuck, you smell good, Saint. Like wood, smoke, booze, and sex. Campfire sex. You ever had that?"

"Is that muscle relaxer kicking in already?" Cash asked instead of answering. No, he'd never had campfire sex. But holy hell, he was thinking about how much he'd love to see Nick stretched out naked with the great outdoors as a backdrop. Cash could kiss wherever the flickering firelight cast dancing shadows on Nick's tan skin. There probably wouldn't be much sleeping under the stars, but it would be a night they'd never forget.

Nick let out a laugh that sounded suspiciously like a giggle. "Maybe they are. Doesn't mean I missed what you did there."

"I don't know what you're talking about," Cash tried.

"Bet you're thinking about campfire sex. You just don't want me to know. Who was he?"

"I've never had campfire sex. Are you happy now?"

"Not really," Nick said heavily. "I'm sad that you haven't experienced it."

Cash nearly pulled up short, but sudden moves probably weren't the best thing for Nick just then. "Have you?"

"No." He sounded so forlorn that Cash couldn't help but smile.

When they reached the great room at the back of the house, Cash turned right toward the expansive suite Harry used to occupy. It would be the perfect space for visiting family members. They'd have their own little area on the opposite side of the home from Cash, giving everyone a private space.

"Don't want to go right," Nick said. He stopped without warning and hissed at the discomfort, proving Cash's earlier assessment had been right. No sudden movements. "I don't want to go right. I want—I *need*—to be near you."

As in Cash's room? There were no guest rooms on his side of the house, which had been a deliberate move on his part. Sleeping near Cash meant in his bed. "Nicky…"

"Please." Nick nuzzled against his neck. "I took a redeye flight, hoping to get back to Denver this morning. I wanted to nap, swap out G-Man clothes for free man clothes, and drive to see you."

"Things didn't go according to plan?"

"Nope. Weather delays, a car accident, and a ridiculously long time at the ER made me more desperate to see you," Nick said. Cash's heart froze at hearing about the accident but melted when Nick said he needed him. "Please don't push me away or put up a wall between us like you sometimes do."

God, had he been so obvious? The pushing and wall building stemmed from the moments when wanting Nick was too much for Cash to bear. His wants and needs didn't matter just then, only Nick's. So they turned left. The only noises came from the suitcase's rolling wheels and Patsy's clicking toenails on the hardwood floor.

Cash knew his house was large, but the hallway leading to his quarters seemed to stretch on forever. He felt like they were in the home stretch once they reached his office, but Nick let out a weary sigh in front of the library next to it that made Cash pull up short. "Need to rest?"

Nick turned his head and looked into the library. "I want to lie on that velvety-looking sofa. Is that the same one you had in your penthouse in Denver? Lost track of how many times one of us got bent over that thing."

"Same sofa," Cash admitted. Only a fool or a glutton for punishment would keep those kinds of reminders around to torture himself. Maybe he was both. "Don't worry. I've had it professionally cleaned since then."

Nick's snort turned into a belch. Cash had to bite the inside of his cheek to keep from laughing. God, he would be so embarrassed if he recalled parts of their conversation.

Cash steered Nick toward the sofa, intending to settle him there before taking a nearby club chair. He'd be down for the count soon, and Cash could retreat to his room for a bit to process everything that had happened and plan for things yet to transpire. Yeah, he had every intention of having a wall in place by the time Nick crawled into his bed. Cash eased him onto the middle sofa cushion, but Nick snagged his wrist before he could step back.

"Don't leave me," Nick said. He possessed an eerie ability to read Cash's mind.

"I was just going to sit over there," Cash replied, pointing to a chair.

"Too far," Nick told him. "I hurt, and you can fix me."

Cash's heart squeezed at the naked vulnerability in Nick's voice. "I'm not a doctor or healer."

Nick patted the cushion next to him. His eyelids were at half-mast, and his face looked more relaxed than Cash had ever seen it. "Please. I want to lay my head in your lap."

Lust struck like a lightning bolt, but Cash tamped it down. Nick was in no condition to consent to anything. Cash questioned if they should even have a conversation since Nick was obviously under the influence of his medication. "I'm not sure that's a good idea."

A wicked smile stretched across Nick's face. "I'll behave. Please, Saint."

Cash was powerless to resist. He sat down on the sofa and stayed still so Nick could position himself on his back. "Do you need to prop something under your shoulder?"

"Nah," Nick said. "I didn't break anything. Some teenager with a newly minted driver's license ran a red light and plowed into the Uber I was riding in. My driver wasn't injured, but his car was mangled to hell. The force of the collision drove my shoulder into the door and dislocated it. The doc reset it for me at the ER. They took an X-ray and performed an MRI. Nothing is broken or torn, just inflamed and sore. I gotta see a physical therapist."

Cash carded his fingers through Nick's hair without thinking about anything other than making him feel good. "Sounds painful."

"I've had better times," Nick said. "But it's given me the excuse I needed to take some time off to heal other damaged things."

Cash's fingers stilled as he considered how to proceed. He was dying to know what Nick meant, but it didn't feel right. He'd hold his question until the morning, but Nick seemed to be on a roll and didn't want to stop.

"My head is fucked up."

"Doubt it," Cash said.

"No, seriously." Nick rolled his head from side to side, shifting Cash's fingers in his hair. "Keep petting." That verb had a totally different connotation, but Cash gave in to Nick's demands instead of arguing with him. "Damn, you're pure magic. You did more for me in five seconds than my doctor or therapist have done in the past eight months."

"What's going on, Nicky?" Cash asked. Fuck propriety. He needed to know the truth.

"My cock is broken. Dead as a dinosaur." Nick opened his eyes and stared at Cash. "But seeing you partially dressed and smiling gave me a little spark. First I've felt in eight months." He sighed and closed his eyes. "My doctor did a complete workup from a physical exam to blood and hormone tests. Nothing wrong with my prostate or testosterone levels. Doc determined the problem was psychological. Apparently, depression or stress can cause these types of issues. He referred me to a therapist to sort out the lifestyle changes I needed to make." Nick's long eyelashes fluttered and their gazes locked again. "Keep those fingers moving."

Cash hadn't been aware he'd stopped. "Sorry."

"I've been seeing a great therapist, and she helped me determine my problems stem from burnout instead of depression. Apparently, the symptoms are very similar, but antidepressants won't help me. I have to figure out what changes I want to make to get my sex life back." Nick sighed. "You know how much I love to fuck, Saint. The desire and drive are there, but I can't reach it. Feels like this vital part of me is locked in a castle protected by dragons. I've never been so miserable in my life."

"I'm so sorry, Nicky. What can I do to help?"

A mischievous smile briefly drove the drowsiness from his gaze. "Slay the dragon. Scale the walls." A big yawn split his face, and he closed his eyes once more. "Maybe just keep touching me like this."

And so Cash did long after Nick fell asleep. He couldn't tear his gaze off the face he loved so much or stop caressing the silky strands of sandy brown hair. Nicky needed him, and Cash wouldn't let him down.

Nick finally stirred sometime around midnight, and Cash guided him to the bedroom and helped him prepare for bed. He carefully eased Nick's arm from the sling long enough to remove his shirt. Cash hesitated before reaching for Nick's jeans once his arm was back in the sling.

"I got it," Nick said. "The next time you strip off my pants, it will be for entirely different reasons."

Cash held Nick's denim-blue gaze and tried not to show how the words affected him. Once Nick stripped down to his underwear, Cash turned down the bedding so he could climb in.

"Christ," Nick said. "These sheets are even softer than the ones at the penthouse. What's the thread count?"

"Twelve hundred."

Nick gave Cash a crooked smile. "Fucking diva."

"And don't you forget it." Cash reached out and carded his fingers through Nick's hair once more. The man practically purred like one of the ranch cats. "Need anything else before you go to sleep. A glass of water?"

"Maybe leave one on the bedside table in case I wake up in the middle of the night. I probably don't need to go stumbling around in the dark until I learn the lay of the land." Just how long had he planned to stay? But that was a question for the morning.

"I'll get you a glass of water. Rest well, Nicky."

He snagged Cash's wrist before he could pull back. Nick brought Cash's hand to his mouth and kissed his palm. "Thank you, Saint."

Nick's eyelids closed, and he was out like a light. Cash brushed the back of his fingers over Nick's jawline. "Yes, Nicky. You've ruined me for other men too."

chapter FOUR

NICK CLAWED HIS WAY OUT OF A WEIRD DREAM AND jackknifed into a sitting position. Unfortunately, his subconscious had been too concerned with survival and forgot about his injured shoulder. The jarring motion sent pain shooting from his shoulder down to his elbow like lightning bolts of misery. Nick's fingers twitched as if he were a puppet and his master pulled on invisible strings. He clenched his teeth and breathed deeply through his nose until the discomfort subsided. Nick turned his fuzzy brain to figuring out where the hell he was. His surroundings were pitch black, and nothing felt familiar until a particular scent combination tickled his nose. Pine, bourbon, and wood smoke. *Cash.*

His memory returned in fractured bits that made zero sense. Nick closed his eyes again and breathed in Cash's scent to stave off the rising panic so he could remember exactly what had happened. *Campfire sex.* The words came out of nowhere and reverberated around his head. The fog eased until he recalled a snippet of conversation. Nick knew damn well that he'd never had sex with Cash near a campfire. *But you sure as hell brought it up to him.* Nick blinked a few more times and his vision adjusted a little better in the dark. Or maybe the cloud cover shifted to let moonlight shine through the wall of windows across from the bed.

He was in Cash's room…alone. If it were daylight, Nick would have a glorious view of the Rocky Mountains. He hadn't immediately recognized the space. Nick had never spent the night there and had only briefly seen Cash's inner sanctum when his best friend had moved into his gorgeous home. Nick lay back down and fisted the soft sheets under his body. His next breath came easier and the one after was almost normal. He scrubbed a hand over his face and tried his best to clear the cobwebs. He reviewed the fragmented memories and shuffled them around until they formed a clearer picture of what happened after he'd arrived at Cash's. The kiss, the rimming reference, and the omelet in the kitchen. Nick trying his best to get Cash to talk about their weekend tryst all those years ago but still coming up short. He'd admitted that Cash had ruined him for other men. Well, he'd said he thought so, which Cash had pounced on. Nick turned the tables on him soon after, and he was almost sure Cash had flirted with him.

Nick growled when he remembered telling Cash about his broken cock, the trips to his doctor and therapist, and his belief that Cash could fix him. "Fuck me." Nick remembered that glorious tingling below that signaled all wasn't lost for him. But Cash had undressed him with impassive hands and tucked him into bed like he would a child. Nick groaned and pulled his pillow over his head. Had he destroyed twelve glorious years of friendship in one night by running his mouth? Maybe he could blame it on the muscle relaxers.

"*Yes, Nicky. You've ruined me for other men too.*"

Nick's breath caught in his throat, and the backs of his eyes stung with impending tears. He hadn't imagined Cash saying that after tucking him in. Life couldn't be that cruel. Fear paralyzed Nick for a moment before he calmed down and willed his limbs to move. He gingerly threw back the covers and sought Cash's hiding spot. Nick didn't think he would sleep in a different room after Nick practically begged Cash to sleep with him. Had his insomnia returned?

Once on his feet, Nick noticed a need more pressing than finding Cash. A soft night-light plugged into the opposite wall helped him find the double doors that opened to the massive closet. Nick pulled them open and soft interior lights came on. Cash had called it smart lighting. He had the brightness programmed to match the time of day. The hardwood floors continued into the walk-in closet, and Nick couldn't help but stop and look around the space. Double rows of clothes racks lined one side, and shoe racks and dressers were on the other. Built-in shelves held folded sweaters and hats in a variety of colors. Cash had placed a tufted ottoman near the shoes and boots. Nick figured it was to sit on while slipping on footwear, but it would make an excellent place to get bent over and fucked. Nick's cock might be hibernating like a bear, but there was nothing wrong with his imagination. If only he could sync the two.

The bathroom was on the other side of the closet, and the lights there also came on when Nick stepped onto the ceramic tile. He noticed the door leading out to Cash's patio sanctuary was slightly ajar. Was he soaking in the hot tub? Nick took care of business and headed out the heavily tinted door. Nick had thought it was odd to have an entrance in the bathroom, but it made sense to Cash's fastidious mind. Chlorine would damage the hardwood in his bedroom, and Cash would want to shower before getting into bed anyway. He'd added a privacy screen outside the door and chosen black glass as an additional safeguard. His crew wouldn't wander back to his private quarters anyway, and the wildlife wouldn't gossip about any naked asses they might witness.

The patio was L-shaped with a small outdoor dining area to the left and a grill and a bar to the right. The sound of bubbling water reached Nick's ears, and he was certain his instincts hadn't let him down. He snagged a bottle of water out of the mini fridge in the bar and rounded the corner. Cash reclined in the hot tub with his head tilted back on the rest and eyes closed. A bottle of red wine and an empty glass sat on the edge of the tub. Cash had chosen subdued lighting for relaxation, and the blissful expression on Cash's face showed it was working. The frothing water called to Nick, but he'd imposed enough already. He was just about to retreat when Cash's gruff voice stopped him in his tracks.

"You just going to ogle me all night, or are you getting in?"

The ER doc had suggested he ice his shoulder several times a day, but the hot tub sounded better. He'd worry about swelling and inflammation later. After setting the water bottle next to Cash's wine, he eased his sling off and set it on the chaise. Nick hooked his thumb in the waistband of his underwear and debated whether he should strip those off too. Cash lifted his head, and his heavy-lidded gaze seemed like a dare. Nick wasn't one to back away from a challenge—real or imagined—and pushed his briefs down his legs and kicked them aside. He didn't strike a power pose or puff out his chest, but he submitted himself for perusal. Cash's fiery gaze blazed a trail down his body, and Nick felt it as strongly as any caress. When their eyes met again, Cash didn't bother to mask his desire. Nick felt wanted and closer to whole for the first time in too long. That warmth stirred low in his belly again, and he vowed to be patient like his therapist had said.

Nick put one foot in front of the other, because sometimes that was all a person could do, until he reached the steps to the hot tub. There was no rail to hold on to, but Nick wasn't concerned about navigating three steps with one arm cradled against his chest. Cash apparently wasn't as confident because he stood up with all the power and grace of Poseidon. Water sluiced down his gorgeous, fit body, putting everything from his lower thighs and up on display. That was when Nick nearly lost his balance on the top step and pitched headfirst into the hot tub. Cash was there before catastrophe could strike. He steadied Nick with two firm hands on his hips, putting Cash's eyes at cock level.

Cash let go of his hips and reached for his free hand to assist him down the steps into the water. Nick tightened his grip on Cash's hand when his feet landed safely on the bottom of the hot tub and followed Cash back to the corner he'd occupied. The seat was large enough for two people, but Nick squeezed in beside him like it was a tighter fit. He loved the friction of Cash's hairy legs against his and bit back a sigh when his little toe brushed against Cash's foot.

Nick didn't know what time it was, and he didn't really care unless Cash was out here hiding from him. "Did I run you out of your bed?"

"No. I fell asleep a little while after you but didn't stay that way for long."

"Insomnia?"

"Too soon to tell." His deep sigh expressed his frustration more than words could. "It's more sporadic than what I've experienced in the past, so I hope it's temporary."

Nick rested his hand on Cash's leg, and his thigh muscles tensed beneath his fingertips. Maybe Nick had surprised him with the brazenly intimate touch after twelve years of platonic interactions. He debated whether to remove his hand for a few seconds, but then he felt Cash relax. It took every ounce of willpower he had to keep still and not reacquaint himself with Cash's body. Nick's fingers spasmed a few times as if in protest, but he behaved himself. "I remember everything I told you, and I don't regret it." He didn't tell Cash that he'd also heard his whispered declaration.

"I'm glad you told me, but I wish you'd done so earlier," Cash replied. "There was no need for you to struggle through this alone."

Nick attempted to lean his head against Cash's shoulder, but their differences in height made the angle awkward. Undeterred, Nick slid a little lower in the tub so he could find the perfect alignment. His hand also shifted on Cash's leg, but at least it was lower and not brushing against his cock.

"I could say the same for you," Nick told him. "You can tell me what's keeping you up at night. Are you having trouble with Salvation Anew again?"

Cash drew in a long shaky breath, but Nick wasn't sure if it was due to his nearness or the mention of the cult. "Nah. They've retreated to their compound and stayed pretty quiet since your brother implemented his genius PR plan."

Nick smiled at the respect Cash's voice held for Rory and the slick way he'd diverted the conversation away from himself. Nick wasn't really in the mood to talk about his boner-killing burnout either. Since Rory was a favorite subject, Nick would table their truth spilling. *For now.* "So many people underestimate my brother, myself included occasionally, which is a big mistake." The guy could move mountains when he was in full-throttle mode, and it was obvious how much the ranch and crew motivated Rory. "I've never heard Rory sound so happy, Cash. I can't thank you enough for that."

Cash covered Nick's hand on his thigh, sliding his fingers between Nick's. That simple touch ignited a spark in Nick's body. Could he stoke it and start a fire? His eyes drifted shut, and he imagined himself sitting between Cash's parted thighs—his back to Cash's front and a hard dick nestled against his ass. The water would bubble all around them as Cash explored every inch of skin he could reach, paying special attention to the inches that had gone dormant. Nick would lean his head back against Cash's shoulder and nuzzle his nose against his neck to breathe his scent in deeper. Cash's caress would be thorough and all-consuming until Nick felt his touch everywhere—even the parts Cash couldn't reach. Wasn't that the mark of a truly skilled lover? You could still feel them inside you even when you were apart like they'd branded you during lovemaking.

"I can't take any responsibility for Rory's happiness here," Cash said, killing Nick's diabolical plan by invoking his brother's name. "Ivan gets a lot of the credit, but Rory is the one who put in the effort. I think he just needed a safe place to work through some things."

"Like me." Nick gave in to his urge to nuzzle his nose into Cash's neck. "God, you smell so good."

"Same stuff I've been using for going on two decades."

Nick had adored his scent then too. "One shouldn't mess with a good thing." He wanted to take the words back before Cash realized cuddling with him would blur the lines they'd drawn. Come to think of it, neither of them had verbally drawn lines. They'd both assumed things by not engaging in sex and had relegated one another to the friend zone.

"Life is interesting," Cash said thoughtfully.

"How so?"

"A near accident brought Rory to the ranch, and coincidentally, an actual accident brought you here."

"There are no such things as coincidences, and I was already coming here. I told you that."

"You were also under the influence of muscle relaxers when you said it."

Nick snorted. "Okay, so they loosened my lips a little, but only the truth tumbled out, even if it was a little embarrassing. *You're* my home, and I've been gone too long."

Cash moved his arm off the back of the hot tub to tug Nick closer, settling his hand on Nick's hip. "Still the pills talking?"

"Nope," Nick said. "Those things wore off. That might be what woke me up, or maybe I knew you were gone." *Great.* He sounded like a needy punk.

Cash stiffened and made to move until Nick pinned him to the seat with his weight. "Let's get you another round."

"No thanks. I'll stick to OTC meds. Aleve will help with inflammation, and it will last twelve hours without making me drowsy."

"I have some of that in my medicine cabinet. I'll—"

"Nope. I want you right here." Nick angled his body and laid his legs on top of Cash's thighs and rested his cheek against Cash's chest. The position put Nick's mouth close to Cash's nipple and his leg brushed up against Cash's erection bobbing in the water. Fuck, Nick wanted the right to wrap his fist around Cash and stroke him until he cried out Nick's name. The same tingling from earlier returned below, and Nick embraced it. *Atta boy. You can do it.* Nick experienced a full body tremble, which created more thigh-to-dick friction.

Cash sucked in a sharp breath and exhaled a needy moan. Nick would swear to every deity there had to be an invisible puppet master pulling the string that made Nick's leg rub against the length of Cash's erection three more times.

"Braggart," Nick whispered in his ear before levering up to study Cash's expression. "You're so damn hard."

Cash turned sky-blue eyes Nick's way, and he saw a myriad of emotions warring in his gaze. He wanted Nick so badly in that moment but was terrified of what would happen if they crossed the line again. "I didn't mean for this to happen." Cash's voice sounded gruffer than usual and tinged with desperation. Was he hoping Nick would finish him off or terrified he would?

"Some of the best things come out of nowhere," Nick said, leaning his forehead against Cash's. Their mouths were scant inches apart. All Nick had to do was lean slightly forward and claim his mouth, but kissing was far more intimate than a hand job. Anyone who said differently was a liar or hadn't been kissed properly in their lives. "Cash." *Baby.* Nick swallowed down the endearment before it caught air. "I could…I *would* really love to make you feel better. I would love to live vicariously through your orgasm."

His Saint trembled all over, and Nick held his breath, waiting for a response. Cash closed his eyes for what felt like an eternity, and when he reopened them, Nick had his answer. *I'm too late.*

Cash tilted his head and studied him, and Nick realized he'd spoken his thought out loud. He searched for a way to minimize the phrase that had echoed in his brain since arriving at the ranch, then realized he didn't want to take it back.

"I'm right, aren't I?" Nick asked. "I'm figuring things out too late."

Something akin to joy flashed in Cash's eyes, but it was gone after the next blink. He shook his head and said, "You're not too late, and that's why I can't take things further with you right now."

Nick cocked his head, and confusion must've been written on his face. Before he could press for more information, Cash made his stance crystal clear.

"I can't do casual with you. Not now, not ever." The sigh that followed was heavy enough to carry the weight of the world. "I won't be able to separate emotional from physical. I'd be all in, and I wouldn't survive the heartbreak when you decided I'm not what you want."

Hope leaped in Nick's heart, and heat pooled low in his belly. Was he hearing Cash correctly? "What if I don't want casual either? Maybe I'm all in too."

Cash leaned forward and kissed him, lingering for several seconds before pulling away. "What-ifs and maybes are risks I'm not willing to take. They're fine for business ventures when it's just money on the line." Cash placed a hand over his heart and removed the veil he kept over his expressions. Every naked, vulnerable thing Cashius Saint Sweeney felt was in his gaze. "You're my heart, Nicky. I can't lose you."

A tidal wave of love and longing washed over Nick, threatening to pull him under. "Would it be better for you if I left?"

"Hell no," Cash snarled. "I want you here. I'm your home, remember? We'll figure this out together."

Nick breathed a sigh of relief. "Fine. But you'll tell the sexy sheriff you're not available."

A wry smile stretched over Cash's mouth just as Nick realized his mistake. "And how would you know Burke is a sheriff?"

"You mentioned it in passing." Nick was pleased with his quick thinking, though Cash's chuckle clearly called his bullshit.

"The sexy sheriff is no threat to you," Cash said, not bothering to keep the humor from his voice. The jets turned off, and Cash sighed. "Time for bed, Nicky. Neither of us will be worth a damn if we don't get some shut-eye."

"My only job is to recover from my banged-up shoulder." *And to sort my shit out.* His feelings for Cash weren't the only revelations. Nick had realized he no longer had a future with the FBI, something that had been his identity since he was twenty-five years old.

"Now who's the braggart?" Cash teased. He gently shifted Nick back onto the seat so he could stand up. They both pretended to ignore the gorgeous erection jutting from his pelvis. "We have a problem."

"Some of us do, Houston, but you certainly don't."

Cash snorted and climbed the stairs, giving Nick carte blanche to ogle his ass and toned legs. Cash had gained a lot of muscle over the years, and Nick loved the way it looked on him. "I only brought one towel."

Nick sighed when Cash descended the external stairs to the patio and his pert ass was no longer visible. "No problem. You dry off first, and then I'll use your towel." He stood up from the water, pulling Cash's attention to him. "Or I'll just walk like this straight to the shower."

They both walked naked as jaybirds and soaking wet to the bathroom. The water heated quickly, and Cash steered Nick inside before following him. The shower was big enough for the Denver Nuggets starting lineup, so Cash had one side of the shower, and Nick took the other. The space between them was too far and not enough at the same time. Nick longed to reach for Cash but took his words to heart. They quickly showered and toweled off before returning to bed. This time, Nick was awake to feel the bed dip from Cash's weight. He expected Cash to remain on his side of the bed, but he spooned in behind Nick instead. Neither of them had bothered with underwear, so they were flesh to flesh. Cash's heart pounded against Nick's back, and Cash's dick throbbed against his ass. It was perfection.

"I'm so glad you're here." Cash pressed a kiss to the back of his neck. "Now stop thinking and go to sleep, Nicky."

"You first, Saint."

Cash's warm chuckle in the dark was the last thing Nick remembered.

chapter

FIVE

CASH SECURED THE LAST BUTTON ON HIS CHAMBRAY SHIRT and dropped his hands to his sides. Nick hadn't so much as moved an inch since he'd left him in bed to shower and get dressed. Cash had woken up wrapped around Nick like a vine and would've rather lost a limb than untangle it from Nick's body. A cooler head prevailed—and not the one that had kept Cash awake long after Nick fell asleep. That particular head was primed and ready to go, damn the cost. Cash recalled laying out his feelings to Nick in the hot tub and knew he'd been right. Decisions made under mental or physical duress could rarely be trusted. Cash would do everything in his power to help Nick but not at the cost of losing him. He'd guard his heart and do his best to keep things platonic while Nick rested and recovered.

Cash nearly broke his own rule moments later when he refilled Nick's glass of water and left a bottle of Aleve on the nightstand. Leaning forward to kiss Nick on the cheek had felt as natural as breathing, but Cash stopped himself in the nick of time. *Talk about sending mixed signals.* He pulled the blankets up over Nick's shoulders to guard against the morning chill. Cash straightened, resisted the urge to brush the wayward strands of hair off Nick's forehead, and headed out of the bedroom.

His dog wasn't anywhere to greet him when he stepped into the hallway, but the smell of baking sweet dough did. Cash smiled as he registered the aroma. The moment the calendar flipped from August to September, Harry broke out the autumnal flavors. She had a particular fondness for pumpkin anything. She'd shown real restraint the prior day by baking banana bread on September first, but Cash figured she wanted to use the overripe bananas. He didn't think Harry would swap the summer decor for fall on a Sunday, but he'd bet money on a complete transformation by midweek.

The sound of Harry's joyful humming reached his ears long before he arrived in the kitchen. She'd always been an upbeat little sprite, but embracing her love for Dylan had amplified her natural happiness to nearly inhuman levels. Cash's smiles turned into laughter as he imagined her levitating off the ground when her body ran out of room to contain the joy. She wasn't the only one who'd caught the love bug on the ranch. If Cash's calculations were correct, Tyler and Owen would be the next people to give in and scratch the itch. Christ, he made it sound like the ranch warranted a quarantine by the CDC. He also sounded like a bitter old man whose squandered opportunities were keeping him up at night. Was that the reason for his recent insomnia?

Cash dismissed that outright. First off, it overjoyed him that the people he held dear were falling in love and building meaningful relationships. And second, he wasn't an old man. Not by a long shot. Pining for Nick wasn't anything new, though it seemed to have reached fever pitch lately. He'd chalked that up to not seeing his best friend for five months. Text messages and phone calls couldn't hold a candle to being in the same room and breathing the same air. Cash just needed to give it a few days, and their relationship would be back to normal. *But what if—*

Cash slammed the door on that thought as he rounded the corner and entered the kitchen. Harry danced in place behind the island while drizzling glaze over dozens of muffins with coffee-cake crumble on top.

Cash was glad he'd cleaned his kitchen mess at two in the morning, not that Nick's car parked outside didn't indicate an overnight guest. The last few times Nick had stopped by, he'd been driving his FBI-issued vehicle. They typically met in Denver when they got together, so only Rory would know the sleek import belonged to Nick. Harry looked up from her task with a smile, and he saw the curiosity in her green eyes.

"Good morning," Cash said casually.

Harry tilted her head to the side and studied him closely. "Are you feeling okay?"

The question caught him off guard, and he fought the urge to look for a reflective surface. Had he forgotten to comb his hair after the shower in his haste to check on Nick? Was the lack of sleep etched on his face? He'd slept great once they'd returned from the hot tub but not for long enough. Broken sleep had always fucked him up.

"Whoa," Harry said, holding up her hand. "You're thinking way too hard over there. I only asked because you haven't harassed me about bringing out the pumpkin spice already."

Cash repressed a relieved sigh and laughed instead. "You didn't give me a chance. I only wished you a good morning."

"That's my point," Harry said. "You usually start off with 'pumpkin already?' Then we debate the appropriate flavors for the 'ber months before you concede and wish me a good morning. It's an entire thing for us. Forgive a girl for worrying."

"There are other fall flavors besides pumpkin," Cash said, taking up his usual stance. "You know I love pumpkin." He snatched a muffin off the cooling rack to prove his point. "If it were up to me, apple cider would be the prevailing flavor for September. I'd settle for pumpkin for October and November, but peppermint mocha takes over on December first."

Harry smiled at the familiar argument. "Do you want to concede now or carry on with tradition until I wear you down?"

Cash peeled the wrapper off the pumpkin muffin as he debated his next step. He took a bite and nearly rolled his eyes back in his head. The pumpkin spice muffin alone was delicious, but the crumble and maple glaze were out of this world. He bowed to Harry and her wisdom, earning a giggle, and continued shoving the muffin into his mouth. Harry poured him a cup of coffee and retrieved the creamer from the refrigerator. He smiled when he saw it was peppermint mocha.

"It's always the right time to enjoy the things you love," she said.

Cash wasn't so sure about mixing pumpkin muffins and peppermint mocha coffee, but he forgot his reticence after the first sip. He recalled Nick seeking him out for comfort and wondered if a little holiday magic was already in the air. *Oh, please. I've been such a good boy.* He took another sip of coffee to hide the smile he couldn't suppress, though Harry resumed glazing the remaining muffins.

"You're up and at it earlier than usual on a Sunday morning," Cash said.

She glanced up. "I love testing out new recipes. Judging by your immediate capitulation, I'd have to say it's a success."

"I'd eat that year-round."

Harry smiled at his approval. "I'm so happy you like it. I've already started adjusting the recipe to incorporate different ingredients. When you find a base you like, it's easy enough to swap out the seasonal elements." She finished drizzling the last muffin, then set the spoon inside the empty glass bowl and carried the dirty items to the sink to rinse. "You didn't tell me we were expecting company. I would've freshened up one of the guest suites and stocked it with essentials."

Cash knew she was curious about the car out front. The only overnight guests they had were the crew's family members, and no one was scheduled to visit for a while. There was no way to hide Nick's presence on the ranch, not that he wanted to, but Cash needed to minimize how many people knew Nick was sleeping in his bed. "That's Nick's car, and I didn't know he was coming," Cash said as casually as possible. "He arrived back from Virginia yesterday and headed straight here." Mostly.

"Rory will be so excited to spend time with his brother," Harry said. "Surely you gave him my suite so he can enjoy his own private oasis." She bustled around doing busy work as she spoke. "I'll find out what Nick likes to eat from Rory so I can make sure he gets some special treats. Find out if he has allergies." It sounded more like Harry was verbally amending her to-do list than addressing Cash until she turned and looked at him. "How long does Nick plan to visit? I'll make sure to stock his suite."

Cash froze with the cup halfway to his lips. He searched for a way to answer her without divulging too much of his personal business. All he could think about was how fucking good Nick looked sleeping in his bed. Harry must've seen at least some of the truth in his expression because her eyes widened briefly.

"Oh. Ohhh. Say no more, boss." Harry mimed zipping her lips.

Awkward. Cash thought it was best to correct the assumptions she'd leaped to but decided against it. Whatever Harry had imagined was probably exactly what his heart desired and feared most. He should've probably downplayed her presumptions but worried he'd just overexplain and make it worse. "Everyone knows you're the real boss around here," Cash told her instead.

"And that's a fact," Rory said. The guy looked rested, in love, and borderline smug when he entered the kitchen. The last one surprised Cash because it seemed aimed at him. Rory had obviously seen Nick's car when they arrived home, but he didn't know Nick had slept in Cash's bed. He was just being paranoid and prickly about his privacy. "And how was my brother last night?"

Cash nearly choked on his coffee. Rory's words didn't hold a hint of innuendo, but his shimmering icy blue eyes were another story. That little shit might not know anything, but he suspected a lot. Nick had been spot-on when he'd said people underestimated Rory, but Cash wasn't one of them. "He's tired from a long day of travel."

Rory leaned his hip against the kitchen island and crossed his arms over his chest. It was a classic what-are-your-intentions pose, but his goofy grin ruined any intimidation factor. Or did it? That smile unsettled Cash more than he wanted to acknowledge. He'd fearlessly challenged the wealthy and powerful to achieve his successes, but facing Rory felt scarier. Nick loved his brother dearly and held him in high regard. Rory's opinion would be important to Nick, so it mattered to Cash too. "I bet he was tired. I assume he landed in Denver and drove here."

"He did," Cash said casually. He debated telling Rory about Nick's car accident, but that would only make Nick's decision to drive to Redemption Ridge more curious. The last thing he wanted to do was encourage the grinning imp in his kitchen.

Rory broke eye contact with Cash to inspect the rows of muffins. "These smell incredible. I'll wait a bit to let Nick sleep in, then take him a few with his morning coffee. He loves anything pumpkin."

"Great," Harry said. "You'll have to tell me his favorite meals so I can fix him something special."

Rory faced Cash once more. "Cash would probably be a better judge. It's been a long time since I've lived with Nicky, and I'm sure his tastes have matured beyond chicken tenders and macaroni and cheese."

Cash couldn't help but grin. "Who doesn't love a good chicken tender and macaroni and cheese?" As far as deflections went, it was pretty lame. "Nick wouldn't want you to fuss over him," he told Harry. "He doesn't have food allergies, and he isn't a picky eater."

"He doesn't like mushrooms," Rory said.

"He didn't use to like them, but he does now," Cash said, recalling the way Nick had wolfed down the omelet. He'd chocked that full of peppers, onions, and mushrooms.

Rory quirked a brow in do-tell fashion, and Cash accepted the challenge.

"Nick changed his mind when he had truffle butter on a steak once."

"Well, damn," Rory said. "I used to love grossing him out with them." After a chuckle, he asked again where he could find Nick. "Maybe I'll jump on the bed the way I used to when I was little."

Cash thought of Nick's injured shoulder and nearly cringed. He quickly pivoted his thoughts to how best to divert Rory's attention, but Harry beat him to it.

She looped her arm through Rory's and pulled him toward the refrigerator. "You'll do no such thing. Tell me all about your trip while you help me prep for breakfast." Harry looked at Cash and made a get-out-of-here hand gesture. He took full advantage of her distraction to beat a hasty retreat to his office. Cash snagged another muffin from the cooling rack. Being the ranch owner had its privileges.

"It was the best trip I've ever taken," Rory said wistfully.

The guy had traveled the world, and Kansas had stolen the top spot? Cash knew damn well it had nothing to do with the location and everything to do with the people, namely the big teddy bear who'd stolen Rory's heart. Cash slowed his steps so he could catch the highlight reel.

"Ivan's mom is so sweet," Rory continued. "I adore her and the fierce way she loves her sons. Ivan and his brother, Innes, razz each other non-stop. It's too funny. No one here would dare talk to Ivan the way his younger brother does."

According to Nick, Rory knew exactly which buttons to push to rile him up too. Cash hadn't witnessed the shenanigans for himself. If the ranch was lucky, they'd get to see Nick and Rory in action.

"Oh my God, Harry," Rory blurted. "You should see Ivan fussing over his little niece. She looked so tiny in his gigantic hands. He cradled her tenderly against his chest and talked to her in the gentlest voice I'd ever heard. *Swoon.* I want to have ten babies with him."

Cash snorted and picked up the pace. He made a quick detour to the library to retrieve his phone before heading into his office. Burke had texted back *No problem* and *I'll hold you to it* almost immediately after Cash had canceled their dinner plans. He felt like he owed his friend a better explanation. Regardless of Nick's presence, Cash needed to let Burke down gently, not through a text. He'd set up the rain-check meal where he could let the guy down. Normally, he wouldn't message people at seven in the morning, but he knew from their conversations that Burke was an early riser.

Cash sat down at his desk and took a fortifying sip of coffee before pulling up his text thread with Burke. He tapped out, *I'm really sorry about last night. A friend showed up unexpectedly. Could we meet for lunch this week?* He set his phone down and picked up the Sunday paper Harry had laid on his desk. Burke replied before he'd read the first headline.

How good of a friend? Burke wanted to know.

Cash chuckled and shook his head. Of course he'd zeroed in on that part. Two could play this game. *Lunch?* Cash asked. The bubble with three dots popped up on his screen, so Cash didn't bother to set the phone down.

I see. Burke followed it with a sad face emoji and, *The lucky bastard. Lunch sounds good. Wednesday?*

They bantered for a few more minutes while confirming the day and time. Burke said Cash could invite his friend. Maybe the sheriff was curious, or maybe he was probing for information. Cash hadn't taken the bait. He told Burke to have a good day and be safe. He was in a good mood when he picked up the paper again. Cash was pretty sure Burke saw the writing on the wall when Cash had replaced what they both knew was a date in Burke's mind with a lunch at the local diner. Cash had squarely friend-zoned him without coming out and saying it. That would happen at lunch because there was no romantic future for them, regardless of what happened with Nick. Based on the teasing tone of Burke's texts, Cash was certain they would be okay.

His good mood shriveled up and died when he read the top headline. A new rash of thefts was occurring in the surrounding community. The interviewed officer remarked that this latest rash mirrored the ones from earlier in the year. Pastor Samuel Jeremiah, though Cash hesitated to use an honorific title for a cult leader, had accused the ranch crew of committing the thefts. Sheriff Burke and several of his deputies were very familiar with the ranch hands since Dylan trained their K-9 dogs. Burke had refused to entertain the allegations without evidence, which had only made Pastor Jeremiah angrier. Cash supposed that was the impetus for the confrontation at the dog adoption event in Last Chance Creek. As Cash had told Nick, the organization had been quiet—too quiet—since then. But how long would that last now that the thefts had started back up?

Burke hadn't said anything to him. Probably because he knew it was a sore subject for Cash. His crew had worked their asses off to build new lives for themselves, and the Salvation Anew assholes didn't care who they hurt with their accusations. The success of the ranch didn't rely on support from the surrounding community, but that didn't mean Cash wanted trouble. He sure as hell didn't want people confronting his men when they went into town. Pastor Jeremiah had garnered attention in the media with his "farm felon" talk. Sometimes all the reporters needed was a catchy moniker to run with a story; the truth be damned. Rory had worked tirelessly to fix all that, and Cash hated to see his hard work going down the drain. Dread sat like a brick in his stomach by the time he finished the article.

Voices and laughter filtered into his office, and Cash realized the rest of the crew had arrived for breakfast. He folded the paper and set it back on his desk. He'd had enough negativity to last a while. Cash wanted to be with the people who'd become his family. When he reached the dining room, Rory was passing out souvenirs to the crew. There was a fresh round of exclamations and guffawing with each revealed gift. Cash understood why when Rory handed him a keychain that said, "What happens in Kansas stays in Kansas." Most of the gifts either played on or outright stole slogans from other states or cities. Rueben got a coffee mug that said, "Topeka: The City That Always Sleeps." Harry got a trucker hat that said, "I left my heart in Wichita." Some souvenirs included famous lines from *The Wizard of Oz*. They were silly little gifts, but everyone loved them.

Once the laughter died down, they grabbed plates and filled them with food. Besides the pumpkin muffins, Harry and Rory served a breakfast casserole that combined hash browns, eggs, cheese, and breakfast meats. Cash took a serving and a half because it was one of his favorite meals, and he helped himself to a third muffin. He could punish himself in his home gym later.

"How was poker last night?" Cash asked once they settled around the table.

He expected the stories to be numerous enough to get them through breakfast, but the replies were brief and general. They all had a great time. Harry and Dylan have a cool place. Finley won most of the chips…again. Cash looked at them, wondering why they didn't embellish like usual, but realized the answer was sleeping in his bed. Of course they'd noticed the sporty sedan parked in front of his house. None of them seemed brave enough to come right out and ask him about it, though he felt the curious glances tossed his way.

"Did you buy a new car yesterday?" Tyler finally asked.

Some of the crew groaned, and others laughed. Wallets came out and several bills got passed to Rueben, who laughed gleefully and tucked his winnings away. Cash assumed the bet was on which of the crew would break first and ask about it. God, he loved the assholes so much, but he wouldn't let his expression give that or anything else away. Apparently Rory wasn't inclined to help them out either because he just sat there with a smug smirk on his face.

"No, I didn't buy a new car," Cash replied.

"An inheritance from an unknown benefactor," Kieran suggested with a smirk.

"It fell through a porthole," Rueben said.

Finley grinned like a lunatic, and Cash braced himself for his guess. Fin's mouth opened, but no words came out because Nick had chosen that moment to enter the dining room. Silence washed over the group. Cash felt the exact instant everyone's gaze pivoted to him, but he only had eyes for Nick. He wore jeans so faded they were nearly threadbare in interesting places. They fit Nick like a second skin, and Cash hated and loved them at the same time. Nick's shirt was so old that it was hard to discern its original color, but Cash remembered. The shirt had been Kelly green. The white screen-printed lettering behind the sling was missing, cracked, or peeling in most places. Cash knew exactly what it said because he'd bought the shirt on his first day of community college.

He'd tucked it away as a cherished reminder of the day that changed his life. Cash thought he'd lost the shirt in a move, but it turned out he'd been a victim of theft. And in more ways than one it seemed. Nick had stolen a huge chunk of his heart that fateful weekend, so why not take his clothes too?

But holy hell, Nick looked so fucking good in it. The hem didn't even reach the waistband of his jeans, leaving a good inch or more of golden skin on display. Cash dropped his gaze and reassessed the jeans. Those threadbare areas looked familiar too. When Nick angled his body to scout the food, Cash noticed the iconic triangle Guess logo was missing. The denim was still a little darker where it used to be. He'd fucking loved those jeans when he'd bought them at the thrift store in town. They'd fit him so well, and he wore them until they were no longer decent to wear in public. Like the shirt, he hadn't been sure when they'd gone missing, only that they had. He'd mourned their loss and wanted to blame the joy of rediscovery on his racing heart. But foolishness was not a key to Cash's success, and he forced himself to admit several truths.

Nick Scott wore the outfit better. With his bare feet and mussed hair, no one had ever looked more beautiful to Cash. The things Nick did to his body were wicked, but it was nothing compared to the impact he had on Cash's heart. And regardless of the speech he'd given Nick in the hot tub, Cash was well and truly fucked. His heart waved the white flag in surrender.

chapter
SIX

INTIMIDATION WAS AN OLD FOE NICK HADN'T FACED OFF WITH IN a long time, but the bastard reintroduced itself with a flare in Cash's dining room. If the emotion were a person, it would stroke the curling ends of its overlong mustache and laugh maniacally at Nick's discomfort. Every pair of eyes was trained in his direction, reminding him of his first day in private school after his mother married Charles Snyder. He'd felt the weight of the students' stares and his new stepfather's expectations. The pressure had been surreal, but it paled to his current circumstances. He hadn't stayed in touch with a single person from his school days, but the people gathered around the table mattered to Cash. Nick wanted to make a good impression, which meant he probably should've dressed better. But his outfit made a statement, even if only Cash understood it.

Nick tore his gaze away from the delicious food and met each of the curious gazes, saving the most important for last. He'd met most of the crew during brief visits but would've recognized the side-betting busybodies by Cash's descriptions alone. He took a moment to introduce himself to everyone, shaking hands with those who extended him the courtesy. Rory popped up out of his seat, wrapped his arms around Nick's waist, and did his best boa constrictor impersonation.

"Leave some air," Nick gasped.

Rory laughed and loosened his grip, but he didn't pull away. "You have some serious explaining to do," his little brother whispered before finally letting go. Nick wasn't sure if Rory meant his presence on the ranch or his injury.

"Looking forward to it," Nick said, but he figured his host deserved those answers first. They'd only scratched the surface the previous night.

Rory gave him one last squeeze before dropping his arms. "I'll make you a plate. Sit down."

"Thank you," Nick said. The only empty seats were the one Rory had vacated and another at the farthest point from the person he needed most.

"Here, take my seat." Rueben rose from his spot immediately to Cash's right. The Hispanic guy in his midtwenties was almost too beautiful to be real. He'd become an overnight sensation when Rory had launched the Redemption Ridge YouTube channel. People were obsessed with his soulful eyes and ridiculously long eyelashes. Rueben was even more gorgeous in person and just as thoughtful as he came across in his segments.

"Don't mind if I do," Nick replied at the same time Cash said, "That's unnecessary."

Nick met Cash's gaze for the first time since entering the dining room. Cash had his mask firmly in place now, but Nick had felt his incinerating perusal earlier. It had been uncomfortable to dress himself, especially in tight clothes, but Cash's reaction was exactly what he'd wanted. It wouldn't be wise to push him, though, so Nick waited for Cash's cue.

Rueben, who'd already stood up, wore a knowing smirk as he volleyed his gaze between the two men. "I insist."

Nick forced himself to look at Rueben. "Thank you."

"It's my pleasure." Rueben emphasized his rolled R, so the word sounded like a purr.

Nick claimed the vacated seat and scooted himself closer to the table. His toes brushed up against Cash's socked foot, and Nick's decision not to push him dissolved. Nick slid his foot under Cash's pant leg to touch bare skin. Outwardly, Cash didn't betray that Nick was playing footsie under the table, but Nick felt a slight tremor beneath his toes. He expected Cash to pull away, but to Nick's surprise, he inched his leg even closer.

Rory set an overflowing plate of food in front of him. "I can't eat all this," Nick said. The shock halted his secret massage, but he kept his foot tucked under Cash's jeans.

"Try," Rory said. "You look better than you did in March, but you're still too skinny." Rory patted him on his good shoulder and resumed his seat next to Ivan.

Cash leaned toward him and whispered, "I'll help." He snagged a muffin off his plate, but there were still two more.

Nick tucked into his food, hoping to make a decent dent. Conversation resumed around the table as the crew caught Ivan up on everything that had happened in his absence. There were a few funny stories about a mean chicken named Bloody Mary and some shenanigans from a horse named Nellie. Nick enjoyed their banter almost as much as the delicious food. When the crew pushed back from the table to start their workday, it shocked Nick to discover he'd cleaned his plate.

Cash chuckled at his astonishment. "We work and eat hard around here."

Nick glanced up and saw that they were alone. "Do you play hard too?"

Cash's nostrils flared. It was the only sign that Nick's question had struck its target. He rose to his feet, and Nick looked his fill before giving Cash his full attention. "I have a few things I want to take care of this morning, but I'd like to show you around the ranch this afternoon."

"I'd love that." Nick stood up with his plate in hand as the crew had done.

Cash took his dishes and stacked them on top of his. "How does coffee on the porch sound?"

Nick sighed. "Like heaven."

"Let's get you set up there," Cash said, then turned to exit the dining room.

Nick followed but stopped suddenly when Cash halted and turned around. With dishes in one hand, Cash backed Nick up a few steps. He hooked two fingers in Nick's belt loop and brushed his thumb over the strip of bared stomach. They might've filled their bellies, but Cash's hungry expression said he craved something else.

"We're going to do so much more than sightseeing today."

Nick quirked a brow. "Yeah?"

Cash moved in even closer. "Oh yeah," he said, voice husky. "I'm going to take you to my favorite secluded place, and we're going to…talk."

Nick snorted and rolled his eyes. "Tease."

"Thief," Cash countered and gave him one last hungry look before he blinked it away. "Come on before they place bets on us."

The snickering and hushed conversation coming from the kitchen suggested that ship had already sailed. Their delay probably wasn't even a minute, but Nick detected some guilty flushes when they entered the room. The kitchen, open and airy, was a vast space, but it looked much smaller with so many people lined up to rinse their dishes and stow them in the dishwashers. Rory and Nick hadn't chatted a lot during his time at Quantico, but each conversation had included tidbits about his ranch life. The process went smoothly, and the guys quickly filed through the kitchen. Tyler and Owen had kitchen duty and hung back to hand-wash the oversized dishes and restore order to the room.

Nick lingered to the side so he wouldn't be in the way and risk someone jostling his shoulder. Getting dressed had hurt him more than he wanted to admit, and the meds Cash had left on his nightstand hadn't kicked in yet. Remembering the gesture put a smile on his face.

Rory sidled up beside him and stopped just shy of bumping into his shoulder. "You might want to cool it, Nicky. You're staring at the boss with a dopey expression on your face."

Nick looked at Rory and thought his brother was one to talk. He'd caught him making moon eyes at Ivan throughout breakfast. Rory was so in love it almost hurt to look at him. During his long drive to the ranch, Nick had made a mental note to have a private conversation with Ivan. His brother had fallen ass over teakettle in love with the foreman, and Nick needed to be sure that Ivan's feelings were genuine. After only five seconds in their presence, Nick scratched that item off his mental to-do list. They were so besotted with each other it nearly gave Nick a toothache.

"You're projecting," Nick said. "You're so infatuated that you see it everywhere you look."

"Is that so?" Rory asked smugly. "Where'd you sleep last night, Nicky?"

Harry swooped in like an avenging angel before he could reply. She handed Nick a cup of coffee, looped her arm through Rory's, and led him away. "Off we go, brat," she said. "You're about to see a new side of me. It's called the pumpkin spice queen."

Nick wasn't sure how much she'd overheard, but Nick appreciated the interference. He and Rory had a lot to discuss, but he wanted the peaceful afternoon Cash had promised him. Then Nick remembered Cash wanted to talk too. What was with all the talking around here? Patsy trotted up to him and let out three sharp barks. "You too?" Nick asked.

She turned around in a circle, but Nick wasn't exactly sure what it meant. "You want to go outside?" It was a safe guess. She barked three more times, which he took to mean yes. "Lucky for you, my lady, I was just headed that way."

Nick didn't risk looking in Cash's direction in case Rory had been right. He didn't want to make Cash uncomfortable in his own home, which was why Nick should move to his own suite. *Fuck that.* Patsy trotted beside him down the long hall toward the front door. Once outside, she dashed down the broad porch steps to the grassy lawn. Nick headed to an Adirondack chair on the side of the house to get a better view of the mountains. A throw blanket rested over the back, and he covered himself up. He should've put on shoes and a long-sleeved shirt to ward against the chill, but Nick was too comfortable to care just then. He sipped his coffee and set it on the matching table next to him. Patsy finished her business and ran to him as if he were a long-lost friend. Cash often took the dog with him to Denver if he planned to stay for more than a night or two, so Nick had been around her a lot. She'd always been affectionate toward him, but she was even more so on her home turf. Dogs were exceptionally sensitive, so maybe she sensed his injuries—physically and emotionally. Whatever the reason, he was grateful for her presence when he sank his fingers into her soft fur. The sun rose opposite of the mountains and set behind them. Nick stroked Patsy from head to tail while watching the shadows shift on the mountain range as the sun rose higher in the sky. It was the most peaceful he'd felt in a very long time, so it didn't surprise him when Cash gently woke him sometime later.

Nick blinked the world into focus, and damn, it was a beautiful day. Blue skies, fluffy clouds, and his Saint squatting down by his chair. "There you are."

Those three words held a special meaning between them. Cash reached up to brush the hair off Nick's forehead. Such a simple gesture, but Nick felt it everywhere. "You still want that ranch tour or would you rather—"

Nick threw the blanket back so fast that Cash had to stand up to avoid getting hit in the face. Patsy barked and pranced. "You heard the lady," he told Cash. "This day is too beautiful to spend it sleeping." Judging by the sun's position, Nick had been out for a while.

Cash chuckled, then leaned down to pick up a wicker picnic basket. "You head inside to get socks and shoes, and I'll get the side-by-side out. Harry and Rory made us enough food to last us a week out on the range."

Nick just bet they did. And he suspected Rory had loaded the basket with presumed aphrodisiacs. There had better be something besides oysters in there, or Nick would find a way to wring his little neck with one hand. He wondered if he'd run into his meddlesome brother and his sidekick when he walked through the house, but Nick didn't see anyone. His shoes weren't in Cash's bedroom with the rest of his clothes from yesterday, so he detoured to the library after grabbing a pair of socks. He located his battered Hey Dudes by the sofa. Nick had hiking boots and tennis shoes in his car, but his favorite casual loafers didn't tie. He doubted Cash would take him hiking in his current condition, so he sat down and put on his socks and shoes. He'd spent the last year in the Bureau second-guessing himself, and it felt good to decide and go with it.

Cash and Patsy were waiting for him by the porch in a black-and-silver side-by-side. The utility vehicle had all the power of an ATV but came with a roll cage, a hard plastic canopy, doors, and seat belts. Cash had stashed the picnic basket in the small bed and buckled Patsy into one of the rear seats. She let out a little Chewbacca-like growl that said *hurry the hell up.*

"Forgive me, ma'am," Nick said as he descended the steps. He tipped an imaginary hat toward her.

"She's no miss," Cash told him. "She's HRH Patsy Ann, Queen of Redemption Ridge." As if to prove his point, Patsy offered a paw when he reached the UTV.

Nick wrapped his hand around her foot and bowed over it. "Long live the queen."

Cash snorted. "Don't encourage her." He stepped on the gas pedal and revved the engine. "Hop in."

Nick climbed in beside Cash and shut the door. Cash took off as soon as Nick snapped his seat belt into place.

"Aren't you going to show me the barns?" Nick yelled over the engine as they zipped past the buildings.

"On the way back," Cash replied. He headed for a well-worn path that disappeared into the woods.

Nick decided not to ask any more questions and just enjoy the ride. The temperature was a good twenty degrees cooler under the dense canopy of trees. Dappled sunshine filtered in, but it was still pretty dark on the path. It was clear to Nick that Cash traveled this way often because he took each veer or turn smoothly without letting off the gas. Nick closed his eyes and leaned his head back against the rest, enjoying the smells of the forest and the breeze against his face. Laughter rumbled from Cash, and Nick opened his eyes.

"You and Patsy were wearing the same expression," Cash said.

Nick really wanted to kiss the smile on his lips, but Patsy let out two quick barks. "You wore it better, my queen," he assured the dog.

Cash smiled at Nick right as they traded the forest for sunshine and blue skies again. Nick couldn't tell if Cash's smile was blinding or the sun just appeared brighter in contrast to the shaded trees. He only knew Cash looked more relaxed than he'd seen in a long time. He couldn't help but recall their previous encounters over the past year or two. Though their conversations and interactions were the same, there'd been an underlying current of tension. Nick just hadn't realized it until the strain was gone. *I'm not too late.* He returned Cash's smile as butterflies fluttered in his stomach and his heart skipped a beat.

The moment didn't last long because Cash needed to focus on driving. Nick tucked the memory some place safe. He wanted that image to be the last thing he saw when he took his final breath. *Oh fuck. I'm acting like Rory.*

He didn't have time for much wallowing as they began a descent to a meadow of sunflowers below. The engine shifted and whined as the vehicle slowed for the steeper angle. The vehicle came equipped with both an oh-shit handle and a fuck-this bar on the dashboard. Nick trusted Cash implicitly and didn't reach for either. If this was a favorite spot, Cash would've traversed it regularly. He'd never put Nick or Patsy in danger by gunning it down the side of a mountain or at least a very steep hill. Faith in Cash and the stunning view below made Nick forget about his temporary concern.

Tall stalks of flowers stretched on for acres, their iconic yellow and brown heads facing the sun and swaying in the breeze. A shimmering stream of water ribboned along the edge of the fields and disappeared out of sight.

"Wow!" Nick exclaimed. The word was a bit underwhelming for the emotion it was supposed to convey. Perhaps the punch was in the delivery.

"I know," Cash replied. "This has always been my favorite view, but it's even prettier since Ivan planted a field of Rory's favorite flowers."

Nope. Nick did not need to have a talk with Ivan. His intentions were crystal clear.

"You've got a pensive look on your face," Cash hollered over the engine. "You know Ivan is crazy about your brother. You don't have to worry about Ivan hurting him."

Nick looked at him and smiled. "I know that. I was just thinking of ways I could enrich your life too."

Cash let off the gas when they reached the bottom of the hill, and they coasted for a bit. He pressed the brake and studied Nick with the most intense expression he'd ever seen. "You breathe, Nicky. That's how you enrich my life."

While the sentiment was sweet, Nick vowed to up his freaking game. "I'd lean forward and kiss you, but I'm not sure if—"

Cash closed the distance and kissed him. Nick didn't even have a chance to close his eyes before Cash withdrew.

"—it's allowed," Nick finished.

Patsy barked three times. "That means yes," Cash said.

Nick grinned. "Then come back over here."

Cash chuckled and shook his head. "We need to do some talking first."

With a deep sigh, Nick accepted defeat. "Feed me first." All he'd accomplished so far was getting dressed, eating, and taking a nap, but Nick felt like he'd run a marathon.

"Happy to oblige." Cash drove a little farther, stopping near the stream. He killed the engine, and Nick got swept up marveling at Mother Nature. The burbling water, sunshine on his face, and breeze in his hair made him forget how hungry he was until Cash announced lunch was ready.

Nick snapped his head toward Cash's voice and was stunned to find he'd already laid out a blanket and unpacked the food. Nick had barely been aware of him leaving the side-by-side. That must've been some daydreaming. Cash ambled over with a concerned look on his face. Nick wanted the smiles back instead.

"Sorry I didn't help. I was daydreaming."

"Don't apologize for breathing it all in." Cash leaned across him to unfasten his seat belt, and Nick took advantage of his proximity to nuzzle his nose against Cash's neck. They stayed that way for a few seconds before Cash eased back with the seat belt in hand. "Let me feed you, then we'll talk."

"And then?" Nick prompted.

"We'll see."

The conversation seemed more significant than any test Nick had taken in his life, and he was not about to fail. Charles Snyder hadn't come into his life until Nick was ten years old, but the business mogul had made a lasting impression. Cash opened the door for him, and Nick swung his legs out. They walked toward the blanket, where Patsy patiently waited for them. When Nick sat down, she belly crawled over to him and pressed her warm body against his. He stroked her fur just as he'd done that morning. The same sense of calm washed over him.

"First my clothes and now my dog," Cash said when he sat across from them.

Nick wanted Cash closer but thought it might be wiser to keep the food between them.

"I didn't consciously plan to steal your clothes that weekend," Nick said. "I'd borrowed them for the one time we left your apartment, and I just never gave them back." Nick remembered they'd sought a certain food that they couldn't get delivered.

"Ah, the bagel run," Cash said. "I remember the errand but not what you wore."

"My tuxedo from the charity event would've drawn a lot of attention," Nick replied. "Funny, I remember what I wore but not where we went." An example of the way they completed each other.

"I'm curious about how they ended up with you in Virginia twelve years later. You said all this stuff came from your trip to Quantico, right?"

If Nick was to get what he wanted—Cash—then he would have to bare his truths. A part of him wanted to point out that Cash had promised to feed him first, and Nick didn't have any food in his hand. But this conversation was twelve years late already. "Yes, I had them with me in Virginia, but I should probably start at the beginning. I took your clothes with me when I left your apartment in Denver. I intended to get them back to you but couldn't part with them." Heat spread up his neck. Nick knew his face was turning pink, but he held Cash's gaze. "They've been with me on every trip I've taken and have become a security blanket. I put them on when I'm stressed, lonely, or just need to feel connected to you." Nick inhaled a shaky breath and dug deeper. He wanted to give Cash a verbal field of sunflowers. "Seeing those clothes in the suitcase this morning was the epiphany I needed. You wanted me to be sure, and the evidence was right there in front of me. No what-ifs or maybes. I've been yours since we met."

Cash's lips parted, and his eyes drifted closed for a few moments. "But your career is in Denver."

Nick knew his time with the FBI had come to a close; he just hadn't severed the connection permanently. He had a few months of salary he could collect while he figured out his future…with Cash. Nick offered a wry smile and shook his head. "Listen, I haven't figured out all the answers on my first day off, just the most important one. Maybe I would've solved all the mysteries of the universe if I hadn't fallen asleep on your porch."

Cash's nostrils flared as he breathed in deeply. "Are you sure, Nicky? I can't lose you."

"I'm positive, and you couldn't shake me if you tried." Nick cocked his head to the side and said, "Now feed me or kiss me."

chapter
SEVEN

THERE WAS ZERO DOUBT IN CASH'S MIND ABOUT WHICH OPTION he wanted to choose. Nick's words and his expression were the signal he'd been waiting for to make his move. Yet he froze. Instead of sweeping the food out of the way and claiming what Nick offered, Cash's brain was trying to figure out how long he'd been in love with his best friend. His single-minded focus came in handy with business deals, but it was mighty annoying just then. Still, once his brain locked on to the point, he couldn't budge from it. Maybe there hadn't been one big event but several important moments that had added to their bond. Their connection grew from a few delicate strands to a sturdy rope capable of—

Woof! Woof! Woof!

Patsy's barking snapped Cash out of his reverie, and he blinked the present scene back into focus.

"There you are," Nick said. He picked up an egg salad sandwich triangle and took a bite, watching Cash as he chewed. "I want it on the record that I wasn't the one who interrupted your freak out." He shoved the rest of the sandwich into his mouth and reached for another triangle.

Cash reached over and lightly smacked his hand. Nick would need that for other things as soon as Cash cleared the air. "I wasn't freaking out." His tight chest and racing pulse mocked him. Okay, so maybe his brain had kicked into analysis mode to distract him from scarier emotions.

"Saint," Nick said, his disbelief stretching out the single word. "You trust me?"

"More than anyone."

"Good." Nick kept his gaze locked on Cash as he shifted all the food to one side of the blanket. "Because I'm coming over there."

Cash stopped thinking and started reacting. By the time Nick crawled across the small gap, Cash was already shifting to a side reclining pose. He reached for Nick before he could stretch his long body beside him on the blanket. Their lips were tentative at first, curious and playful. That lasted until Nick nipped Cash's bottom lip and tugged on it. Cash fisted Nick's hair so he'd let go and took control, pushing his tongue inside Nick's mouth. Cash relaxed his fingers and cupped the back of Nick's head to make sure he didn't escape. Nick growled low in his throat and sucked on Cash's tongue, making him think of other things. It had been nearly two years since he'd been with someone, and he'd craved Nick for too long. Cash was dry timber to Nick's spark. Arousal spread through him like a wildfire as his blood rushed south. Each twirl of their tongues stoked the flames higher and higher.

Nick used his good arm to roll Cash to his back and straddled his waist. There was no way in hell Nick didn't feel Cash's erection. It had been a long time since he'd been embarrassed about getting hard, but—

Nick broke their kiss and sat up. "You're overthinking it again, Saint. That will make me question my prowess more than my ability to get fully erect right now." Nick rolled his hips forward and created the perfect amount of friction where Cash needed it most. Leaning forward, Nick placed his hand on the blanket next to Cash's head. "Don't hold back. Let me have this. I want to kiss you everywhere and enjoy your body like it's the first time. I need to hear, feel, and smell your arousal." Nick continued to rock against him and lowered his head to Cash's ear. "You're so hard for me. Give me all of you."

Cash emitted a soft whimper before Nick swooped down and claimed his mouth in a branding kiss. Then there was no capacity for worry because all Cash's focus went to the pleasure building in his core. He reluctantly tore his mouth away from Nick's. "I'll come if you don't ease up," Cash whispered.

A wicked smile greeted his confession. "We can't have that." Nick stilled his hips, and Cash wanted the delicious friction back. Before he could complain, Nick sat up straight, untucked Cash's T-shirt from his jeans, and rucked the material up to his armpits. "Christ, you're sexy."

Nick didn't wait for Cash's reaction before inching down and leaning over Cash's chest. A breeze whistled through the field of flowers and brushed over his bared skin like a caress. Goose bumps popped up all over, and Cash's nipples hardened. The heat from his lower belly expanded like a giant blush.

"Are you still really sensitive here?" Nick blew across Cash's nipple, causing him to tremble. "That's a yes." He teased the tight bud with the tip of his tongue, then alternated between sucking and rasping his teeth over it. Cash hardly recognized the needy moans escaping his own mouth. He thrashed his pelvis upward, seeking the glorious friction he needed to find release. Nick ripped his mouth away and smiled down at him. "I'd planned for you to come in my mouth." Nick snapped his hips forward, making Cash arch his neck. "But I can get you off like this." The urge to close his eyes and just let the passion sweep him away was strong. But this wouldn't just be anyone's mouth on his cock nor would he be staring into any old pair of blue eyes. This was Nick—the man he'd loved since…forever. What did it matter when, why, or how Cash fell in love with his best friend? He would not squander the moment he'd ached for by living in his head instead of in the moment.

So Cash met Nick's scorching-hot gaze and reached down to still his hips. "I want your mouth."

Nick's chuckle was dark and wicked. "In due time."

He leaned back down and kissed a path to Cash's other nipple. He added more suction, teeth, and wet tonguing before inching his way lower. Nick took his time mapping out every inch of exposed skin and rubbed his face against Cash's happy trail. "I've been wanting to do that since I saw you standing partially dressed on your porch last night. I'm so fucking hot for you."

Cash fisted his hand in Nick's hair and pulled until their gazes met. "Prove it. Suck me off."

Keeping eye contact, Nick stuck his tongue out and dipped it into Cash's belly button. "I only have one good hand. Gonna need you to take your dick out and feed it to me."

Cash nearly broke a world record when unbuttoning his fly. Nick eased up so Cash could shuck his jeans and underwear to his knees. He felt absolutely carnal as he lay there partially dressed and stretched out for Nick. The sun kissed parts of his body he hadn't exposed to daylight for a very long time.

"God, you make me hungry." Nick's sexy growl wasn't for the food Harry and Rory had packed. He inched down until Cash's thighs supported his chest. Nick hovered over the drooling erection but kept his gaze locked on Cash's face. "Feed it to me. Slowly."

Cash fisted his dick and offered it to Nick, who swirled his tongue around the leaking tip.

"Tastes so good," Nick groaned. He sucked the crown into his mouth and used his tongue to massage the sensitive spot beneath the head.

Cash wanted to close his eyes and bask in the incredible sensation of Nick going down on him, but he didn't want to miss a single expression that crossed his gorgeous face. Need quaked inside him, making Cash desperate for more. Nick looked content to roll his tongue around and suck on his cockhead for eternity. He'd said to feed him. Cash used one hand to guide Nick's head down and the other to push his cock deeper into Nick's eager mouth. A wicked chuckle reverberated down the length of Cash's erection as Nick took him down. Nick eased off to tease the tip before descending again. This time, he didn't stop until his nose pressed against Cash's trimmed pubic hair. Nick made a muffled gag and breathed deeply through his nose. Christ, Cash had forgotten just how well Nick could deep throat him.

"I need to come," Cash groaned.

Nick swallowed, and his throat massaged Cash's cockhead.

"Fuck," Cash moaned. "Nick, baby, I—"

Nick eased up slowly until the tip slid from his slick lips. "Say it again."

"Baby."

Nick's eyelashes fluttered, and a flush spread across his face. Cash knew what he wanted—needed—and said it a third time. Nick swallowed Cash's dick back down, hollowing his cheeks with the force of his suction. Christ Almighty. Cash nearly levitated off the blanket when Nick bobbed his head up and down his erection. Saliva and precum made fantastic lube, and the slurping sounds Nick made had Cash's balls tightening in warning.

"Pull off…if…you…"

Nick didn't slow or spit him out; he redoubled his efforts until Cash came down his throat with a hoarse cry. Nick continued to suck and lick his cock until he reduced Cash to a muscleless heap on the blanket. Cash stared up at the face he loved dearly. Nick's eyes shone with joy and pride. His cheeks were pink from exertion, and his swollen lips glistened with saliva and spunk. Cash pushed up to his elbows and kissed Nick, tasting himself on Nick's tongue. Now that the immediate passion had subsided, Cash's earlier concern returned.

"Oh no," Nick said, shaking his head. "You're overthinking again. Why don't you tell me what's bothering you?"

"I feel selfish letting you pleasure me without reciprocating."

"If the situation were reversed, what would you do?" Nick asked.

Cash thought the asshole looked a little too smug and really hated to agree with him. "I'd stretch you out and make you feel good." The truth earned Cash a long, hungry kiss.

"I craved your taste and your happiness more than anything else. There are other ways for us to be intimate. I'd love to feel your hands and mouth on any part of my body you'd like to touch."

Cash cupped Nick's face and brushed his thumb over Nick's cheek. "It's your love language."

"I'm not sure what that is, so I'll take your word for it."

Cash spent the next thirty minutes stripping Nick down to his underwear and proving just how much he loved being touched. Nick didn't get fully erect, but he'd cheered when he achieved a half chub.

Shoving his underwear to midthigh, Nick trailed his fingers over his flesh. "Isn't he a beauty, Saint?" He told Cash it was the hardest he'd gotten in eight months.

"Perfection," Cash said.

He licked and kissed Nick's semierection to show his adoration. Then Cash rested his head on Nick's thighs and took his dick into his mouth. He'd just meant to lie there for a moment, but the warmth of the sunshine and the bone-melting orgasm made his eyelids too heavy to keep open. When he came to again, Nick's cock lay flaccid against his pelvis. It was still perfection in Cash's eyes. Nick and Patsy were sound asleep too. The egg salad sandwiches were gone, and it was a toss-up who'd eaten them. Both were probably an option, but Cash had a sneaky suspicion his dog had devoured them as soon as the humans had fallen asleep. If so, she would get extremely gassy. Her furry ass wouldn't be sleeping in his room for a second night in a row, and he didn't care who got pissy about it.

Cash's cell phone rang, startling him and the nappers. Nick jack-knifed into a sitting position, then recalled his injury with a grimace and foul language. Cash rooted around in the blanket until he found the phone. Seeing Owen's name on the caller ID surprised him. The guys rarely called him unless Ivan was unavailable. Technically, their foreman was still on vacation, so it made sense Owen would turn to Cash if a problem came up.

He accepted the call. "Hey, Owen. What's up?"

Surprise turned to fear when Owen blurted, "Tyler's in trouble and needs you."

Cash immediately set to straightening his clothes at hearing the urgency in Owen's voice. "What's wrong? Is he hurt?"

"No," Owen said, then released a soft moan. "Well, I don't know. He got arrested."

chapter
EIGHT

NICK DIDN'T KNOW WHO CASH WAS TALKING TO OR WHAT had happened, but he didn't need to rely on his Bureau training to know it wasn't good. Cash's voice had been urgent when he'd asked about potential injuries, and the response produced a crestfallen expression Nick never wanted to see again. His shoulder throbbed like a son of a bitch, but he ignored it as he propelled himself to his feet with his free hand. He kept an ear trained on Cash's half of the conversation and pieced together that someone had gotten arrested.

"Owen, where are you now?" Cash asked.

If Owen was the one calling, that meant Tyler was probably the one in trouble. Cash had mentioned they were inseparable, two halves of a whole, and Nick had seen that firsthand at breakfast. They completed one another's sentences and moved together as if choreographed. Nick also recognized that Owen was in love with Tyler, who was clueless about the depth of his friend's affection. Nick suspected Tyler's devotion ran deeper than friendship too, even if he hadn't fully figured it out yet. Nick would be the first to say ignorance is not always bliss in situations like this. He felt a vested interest in the outcome of their relationship, and the first step would be to get Tyler out of jail. What the hell could that kid get arrested for anyway? He seemed like such a sweet kid, maybe a little derpy at times but endearingly so, kind of like a golden retriever.

Patsy woofed once as if she'd read his mind. Her expression was as anxious as Cash's voice. Patsy clearly didn't like it when her favorite human was upset. Nick reached down to pick up his discarded jeans and scratched her ears to calm her. "It's okay, girl," he soothed. "We've got him."

Cash was alternating between uh-huhs and okays and sounded a little calmer. Nick held his sling out a little to help balance his upper body as he slid his first foot into the denim, then the other. "Nick, wait for me to help pull up your jeans. You're about to topple over."

Nick snapped his head up and met Cash's shocked gaze. He'd just revealed their relationship status to one of the biggest gossips on the ranch. If Cash was lucky, Owen was too distressed to comprehend what he'd heard. Cash mouthed "Sorry" as he stepped over to assist with the jeans. Nick just shrugged because he'd hire a skywriter. Cash was the one who would struggle with the ranch crew knowing his business.

"Just hang tight, Owen," Cash said into the phone. "Head over to the diner and hang out there until Nick and I arrive."

In less than twenty-four hours, Nick had gone from *me* to *we*, and it pleased him immeasurably. Once Nick tucked everything away, Cash disconnected the call and turned his attention to pulling himself together. He put on his socks and shoes, then started repacking the picnic basket. The container that had held the egg salad sandwiches was empty. Nick was almost positive Cash hadn't eaten them, and he knew damn well he hadn't. He glanced over at Patsy, who wore an innocent wasn't-me expression. Nick quietly put the lid back on the container and stacked it in the basket without ratting on her. She had offered him more comfort than one man deserved, so keeping quiet was the least he could do. Nick winked at the dog and was positive she understood.

"Which one of you ate all the egg salad sandwiches?" Cash asked. So he had noticed the empty container.

"We're not telling," Nick replied, darting a conspiring glance at Patsy.

"Okay," Cash said. "Looks like I'm sleeping alone until I get a verbal confession or flatulence gives someone away."

Nick pointed at the dog and said, "She did it." Patsy's expression didn't change, but Nick figured she'd get even. When Cash turned around, he shrugged as if to say *what could I do?* No grace was given.

Once the food and blanket were in the basket, they loaded it in the side-by-side. Cash wore a pensive expression as he drove, and the trip back wasn't nearly as fun for many reasons. The lighthearted mood was gone, and Cash had to be much more aggressive to make the climb to the ranch. He drove the vehicle full throttle like his racing days. Nick gave up looking brave and grabbed the fuck-this handle on the dashboard in front of him.

Cash didn't ease up once they crested the hilltop and entered the woods. The forest rushed by them in a green and brown blur. Nick was eager to find out what the hell had happened but waited until they wouldn't have to yell over the engine. Cash sped through the barnyard and screeched to a stop near the front porch.

"I just need to put Patsy and this stuff in the house." The dog responded with two sharp barks. "Don't sass me, young lady. In you go."

The border collie's head hung low, and her tail drooped as she followed her human. Cash returned moments later with a key fob in his hands. He pushed a button, and Nick's BMW beeped twice. Cash scowled and looked at his hand.

"I didn't mean to grab your keys," he said.

Nick didn't allow anyone to drive his car, a playful point of contention between them. "She's closer and will get us to town faster than a lumbering pickup."

"It's not lumbering when I drive it," Cash said as he led the way to

Nick's sleek sedan. "Though I have wanted to drive this bad girl since you bought her."

The engine fired up with a throaty purr that made Nick want to shimmy in his seat. He watched as Cash familiarized himself with the car's bells and whistles. He adjusted the seat, mirrors, and steering wheel before putting the car in reverse.

"You look damn fine driving my car." Nick's voice did a good impression of the engine's throaty purr. "I'm going to buy you some black leather driving gloves."

Cash smirked and glanced over at him. "I'm going to drive you."

Nick sucked in a sharp breath. God, he wanted that so much. It wouldn't matter if he couldn't get hard or climax. Just imagining Cash's dick inside him again was enough to make him shiver. Nick wanted—*needed*—the connection, to give his body to Cash and witness him take pleasure… Fucking yum. Nick shivered again.

"Need me to turn the AC down?" Cash teased.

"You damn well know how much I love getting on my knees for you," Nick fired back. If Cash was going to play dirty, he'd do it too. "Now that the whole ranch is going to know about us, I won't have to worry about keeping quiet while you plow me."

Cash puffed up his cheeks and blew out a harsh breath. "I can't believe I was so careless."

"That phone call rattled you good," Nick replied. "Tell me what Owen said instead of acting like me."

Cash glanced over at him with a scowl. "How am I acting like you?"

"You used sex or sexy banter as a distraction device."

Chortling, Cash shook his head. "That is your MO."

"Yeah, it is. My therapist helped me sort that out." When the thrill of the hunt and sex with nameless strangers had lost their appeal to Nick, he hadn't found a different stress reliever. His agitation had just built until he'd burned out, silencing his libido completely. *Temporarily.* Nick refused to believe his condition was permanent. Panicking, he'd learned the hard way, would only delay his recovery.

The engine downshifted as Cash slowed to take a twist in the road. Nick looked over to see if he appreciated the sexy way the Beemer hugged the curves. Instead of a joyous smile on Cash's handsome face, Nick saw a scowl. Obviously, the situation with Tyler had Cash stressed out, but he knew that wasn't the reason for his displeasure. Then Nick realized Cash was overthinking his arrival at the ranch again.

"Huh-uh," Nick said.

Cash glanced over. "What?"

"Now you're resorting to your brand of distraction by overanalyzing my words and gestures. You're looking for ulterior motives or any little excuse you can latch onto to justify your fear. I'm an open book, Saint." And after they dealt with Tyler's situation, Nick would bare everything to Cash.

Cash sighed heavily and laid his right hand on Nick's thigh. "You're right. I do trust you, Nicky. I've just…"

"Wanted this for so long. Me too." Nick reached over and laid his hand on top of Cash's. "I was just a tad slower than you were, I think."

Cash rotated his wrist and threaded his fingers between Nick's. "You think?"

"Well, I'm not flattered by your tone," Nick teased. "It implies I'm dense."

Cash's lips quirked, but the half smile didn't linger in light of the uncertainty with Tyler. "I think we were both a little dense." Cash squeezed his fingers. "Or maybe the time was never right before now. Maybe we need to stop thinking about why it didn't work out before and focus on how it could now."

"I'm game if you are," Nick told him. "Now bring me up to speed."

Cash sighed deeply again. "All I know so far is that Tyler got arrested. Owen was too distraught to say much beyond that." Cash let out a little growl. "People think my mission is nuts. They think these guys are destined to become repeat offenders." Cash's voice rose, and his tone went from mild to spicy.

"Not me," Nick said quickly, hoping to douse the heat like a glass of milk. Anger wouldn't get Cash the outcome he wanted, and he'd be upset later for his loss of control. "I've just met Tyler today and have no clue what crimes landed him in jail, but I feel confident going out on a limb to say there's no way in hell he willingly committed a crime since breakfast."

"Thank you." Cash's words were heavy with gratitude and relief. "I hope this is all a simple misunderstanding I can clear up quickly."

Nick hoped so too, but he wasn't holding his breath.

"Tyler comes across as a goofball, but there's depth beneath that affable facade. He's starting to figure a lot of things out about himself, and I know the truth scares him. I've been there." Cash sounded so dejected and like he was putting the cart before the horse. That wouldn't serve any of them well.

"So have I," Nick replied. "We'll figure this out. Let's find out why he got arrested, and then you can call a good lawyer."

"I'll call an *excellent* lawyer," Cash growled.

That's my guy. Nick briefly wondered why he hadn't spoken that thought out loud. Maybe because navigating this new aspect of their relationship felt a little like tiptoeing through a minefield. It might've helped if they'd had a deeper conversation before Nick sucked Cash off. *Nah.* Nothing could make him regret pleasuring Cash in his favorite spot on the ranch. He would turn the moment into his go-to place during meditations. He'd feel the warm sun and breeze on his skin, the tug of fingers in his hair, and the expression of pure bliss on Cash's face as he climaxed. Nick would relive those moments anytime stress threatened to wreck his recovery.

"If Burke isn't already there, I'm going to call him in," Cash said.

Stressful times like now. He'd forgotten all about the sexy sheriff. He could handle this one of three ways: fixate on the almost date, play it cool during introductions, or stake his fucking claim. Nick's lips quirked up as he settled on the right option.

"Don't make me turn the car around." Cash's stern voice interrupted

Nick from scrolling through his options on claim staking. It also sent a tingle down Nick's spine that lingered in his balls.

"What did I do?" Nick asked. He couldn't seem to wipe the smirk off his face, no matter how hard he tried.

"You are not going into the sheriff's department and engaging in a pissing contest with Burke," Cash replied, proving the mind reading went both ways.

"I agree it wouldn't be appropriate today."

"Not *any* day," Cash countered.

Nick sighed. "My dick will stay in my pants." There were other ways to get his point across.

Cash grunted but let it go as they pulled into town. Nick didn't like the tense set of his shoulders as he smoothly parallel parked the car down the street from the diner. Owen was leaning against the front of the building and watching the road coming into town. He probably didn't expect them to arrive in Nick's car, so he reluctantly let go of Cash's hand to lower the window. Nick stuck his arm out and waved to get Owen's attention and retracted it once the younger man noticed them.

Nick rolled the window back up and covered the hand Cash had left on his thigh. "Hey." Once Cash met his gaze, he said, "Do I have dry cum on my face?"

Cash growled low in his throat, but he inspected Nick's face for evidence of their debauchery. "You're good to go," he said, right before Owen opened the door behind Nick.

"Sorry about that," Owen said. "I was looking for Cash's truck." He sounded much calmer than Cash had described. Maybe knowing the boss had Tyler's back was the assurance Owen needed to regain his composure.

"No problem," Cash replied as he merged into traffic. To Nick's surprise, Cash resettled his hand on Nick's leg. "I grabbed the wrong keychain and didn't want to waste time going back inside."

"Appreciate you, boss," Owen said. "Sorry I was so rattled when I called you. Probably couldn't hear a word I said."

"Not much beyond Tyler getting arrested," Cash admitted. "And don't apologize for caring about people, Owen."

"Especially not your best friend," Nick added. "Can you tell us now what happened?"

"Honestly," Owen said, "I don't really know anything more. We'd come to town for a bite to eat and to do some shopping. My mama's birthday is coming up, and I wanted Hope to put together a goodie basket for her so I could get it shipped out."

Brave man. Nick had heard all about Hope's shenanigans and was looking forward to meeting her.

"Anyway," Owen said, "Hope's openness about sex and masturbation embarrasses Tyler a little, so we split up."

Nick nearly choked on his saliva. Seemed Cash had left out some major details during story time.

"When I left her shop," Owen continued, "Tyler was up against the truck in handcuffs with a deputy patting him down. I froze in complete shock, and that's when Ty noticed me on the sidewalk. He shook his head real subtle…like a signal. When I still stood there like an idiot, he mouthed 'Go' at me. The deputy was too busy to notice, so I turned and hightailed it out of there. I ducked into an alley between businesses and called you."

"I'm glad you did," Cash said. "Wish I knew what the hell they arrested him for, but I guess we're about to find out."

They arrived at the sheriff's department a few minutes later, and Cash heaved a relieved sigh. "Good. Burke's here."

Nick swallowed his possessive snarl and forced his face to remain neutral. Cash gave his leg an encouraging squeeze before retracting his hand. They parked and made a beeline for the front door. Nick recognized the impressive man talking to a deputy at the rear of the station. As if he sensed Cash's presence, Seth Burke looked their way. He held up a hand to interrupt the deputy, said something to him, and immediately headed in their direction. The photos and videos on the internet, though very impressive, didn't do the man justice. He was much taller in person, or maybe his white Stetson just made it seem so. Burke's movements were more an amble than a stride, but his posture and demeanor made it clear he was the man in charge. It reminded Nick of Timothy Olyphant's portrayal of Raylan Givens in *Justified*.

Burke's eyes never left Cash as he moved through the station, and Nick fought the urge to whip his dick out and get a head start. The tall sheriff stopped in front of the trio and seemed to notice Nick and Owen for the first time. Cool gray eyes assessed and dismissed Owen before landing and lingering on Nick. *I'm your cockblocker, asshole.* Burke briefly narrowed his eyes before forcing his attention back to Cash. "I was just about to call you," he said. His voice was solemn and professional but not unkind.

Cash made quick introductions. He referred to Owen as a member of his crew and Nick as his friend. Burke shook Owen's hand first before extending the gesture to Nick. Seizing the opportunity, Nick wrapped his hand around Burke's in a bone-crunching grip that said *back off! He's mine.* Burke's narrow-eyed gaze replied *fuck up, and I'll swoop in.*

Once they understood each other, the two men broke the exchange and stepped back. The machismo made Cash sigh and roll his eyes, but Nick was relieved to see Owen smiling a little. Yeah, the rest of the ranch would definitely hear about this.

"Let's head back to my office," Burke said.

Cash turned to Owen and said, "Would you mind hanging out here for a few minutes? I have some things I'd like to say to Burke in private."

Owen shrugged and took a seat.

"What about him?" Burke said, tipping his head at Nick.

"He's with me," Cash replied.

"I'm with him," Nick echoed.

"Ah," Burke said. "Got it."

Good.

Burke turned to lead them to his office, and Nick leaned close to Cash. "See? No dick measuring involved."

Cash nudged him with his elbow before following the good

sheriff. Nick was extremely curious about what Cash wanted to say to Burke out of Owen's earshot. Burke didn't take long to get right to the point.

"Deputy Hines was walking down the sidewalk and noticed tools matching the description of stolen items in the bed of Tyler's pickup truck."

There was so much wrong with the statement that Nick opened his mouth to cut him off, but Cash reached over and squeezed his thigh. Burke's eagle-eyed gaze noticed the gesture, which was the only reason Nick let it fly. Cash, it seemed, was not so inclined.

"Burke, you expect me to believe your deputy was just strolling by a Redemption Ridge pickup and looked inside the bed without provocation? And these stolen tools just happened to be out in the open for him to find? Don't you find that odd? I also want to know how the deputy knew they were stolen tools. Were they rare?"

"The items had the owner's name written on them in black marker," Burke replied calmly. "He's a contractor and labeled his equipment for easy identification on crowded jobs. Hines phoned the station and confirmed the serial numbers were a match from the police report."

That information sounded pretty damaging, but the seizure itself was sketchy. Nick wasn't willing to be silent any longer. "A good attorney will have this thrown out," he told Cash. "The deputy still needed just cause to search an open truck bed."

Burke cocked his head to the side. "Just what is it you do, friend Nick?"

"FBI. Special Agent in Charge."

"I see," Burke replied, sounding unimpressed. "But I don't agree. Items left out in the open are fair game."

"He needed a search warrant," Nick argued. "If they'd been inside a locked car, your deputy wouldn't have been able to break the window to inspect the serial numbers. He would've had to get permission from Tyler or get a warrant to search."

"They weren't in a locked car. They were right out in the open for my deputy to spot."

"You mean the deputy that had to leave the sidewalk and lean against the truck or even stand on tiptoes to see inside the bed?" Nick asked. "These are tall trucks, not low-riders. The whole situation sounds fishy. I like our chances with a judge."

"Guess we'll see," Burke said, crossing his arms.

"I don't want it to get that far," Cash said sternly.

"You're right," Nick replied. "Let's discuss this with the county prosecutor."

"I don't want to do that either," Cash said. "Nick, I can prove Tyler didn't steal those tools, thanks to your buddy at the Bureau."

"How?" Nick and Burke said together.

Cash chuckled nervously and licked his lips. "When the first theft occurred months ago, Samuel Jeremiah from Salvation Anew went to the press and accused someone from my ranch."

"That guy." Burke's irritated growl raised his standing with Nick but only slightly.

"My crew has had some unpleasant interactions with the group even before the incident at the pet-adoption event. Nick put me in touch with someone at the FBI who investigates cults, and he gave me some invaluable advice to protect myself and the crew." Nick got the impression this was the part he didn't want Owen to overhear. "I installed tracking devices in every ranch truck, including my own, and can pinpoint exactly where the vehicles have been. I've also documented each reported theft and cross-referenced my vehicles' locations during those incidents."

Burke exhaled slowly, and Nick could tell he was relieved. "Does your crew know about the devices?"

"They don't. I worried they'd misunderstand my motives. I think in the long run it worked out better for them. You can't accuse them of working around something they didn't know existed."

"What about personal vehicles?" Burke asked.

"Only Finley and Harry have their own vehicles, but neither has a record and aren't as much of a target."

"Did you bring any of this evidence with you? I'm willing to release Tyler into your custody without booking him while we investigate further."

Cash shook his head. "Owen said Tyler got arrested but didn't know what for, so I didn't come prepared. If you can give me the theft dates, I can get you what you need?"

"This theft was back in May," Burke said.

Nick snorted. "And you guys thought Tyler was just carting the stolen tools around in the back of his truck for over three months? Sounds like someone planted them."

Burke scowled at Nick. "Are you accusing my deputy of planting evidence?"

"No, Sheriff, I'm not." Nick's gut told him the cult was behind this, but he'd love to know what made the deputy decide to look in the truck's bed.

"Receiving stolen property is also a crime, Agent Scott. Surely, they teach you that at Quantico."

Cash held up his hand before Nick could reply. "Enough." His stern voice did funny things to Nick's insides. Maybe Cash could raise his libido from the dead faster than he'd hoped. The cock whisperer. "How about I voluntarily share all the data I have? I can transfer everything to a flash drive."

Burke pushed back his chair and said, "Let's go."

"Go?" Cash asked.

"I want to see the files and setup with my own eyes," Burke said. "That way no one can suggest I gave Tyler a free pass because of our *friendship*."

Nick knew the sheriff was correct, but that didn't mean he had to like it. Inspiration struck as Nick and Cash stood up too. "Do you mind giving Cash a ride to the ranch, Sheriff?"

"Of course not."

Nick turned and met Cash's curious gaze. He wanted to accomplish two things with his suggestion. First, Nick wanted to check the stores closest to the truck for security cameras, and then he wanted Burke to know he didn't intimidate Nick in the least. "I'll help Owen finish his errands, and we'll meet you back at the ranch once you get Tyler out."

Cash knew he was up to something but didn't push. "Okay."

And because he was a petty bitch, Nick kissed Cash softly before leaving the sheriff's office.

chapter
NINE

TYLER LOOKED LIKE A WHIPPED DOG WHEN A DEPUTY ESCORTED him to Burke's office nearly two hours after Cash received Owen's call. It had been one hundred and fifteen minutes of tension that Cash was eager to put behind him. The silent trip to the ranch with Burke had been pure hell. Cash kept waiting for him to ask about Nick or comment on his possessive display, but he'd said nothing. Somehow, that made the situation worse. Once at the ranch, Burke had been all business, which was the appropriate tone considering the situation. Cash just missed the friendly twinkle in his friend's eyes and the easy camaraderie they felt in each other's presence. But if he were honest, the easiness had dissipated each time Burke asked him out.

Cash should've been up front with Burke the first time it happened and admitted he was hung up on someone else. But Cash hadn't been willing to admit it to himself, let alone to Burke. He thought he could bury his unrequited love in the basement of his soul through sheer willpower. Then said love showed up, threw open the door with a few words, and let all his feelings out. Cash had been foolish in so many ways. He just hoped it wasn't too late to salvage his friendship with Burke. But he'd have to worry about that later. Tyler's well-being came first. Though Ty didn't wear cuffs or shackles, he moved as if he did. Dread and shame hung over him like a rain cloud, but Cash carried a big umbrella.

"Ty." Cash gentled his gruff voice as best he could.

The younger guy snapped his head up and his eyes went wide with surprise. Had he not expected Cash to come to his aid? "I didn't steal anything, boss."

Cash crossed the room and placed both hands on Ty's shoulders. "I know you didn't. I've come to take you home."

Tyler looked from Cash to Burke, then back. "You mean it? They're not keeping me until my arraignment? You can deduct whatever bail money you paid from my paycheck," Tyler added in a rush. "If that's not good enough, I can call my folks and see if they'll help."

Cash pulled Tyler into his arms and hugged him tightly. The younger man stiffened for a few heartbeats before melting into his embrace. Ty released a muffled sob against Cash's shoulder before pulling himself together and stepping back.

"There's no bail to pay back and there won't be an arraignment," Cash said.

Thanks to Nick, Owen, and a certain feisty redhead who'd rallied the business owners on Main Street.

Cash's compiled data impressed Burke, but he said it only proved the Redemption Ridge trucks weren't nearby when the thefts occurred. He'd suggested that Tyler could've ridden there with someone else. Cash explained that Tyler went nowhere without Owen and vice versa. They weren't close to anyone outside the ranch's tight inner circle, and they didn't own their own vehicles. Burke dismissed the logic and said he could charge Tyler with receiving stolen property. Cash had countered that Tyler didn't need to purchase or receive stolen property because every tool he needed was available on the ranch. Both men had dug in their heels as tension rose between them until a young deputy alerted the sheriff to a problem in the lobby.

The problem turned out to be seven business owners from Main Street led by Hope. They were armed with security camera footage that painted a vivid picture and cleared Tyler of all charges. Judging by Ty's reactions, he hadn't known about his vindication when the deputy brought him to Burke's office.

"Tyler." Burke's voice was authoritative as ever, but he'd softened the edges just the slightest bit.

The younger man turned to face the sheriff. Tyler's spine stiffened and rapt attention replaced the hangdog expression from earlier. "Sir." Cash wouldn't have been surprised if Tyler had saluted Burke.

The sheriff gestured to the two chairs in front of his desk. Tyler took one, and Cash sat in the other. "You've been set up," Burke explained.

Tyler's eyes went wide again, and he bounced his gaze between Cash and the sheriff. "Me? I don't know anyone who'd want to do that."

But Cash did, though he didn't know how he'd prove his suspicion.

"How do you know I was the target?" Tyler asked.

"Well, I can't prove they were setting you up specifically," Burke replied.

Cash realized the sheriff's thoughts were following the same path as his, but he kept his mouth shut and let the man speak.

"I want to show you the footage from Main Street to see if you recognize the person who placed the stolen goods in the truck bed," Burke said. "Mr. Sweeney already watched the clips and didn't recognize the guy."

Mr. Sweeney, huh? So that's where they stood.

"Okay," Ty said hesitantly. "Gotta tell you, Sheriff, I only really know the people on our ranch. Unless this person works at a store or restaurant in town, I won't recognize them."

"It's worth a shot," Burke said.

"I'll do anything I can to help." Tyler's eagerness was one of his most endearing traits.

Burke turned his computer monitor around so Tyler could see it better, then cued up the first clip. It showed a slender man wearing a white long-sleeved T-shirt, jeans, and cowboy boots walking down the street with an oversized canvas bag. The guy wore a ball cap pulled down low over his forehead and kept his profile toward the cameras, even when he dumped the tools into the bed of the truck. Burke paused the video and zoomed in.

"I'll be damned," Tyler whispered.

"Do you know him?" Burke asked with urgency.

Tyler shook his head. "Sorry. I was just shocked by his boldness."

Burke continued playing the video clips to show the man walking down the sidewalk. He discarded the canvas bag in a trash can and continued toward a parked sheriff's cruiser. They watched as the man approached a deputy who exited the diner with two large sacks of food. He gestured animatedly toward the parked truck, now out of frame. Burke paused the action again. The security camera footage came from across the street, so he zoomed in again to look for any identifying features like scars or tattoos. The only feature that stood out to Cash was the man's nose. It had a slight bump on the bridge as if it had healed poorly after an injury, which gave the nose a hooked appearance.

"Sorry, sir," Tyler said. "I can't help you. I've never seen that man before in my life."

The sheriff sighed. "I'll keep working on this. Can you think of anyone who holds a grudge against you?"

"Me personally or the ranch?" Tyler asked. "Because I've never exchanged a harsh word with anyone." He scrunched up his face. "Well, a few of the guys from Salvation Anew said some shitty things to me once in town. I just ignored them and kept walking." Tyler looked at Cash. "Do you think they're behind this? The logo on the truck doors clearly identifies it as ours. Could this have happened to any of us who drove into town? We're here often enough. Dude could've just been waiting for the opportunity."

"That's for me to figure out." Burke's voice had regained its sharp edge, and he locked his gaze with Cash's in a warning. He didn't want Nick interfering more than he already had with the errands that had caused him to part ways with Cash earlier. "You've been as helpful as can be, but I'll take it from here."

Tyler held up both hands in surrender. "Fine by me, sir."

Burke arched a brow at Cash, who grinned to let the sheriff know he'd received the message. Now he just needed to convince his…um… Nick to stay out of it. Burke stood up and said, "I'll walk you out."

Tyler didn't let on if he thought that was weird. Then again, he was probably too eager to leave the station to pick up on nuance. Burke had ordered Tyler's truck to be returned, and a deputy had parked it in front of the station for them.

"You mind driving?" Tyler asked Cash when Burke held out the keys.

"No problem."

Cash mentally braced himself for an accusation or snide remark once Tyler climbed into the passenger side of his vehicle and shut the door. Instead, Burke chuckled as he dropped the keys into Cash's open palm.

"You know," he said, crossing his arms, "you could've just told me you were in love with someone else. I wouldn't have been upset." Burke tipped his head to the side. "I think I already knew but continued to hope I had a chance." With a heavy sigh, he added, "Tell that arrogant asshole that you and I are still having our weekly lunches. I'm not losing my friend over this."

Cash's muscles unclenched, and relief flooded his body. He reached over and clasped Burke's shoulder. "I'll see you Wednesday at one, Seth."

"Looking forward to it." The twinkle returned to his gray eyes. "Hey, Cash," Burke called out before he could open the driver's door. "Be careful and stay alert."

Burke's caution held an ominous tone, but Cash tried to smile through his unease. "Will do."

Tyler said little on the way home. He appeared to lock himself down tight, though Cash caught a telltale shiver every once in a while. Cash's mind was in a million places too, so he embraced the quiet instead of trying to guess the assurances Tyler needed to hear. Owen would know the perfect way to reach Ty just as Nick would calm the tumultuous feelings troubling Cash. They were going home to their respective people, and that was better than idle chitchat.

Tyler didn't launch himself out of the truck when Cash parked it in the usual space next to the barn. He turned solemn eyes on Cash and said, "Thanks for coming for me."

Cash laid his hand on Tyler's shoulder. "Always, Ty. And I mean that. There may come a day when your dreams take you away from the ranch, but I'll always be just a phone call away."

Tyler's lower lip trembled for an instant before he stiffened it. "Landing in lockup was the best thing to happen to me. It forced me to get clean. I found Owen. Then I met you." Tyler took a deep breath and scanned the ranch for a few moments before meeting Cash's gaze. "This ranch and the people on it mean everything to me."

"And all of you enrich my life in ways I never dreamed possible," Cash told him.

"I'll never be able to repay your kindness, but I promise to never betray it." Tyler puffed up his cheeks and blew out slowly.

Movement in his periphery caught his attention. Cash glanced out the rear window and saw Owen and Rueben advancing on them. "Heads up. Incoming."

Tyler looked in his side mirror and smiled as he removed his seat belt. "My favorite welcome wagon." He opened the door, and Owen was on Ty as soon as he stepped down.

"It's about time," Owen said as he hoisted his friend off the ground. He didn't quite do a romantic hero spin, but it was pretty damn close.

"I was just about to mount a posse and bust you out of there," Rueben said. He swooped Tyler up as soon as Owen set him down.

Cash released his seat belt and eased from the truck. Rueben and

Owen were speaking over each other and peppering Tyler with questions. Cash shook his head and headed toward the house.

"Oh my gosh," Tyler said. "One at a time."

"Why did it take so long to get you out?" Owen asked.

"It's a long story," Tyler replied. "I'll tell you all about it."

"How sexy was Burke when he had you in handcuffs?" Rueben asked.

"Sounds like the thought's crossed your mind a time or two," Tyler said.

"Maybe three," Rueben replied slyly.

The trio laughed and headed toward their cabins. Cash wasn't sure if Rueben was serious about his crush on the sheriff, but he thought it was cute. Stranger things had happened. Neither his man nor beast greeted him when he entered the house, though he suspected they were together. Patsy sensed Nick's emotional turmoil and wanted to mother him. He kicked off his shoes and walked silently through the house in his socked feet. The kitchen, living room, and library were empty, so he continued back toward his bedroom. He eased the door open in case Nick was napping, but only the dog was zonked out. Her front paws twitched like she was chasing something in her sleep. Nick lay sprawled on the bed, reading a paperback book. He still wore Cash's T-shirt but had swapped out the tight jeans for a pair of black sweats. Must've been a damned good book because he didn't hear Cash enter the room. Nick stared intently at the pages in front of his face and licked the corner of his mouth.

"Whatcha reading?" Cash asked.

Nick flinched and fumbled the book but caught it before any harm came to his handsome face. He pushed himself into a sitting position and laid the book on the other side of his body. Didn't Nick want him to see what he was reading? Cash noticed the canvas shopping bag sitting on the bedside table. Hope's white label stuck out in stark comparison to the purple, further proving that Nick was the one behind Hope's rally.

"I really wish I'd been there when you met her," Cash said with a smirk as he gestured to the tote.

Nick laughed and rubbed a hand over his face. "God broke the mold after she was born."

Cash eased toward the purple bag to see what he'd picked up during his excursion, but Nick pulled it away from him.

"How about show and tell? You tell me everything that happened with the sheriff, and I'll show you what I bought from Hope's store."

Cash walked to the bed, and Nick eased over to make room for him.

"By the way," Nick said before Cash could start his story, "I'm nearly positive there's no need to ban Patsy from the room." He waved his free hand in front of his face. "Pretty sure she's already expelled all the gas from the egg salad sandwiches."

Cash chuckled and shook his head. "I know that dog, and I'm pretty sure she's just getting started. No man or beast is going to gas me out of my bedroom."

Nick tapped his temple. "Noted."

Cash stretched out on his side to face Nick, who still lay on his back. "The situation with Tyler was stressful and awful, but knowing I got to come home to you made it so much better." He gave Nick a sweet kiss before he launched into the story.

Nick narrowed his eyes and interrupted Cash when he started with their return to the station. "He didn't make a single remark about my chest thumping?"

"Burke got your message loud and clear."

"Yeah?" Nick asked. "What did he say?"

Cash cut him off with another kiss. "All in due time." Nick circled his forefinger in the air as a gesture for Cash to speed up. He went through the conversations they had about Tyler's potential role after Burke accepted none of the ranch trucks were involved. "Just when I was about to lose my cool, in marched Hope and her brigade of do-gooders."

"Concerned citizens," Nick amended.

"Thank you for doing that," Cash replied. "I'm not sure Tyler would've gotten out of there tonight if not for those videos." Cash told him the rest of the story and finished with Burke's message for Nick.

"I deserve the arrogant asshole remark," Nick said. "How do you feel about me pissing on your leg before you go to town?"

"Hell no."

"Can I sit in a nearby booth?"

Cash tilted his head. "You're not really jealous, are you?"

Either the question or Nick's unspoken answer made him uncomfortable, not full-on twitchy but close. Nick met Cash's gaze and held it for a long time. "Only with you," he finally said. "I've never cared about anyone else enough to bother with such a primitive emotion. I'm not really sure I like it." He sighed. "And I'm sorry if my Neanderthal routine embarrassed you today. This is my problem to deal with, and I will add it to the list. If it's all the same to you, I'd rather put most of my attention on firing Ole Sparky back to life first."

Cash rested his head on Nick's good shoulder and rested his palm on his tight stomach. "I need to make a confession."

"Need an attorney or priest first?" Nick teased.

Cash pinched the skin just above Nick's waistband. His stomach muscles tensed, reminding Cash that Nick was ticklish there. It probably wasn't a good time to make him flinch or shake. He eased his hand down lower and just kept going until the tips of his fingers dipped beneath his waistband. Cash's fingertips didn't encounter underwear, only smooth skin. "I thought it was really fucking hot."

"Huh?" Nick asked breathlessly.

"The caveman routine," Cash said as he trailed his fingers across Nick's pelvis from left to right.

Nick groaned long and low. "Don't stop."

Cash leaned in and kissed his neck. "Never."

"I want to feel you inside me," Nick said. "I want to watch you take pleasure from my body again."

Cash's fingers stilled, and he forgot to breathe for a few seconds. The visual sent a spike of lust straight to his dick until he thought of how painful that could be for Nick. Penetration was often uncomfortable even when you were aroused out of your mind. He wouldn't use Nick that way. He would wait until Nick had healed. "And you will, Nicky."

"Now?" Nick's whimper nearly made Cash take back his unspoken promise.

"I won't hurt you like that," Cash said. "There are many ways to be intimate that won't cause discomfort or make you feel used."

"I'm begging you to use me," Nick whined.

"Not like that, baby. Please don't ask that of me. I crave so much more from you than sexual release."

Nick turned his head, and Cash had to pull back to see his expression. Nick's dark blue eyes sparkled like sapphires. "I figured out your love language."

Cash smiled. "Did you now?"

Nick nodded, looking smug as hell. "I bought a book on the subject from Hope's store."

"What else did you buy?"

"I see you trying to change the subject," Nick said. "I'll do the showing my way." He covered Cash's hand and pushed it down lower to rest on Nick's cock. "Touch is definitely my love language, and yours is quality time."

Cash struggled to define the pleasure coursing through his veins. It wasn't arousal, though that was present too. This euphoria had more to do with being seen and understood.

Nick took in a shaky breath. "No fucking wonder we couldn't get this right. I've been too busy or far away to give you the quality time you need, and I didn't have your hands on my body."

Cash grazed his fingertips over Nick's cock and cupped his balls. "We're already making up for lost time."

Nick closed his eyes, bucked against Cash's palm, and fucking purred. After a few moments, he met Cash's gaze again. "I bought a variety of lubes and a men's supplement that's supposed to promote healing and improve all aspects of my life. All-natural stuff."

Cash's hand stilled but remained on Nick's crotch. "You had enough time to shop for books, sex aids, and male supplements while organizing Tyler's rescue?"

"I introduced myself to Hope and explained Tyler's situation to him. She was the one who rallied the shop owners while her husband watched the store. I bought one book, several lubes, and a single bottle of supplements from him. Gotta give him credit. He didn't blush once."

"If Gary were the blushing type, he'd be perpetually red," Cash replied.

They lay intimately entwined on the bed, touching and talking until a horrendous odor made them gag.

"Told you she was just getting started," Cash said as he launched off the bed to turn on the ceiling fan. He narrowed his eyes and studied the sleeping dog. Cash was prepared to toss her out on her fluffy ass, but Nick had other ideas.

"Don't you even think about it."

"I thought you said dinner would be a quiet affair," Nick said when they stepped out into the hallway a few hours later. They'd dozed in and out for a few hours, waking up to touch, kiss, and caress before nodding off again. The din from the kitchen and dining room was a rolling thunder of animated voices.

Sundays on the ranch were casual. Rory or Cash usually heated one of Harry's premade casseroles in the oven and served it up to those who ambled over to eat. Some guys hung out in their cabins and ate leftovers on Sunday evenings. But Cash had told Nick he'd help pull his pants up in earshot of Owen, and he'd kept his hand possessively on Nick's leg with Owen in the back seat of the car.

"I should've known better," Cash muttered, fighting back a smirk. He debated how to handle the situation—give those nosy Neds something to talk about or keep it cool and leave them guessing?

Nick must've read his mind because he said, "How do you want to play this?"

Cash stopped in the hallway, backed Nick against the wall, and planted a hard kiss on his lips. "For keeps," Cash said when they pulled back, breathless and wanting.

Nick held up his hand with his pinky extended. Cash snickered and curled his finger around Nick's. The pinky promise was ridiculous but endearing as hell. "Listen," Nick began, "I know how private you are, and I don't want you sharing anything that makes you uncomfortable."

Cash thought about it for a second. "I am a private man, but I've honestly had nothing to share with the guys. I was just a sad, lonely man living vicariously through others."

Nick cocked his head to the side. "You forget I've seen how people respond to you in a crowd. They practically devour you with their eyes and offer themselves up on a silver platter."

"But I haven't nibbled in over two years. It was like settling for a burger when I really wanted a steak."

Nick hooked his finger in Cash's belt loop and pulled him closer until their mouths almost touched. "You'll never have to eat burgers again."

"That's a pity," a male voice said.

Cash and Nick jerked apart like naughty teenagers and whirled to face their interloper. Dylan grinned like a lunatic at the end of the hallway.

"Tomorrow's Labor Day, and I planned to grill my gourmet burgers with all the fixings. Guess I can come up with a different menu." His wry grin said he knew damn well they weren't really talking about food.

"Will there be bacon for these gourmet burgers?" Cash asked.

"All the fixings must include bacon," Dylan replied.

Cash could practically taste the crispy, salty meat. "Nick likes avocado slices."

"Noted," Dylan said. "Dinner's ready. Come eat while it's hot. Harry made million-dollar spaghetti." With that, he spun around and ducked back into the kitchen. Dylan knew that would get him moving.

Cash grabbed Nick's hand and tugged him down the hallway.

"What makes spaghetti worth a million dollars?" Nick asked.

"It's baked spaghetti with a cheesy layer in the middle."

"Like lasagna?"

"Sort of," Cash replied. "I think there's cream cheese in there too."

Nick groaned and stepped up the pace. "Sounds good to me. I'll carbo load and sleep like the dead tonight."

A hush spread over the kitchen when Nick and Cash stepped into the room, still holding hands. "Oh, get over it," Cash told them. No one moved or practically breathed for a few seconds. Then the group exhaled collectively and started talking at once as they helped Harry carry the food to the dining room.

She'd tossed one of her delicious salads together and made several loaves of cheesy garlic bread. On her way out of the kitchen, she leaned close and whispered, "Happy for you, boss. I hid another loaf of banana bread in the pantry." Harry winked and continued toward the dining room.

Nick squeezed his fingers, and Cash turned to face him. "You've created the most incredible atmosphere with your family."

"Thank you."

And they were his, which is why he should've trusted them with the truth about the damn trackers when he'd installed them. Cash couldn't go back and change the past. He could only explain his decision, apologize for the subterfuge, and promise to be more transparent if faced with a similar choice in the future. Cash waited until the animated chatter about Tyler's arrest settled into focused eating and furtive glances in his direction. He set his fork down and told them everything. Cash saw a brief look of hurt cross Ivan's eyes. The big guy was used to being included in every decision regarding the ranch, but his subtle nod let Cash know he understood.

"I'm sorry I didn't tell you," he explained. "I just didn't want any of you to think I suspected you of the thefts or anything else nefarious. I've never wanted you to feel micromanaged the way you were in jail. I hope you can forgive me." Cash's heart fell when no one spoke or moved for several moments.

"I'd still be in the county jail if not for you installing those tracking devices," Tyler said. "No one would've bothered to check storefront video footage to catch that jerk planting evidence in the truck."

Cash didn't agree. Hope would've approached her fellow business owners once she found out, but it could've been too late. Most security systems recorded over stored data after a set period. Regardless, Cash appreciated Tyler's support. "Thank you."

"You've never let me down," Rueben said. "Not one time. I can't imagine where I'd be without the opportunities you've given me."

A chorus of agreement echoed around the table, even Finley, who'd never been in jail a day in his life. But the ranch was where he'd met the man he loved, so Cash could understand why he felt that way.

"There's nothing to forgive," Dylan told him firmly. "You give us so much, and it's fine if you keep something to yourself."

Cash suspected Dylan meant more than the tracking devices because Owen's cheeks turned pink. Cash winked at him to let the guy know it was okay if he engaged in a little harmless gossiping. "Thank you all." His voice sounded extra gritty with the added emotion weighing down the words. Cash cleared his throat. "You all mean more to me than you'll ever know."

Harry wiped tears from her eyes. "It's getting way too heavy in here, and absolutely no one is eating my food."

"You heard the boss," Cash said. "Get those forks moving."

Laughter echoed around the table before everyone dug back into their meal. Nick ate two helpings while fielding some questions from the crew about his years with the FBI. It was a subject they'd need to broach, just like their suspicion about who was behind the planted evidence in Tyler's truck. But Cash decided not to dwell on either topic. He led Nick back to his suite after they took their dirty dishes to the kitchen. Talking was the last thing on his mind after a tumultuous few days, so he was relieved when Nick picked up the remote control. Normally, they'd debate what they would watch, but Nick went straight to *Heartstopper* season two.

"How'd you know?" Cash asked.

"I saw the show listed under the Watch it Again category and tried it myself."

Cash looked over at him. "And?"

"I wish I'd had characters like these when I was younger," Nick replied. "It's a great cast and a timeless story. I'm excited to see season two."

"Push Play, then."

They only watched three episodes before Nick asked if they could hang out in the hot tub for a little bit.

"As long as you keep that shoulder out of the hot water," Cash said. "You need ice to help with inflammation."

"I promise to ice it after a good soak."

Cash would see to it. He poured himself a glass of wine, and Nick grabbed a beer. It didn't get better than bubbling hot water beneath a blanket of stars and the promise of sleeping beside Nick again.

And then Nick kissed him.

chapter

TEN

Waking up naked in Cash's arms was both heaven and hell—the former because Cash's morning wood wound up nestled between Nick's butt cheeks; the latter because Cash's misplaced sense of chivalry prevented him from acting on his arousal.

"Please," Nick begged.

"No," Cash returned.

Please. No. Please. No. Please. No. And so it went until Friday morning, when Nick tried another tactic.

"You're so fucking hard for me." Nick's thick voice sounded more like a taunt than an observation in the predawn hours. The awareness turned his insides to molten lava, which spread outward from his belly until he burned from his scalp to his toes. Nick rocked his hips back and reveled in Cash's needy moans. "It would be a shame to waste something so perfect."

Cash's hand tightened on Nick's hip. He thought it was to stop Nick from rubbing against him, but then Cash thrust upward, notching his cock higher along Nick's crease. The groan that rumbled from Cash was all the encouragement Nick needed. He'd make his man blow his load by hook or by crook.

"Baby," Nick crooned, tightening his glutes to massage Cash's shaft. "I need to please you and feel the power coursing through your body as you get off. Want to feel your cum on my skin. Need to smell you, Saint, so I know I'm yours."

Cash slid his arm low around Nick's waist and pressed his warm palm to Nick's abdomen. Between the warmth flooding his insides and the heat pressing against his flesh, Nick thought he could burn to ash right there in Cash's bed. If they were to be his last moments, there was no other way he wanted to go out.

"I won't hurt you," Cash whispered before kissing the shell of Nick's ear. He rolled his hips again, and Nick felt the glide of precum along his crease.

"Denying me your pleasure hurts me," Nick replied. "I'll just put undue pressure on myself to recover, and the added stress will cause a setback." The statement wasn't part of the hook or crook pledge. It was an earnest plea from Nick's heart. "I don't need penetration, baby. Grab the lube and rub one out between my thighs."

Cash didn't move, didn't even breathe, for a few seconds before he released Nick and rolled toward his side of the bed. It was still pitch-black in the room when Cash yanked the bedside drawer hard enough to pull the entire thing from the table. Cash cursed a blue streak as the contents crashed to the floor. It was both one of the best and worst moments in Nick's life. The best because he'd rendered this elegant man to a savage beast. The worst because said beast wouldn't be wearing out his ass the way Nick truly craved. Cash turned on the bedside lamp and soft light encircled the bed.

Nick blinked to adapt, then rolled onto his back to see what was going on. Cash was on his knees with his ass in the air as he leaned over to pick items up off the floor. Nick reached between his toned thighs, cupped Cash's taut balls, and rolled them in his hand. "Lube, baby. Leave the rest for later." Cash righted himself, braced his palms on the nightstand, and rocked back into Nick's touch. "Do you want to straddle my face? I can eat you out and jerk you off."

Cash lost his balance and nearly pitched off the bed. "You're trying to kill me, right?"

Nick chuckled. "C'mere, Saint. Quit stalling."

Cash repositioned himself to lie on his side while Nick rolled over and presented his ass. "Won't last long."

"And whose fault is that?" Nick playfully chided. "I sure as hell didn't ask you to abstain like a monk."

Cash nipped his good shoulder as he drizzled a thin line of lube along Nick's crease and taint. A moment later, he heard the telltale signs of Cash slicking up his dick. Nick expected him to begin frotting when Cash separated his ass cheeks, but Cash circled Nick's pucker with his thumb instead. Around and around the wrinkled rim, stopping only to tap the center.

Nick growled in frustration. "Fucking tease." But there was no heat in his words, only longing.

"You're so perfect for me, Nicky. I'll never want anyone the way I want you."

Key parts of Nick's psyche had been hidden away for a while. He'd mounted a rescue and located the locked iron door but couldn't open it. Nick closed his eyes and gave himself over to the moment. Cash's sexy voice and tender caresses filtered into his soul like wisps of smoke through the door's keyhole, sparking life in the barren space. Tears burned the back of his eyelids and his chest swelled with joy.

"Touch me," Nick begged, though he didn't instruct where.

Cash knew. He always did. Sliding his hand around to cup Nick's cock and balls, Cash shuttled his erection between Nick's closed thighs. The rasp of Cash's cockhead over his anus and against his taint drove Nick fucking nuts. Cash's caresses and thrusts started out tender, almost soothing, but quickly escalated in intensity.

"I'm going to come," Cash snarled in his ear.

"Glaze me like a donut," Nick panted.

Cash eased from between Nick's legs and got to his knees. Nick carefully rolled onto his back and lifted his legs toward his chest, exposing his hole. Cash positioned himself at Nick's ass and shuttled his hand up and down his cock. The ferocious expression on Cash's face made Nick's pucker quiver. Cash reached forward with his free hand and massaged Nick's hole, only pulling back when he started to come. Hot semen splattered against Nick's asshole, taint, and balls. He couldn't wait until it painted the walls of his tight channel.

When he lowered his legs, Nick noticed he'd achieved an impressive three-quarter boner that promised *soon*. He couldn't resist reaching down and tracing its length with a few fingers.

Cash leaned forward and kissed the head of his cock before easing off the bed. "Don't you dare call him Ole Sparky again," he called out as he restored order to his bedside table. "That's what they nickname electric chairs."

"Fine. He'll be known henceforth as Spiffy Stiffy."

Cash snorted from somewhere in the closet or bathroom. Nick was content to stretch out in bed with his almost erection and his glazed donut. The underlying panic Nick had pretended wasn't there, or was under control, eased up. Cash returned with a wet, warm washcloth and lovingly wiped Nick's cock, balls, and ass.

"Hey, I was still enjoying that," Nick groused.

Cash tossed the rag onto the floor and eased onto the bed. "You'll enjoy this more." He splayed Nick's thighs apart and lay flat between them. Cash licked a path along Nick's shaft and sucked it into his mouth. The heat was incredible, and Nick moaned.

"I don't think I can yet." But he used his free hand to anchor Cash in place.

Cash eased off and met Nick's gaze. "This isn't about orgasms or hard-ons. I'm just speaking your language, baby. Let's try to get some more rest." Cash nestled his shoulders between Nick's thighs to lie flat.

Then he rested his cheek on Nick's pelvis, put Nick's cock back in his mouth, and closed his eyes.

Nick carded his fingers through Cash's hair, closed his eyes, and imagined that damn iron door to the room beyond. Cash's earlier caresses felt like wispy smoke tendrils through the keyhole. But these wet, passionate kisses were bright shafts of sunlight, piercing the gloom and despair. Smoke and bright light created fog, but it was better than bleak darkness. His last coherent thought was, *Hang in there, Spiffy Stiffy. The cavalry has arrived.*

It was after ten o'clock when Nick entered the kitchen in search of breakfast leftovers. He'd hoped to sneak in and out unnoticed but no such luck. Harry and Rory were sitting at the kitchen island, sipping coffee and looking at something on a laptop. It reminded Nick that he'd left his computer in the library and it probably needed charging. He made a mental note to take care of that after breakfast so he could do some covert research on Salvation Anew and the Samuel Jeremiah guy at its helm. Cash had passed along Burke's message that he didn't want interference, but Nick didn't trust Cash's safety to just anyone. He'd hoped Cash would come back from lunch on Wednesday with news other than the meatloaf had been dry and the mashed potatoes too wet.

Cash had read his mind, kissed his mopey face, and retrieved the rest of Nick's belongings from the trunk. He'd put Nick's gun and badge in the office safe and found space for all Nick's clothes in his dressers or closet. Nick had observed and made lewd suggestions about what they could get up to on the oversized tufted ottoman in the closet. Though he had his own clothes and toiletries, Nick still went for Cash's stuff every morning. On some level, he knew he was acting like a smitten teenager, but he didn't fucking care. He just enjoyed smelling like Cash and feeling his clothes against his skin.

Rory noticed his presence first and looked up. His little brother scanned him from head to toe and didn't bother trying to quell his knowing smirk. Rory had been aware of his feelings for Cash before Nick was willing to recognize them. They'd had a lot of time to reconnect, and it reminded Nick of when they were little boys. They talked a lot and Nick felt like he was really seeing his amazing brother for the first time.

"Morning, Nicky."

He braced himself for jokes about sleeping late, but they didn't come. Rory knew something was going on but didn't press. Nick couldn't remember the last time he'd slept so late. His body clock usually had him up at five thirty. And he had been up that early, but he'd fallen back to sleep…with his dick in Cash's mouth. He zombie shuffled over to the coffeepot and poured a glass of strong, black coffee. Nick took three drinks before he could manage a simple, "Morning."

"There's a plate of food for you in the microwave," Harry told him.

Nick saluted her with his mug. "Thanks. You're an angel."

Harry snorted. "Hardly. And don't thank me. Cash is the one who made it before the Neanderthals ate everything."

"I don't want to take food out of someone's mouth. They work hard around here, and I just…" Take up space and steal their air. *Great*. He'd reached the pity party phase of his recovery.

"I make enough to feed two armies. Don't you worry about a thing," Harry told him. "We're so glad to have you on the ranch."

"Not as happy as I am to be here." Nick opened the microwave to inspect what yumminess he had in store and nearly choked on his sip of coffee when he saw the glazed donut on the side of the plate. The memories of that morning came flooding back, and he was grateful his back was to Rory and Harry. It spared them from seeing what surely had to be a lecherous grin between bites of pastry while the food reheated in the microwave.

"Would you think I'm rude if I just stand at the counter and eat?" Nick asked. "I've been sitting and lying down too much."

Harry waved away his concerns and continued working.

Nick enjoyed watching Harry and Rory interact because they fed off one another's energy. He couldn't remember the last time he'd seen his little brother so happy. Maybe before their mom died? Maybe never. Rory was clearly in his element and thriving. After Nick finished eating, he rinsed his dishes and put them in the dishwasher. He ruffled Rory's hair like old times on his way out of the kitchen.

"Paybacks will be hell after you recover," Rory said as he straightened his hair.

Nick still had one more week in the sling before he could start physical therapy. He needed to find a facility close by to knock that off the list. Cash's office door had been shut when he walked by on his way to breakfast. He'd heard Cash's voice and figured he was on a phone call or Zoom meeting, so Nick didn't interrupt him. The door was open now, and he didn't hesitate to poke his head inside. Cash looked up from typing and smiled. He wore a pair of black glasses that made him look even sexier. The mouth that had been wrapped around his dick spread into a warm smile.

"Good morning," Cash said. "I saved you a plate of food."

Nick eased into the room and shut the door behind him, earning a bigger grin. "I already enjoyed it. Thanks for the glazed donut." He'd kept the innuendo out of his voice, but he could tell Cash received the message loud and clear. Nick walked around to Cash's side of the desk and sat on the edge directly in front of him. Cash placed his hands on Nick's hips and tipped his head back for a kiss. Nick leaned forward and took his time teasing Cash's lips open and tasting his mouth before straightening back up.

"What's on your agenda?" Cash asked.

"Charge my laptop and find a local physical therapist. Take a nap." Both his brain and injured body needed the rejuvenating sleep. "Once I get some mobility and strength back, I can do more stuff to help around here." He'd tried to lend his good hand, but everyone shot him down. "Earn my keep."

"You don't need to earn anything," Cash said. "But I'd be going out of my mind if the roles were reversed, so I'll try to think of something."

"Appreciate it." Nick slid off the desk to his feet. "I'll get out of your hair so you can get back to work. A minute wasted is a million lost."

Cash snorted. "Hardly." He snagged Nick's hand before he could get too far. Cash's baby blues smoldered with intensity. "I want to take you on a date."

It would be their first. "I would love that."

"Where would you like to go?" Cash asked.

Nick nearly said Cabo San Lucas but realized Cash might take him seriously. "You pick. I will love any place as long as you're there."

Cash blessed Nick with a smile that was both angelic and devious at the same time. Just what idea was forming in his brilliant brain? "One more kiss," Cash said.

Nick obliged and left Cash glassy-eyed and needy. He headed to the library, plugged in his laptop, and got comfortable with it on the couch. Nick had truly intended to look for a physical therapist, but when he pulled up the browser, he typed in Samuel Jeremiah's name instead. Several articles came up from area newspapers, blog posts, and news channels. Nick hovered over the top link for a few seconds before clicking it. Burke had made his stance clear to Cash, who'd relayed the messages to Nick, but what they didn't know wouldn't hurt them. Nick put on his headphones and clicked the first video.

Two hours later, he'd reviewed everything twice. The first pass was just to get a feel for the things being reported. The second time, he wanted to read or watch the order in which things got reported. In doing so, an obvious pattern had emerged. Samuel Jeremiah and Salvation Anew put all their energy on attacking the casinos and drinking establishments until they garnered media attention. After that, Jeremiah only frothed at the mouth over Redemption Ridge. Nick needed to know who this Samuel Jeremiah guy was, where he came from, and why he had an ax to grind against Cash. He had the tools at his fingertips to do it but was technically on leave. That would raise some major red flags, which he wanted to avoid.

Nick retrieved his phone from his pocket and dialed his closest friend and ally at the Bureau, Andi Spitz.

"You're supposed to be on leave, Nick," Andi said when she picked up.

"I am, and that's why I'm calling you."

Andi sighed dramatically, and Nick pictured the eye roll that accompanied it. "Hang on a minute." He heard her high heels clicking as she hurried. A door swung open, more rapid footsteps, and then creaking hinges.

"Are you taking me into the bathroom?" Nick asked.

"Yes. I sensed you needed to ask a favor you might not want overheard."

"This is why you're my favorite," Nick told her.

"These bullshit lines are why you're single," Andi shot back.

Nick didn't bother to correct her and got straight to the point. "I've just got a terrible feeling about this guy," he added once he finished.

"Samuel Jeremiah sounds unstable at best and downright unhinged at worst. I'll see what I can find out for you, but I'm really swamped right now." Andi lowered her voice and added, "They're keeping me on a pretty tight leash at the moment."

A wave of guilt washed over him because it was her willingness to assist him that had landed her in hot water. And there he was, doing it again. "I'm—"

Andi cut him off with an impatient growl. "Do not apologize one more time. We did the right thing then, and I'd bet good money you're doing the right thing now. I've got your back, Nick."

"Thanks." Relief flooded through him, easing his tense muscles. "And, hey," Nick said before she could disconnect, "is your brother still looking for instructors at the police academy in Colorado Springs?"

"He is," she replied. "You know someone who's interested?"

Nick expected saying goodbye to this dream would be harder, but all he felt was solace. "Yeah, I do. Can you tell me the best way to get in touch with him?"

chapter
ELEVEN

CASH HEARD THE SHOWER RUNNING WHEN HE ENTERED the bedroom suite. The image of Nick naked and wet was almost more than he could resist, but he was in a time crunch. An idea for a perfect date had popped up in Cash's head almost immediately that morning, but it had taken a bit of finagling to make the arrangements. Cash rarely used his clout to get his way, but he would've done so to make this date perfect. Luckily, everything clicked into place with a little extra effort and money. Seeing the look on Nick's face when he realized what they were doing would justify any cost.

By the time Nick strolled into the bedroom, Cash was zipping up the oversized weekender. He glanced up and froze. Nick's hair was several shades darker when wet and stood out in every direction. The towel he'd rubbed over his head was now wrapped haphazardly around his waist. One faint breeze and that sucker would drop to his feet. Cash wanted to help the towel along its way, but they'd be late if he touched Nick right then.

Nick darted a glance at the overnight bag on the bed, then back to Cash. His gorgeous lips turned down at the corners briefly before Nick recovered. "Packed bag and a scowl on your face. What's wrong? Did you get called away on business?"

Cash shook his head rapidly as if he could clear his face of an expression like it was an Etch A Sketch. "Nothing's wrong," Cash replied. He laid his hand on top of the bag and added, "This is for both of us. The scowling is because I don't have time to toss that towel to the floor and do the things I want to do to you."

Nick dropped both hands to his waist, opened the towel, and showed off every glorious inch of his toned body. He was still five or ten pounds below his normal weight, but Rory and Harry's cooking would fix that in no time. They'd gotten off to a great jumpstart already and Cash planned to pick up the ball and run with it during the sentimental weekend he'd planned. The reminder stopped Cash before he could start toward Nick. Cash released a frustrated growl instead.

Checking his watch, Cash said, "We need to be on the road in fifteen minutes. Need help getting dressed?"

Nick reached for the folded clothes he'd laid on the bed. "Nope." He gripped a pair of hunter-green briefs in both hands and held them in front of him.

"Where's your sling?"

"I found a highly rated physical therapist in Colorado Springs. I scheduled my initial appointment with Heather next week, and we had a brief Zoom call once she received my records from the hospital. She discouraged me from using the sling twenty-four seven. My shoulder could freeze up and cause more damage than using it at my comfort level. Heather also emailed a few exercises I can do until my appointment. She advised me to only use the sling when I'm fatigued or need added stability."

"Where is it, and I'll add it to the bag?" Cash asked.

"On the bathroom vanity." Nick looked at the bag again. "Did you already pack clothes for both of us?"

"I did," Cash replied. He stopped and gave Nick a quick kiss. "All you have to do is get dressed. I've taken care of everything else."

"No one has whisked me away before."

"Get used to it," Cash called over his shoulder.

He grabbed the sling and retraced his steps. Nick stood by the bed in just his underwear and rummaged through the bag.

Cash stepped beside him and gently nudged Nick out of the way. "Huh-uh. Get dressed."

Nick rolled his eyes and reached for his jeans—er, Cash's jeans. He'd noticed Nick wore his clothes instead of his own. It was startling how much the simple gesture moved Cash. "I noticed you packed all the lube I purchased from Hope."

Cash cocked his head to the side. "Do I look like an idiot to you?" He scrunched up his face as he considered the twelve years spent dancing around one another instead of with each other. "Don't answer that."

Nick laughed and pulled his jeans on. Cash sat down on the bed and tried not to whine pitifully as he covered up his gorgeous body. A text came through his phone informing him of the helicopter's ETA. He got up and retrieved two light jackets from the closet.

"So we're not going someplace hot and sunny?" Nick asked, reaching for a lightweight ivory sweater.

"Not this time."

The men both lavished love on Patsy, who looked pissed that she wasn't going with them. She actually loved riding in a helicopter, but Cash needed to give his full attention to Nick this weekend. Quality time wasn't just something Cash craved from Nick; Cash wanted to give an abundance of it to Nick also.

Cash unlocked the BMW with the key fob, and Nick laughed.

"I see how it is."

"You wear my clothes," Cash countered. "Better than I do, I might add."

"Not possible," Nick said as he opened the passenger door.

He got buckled in while Cash stowed the bag and climbed behind the wheel. The sun was barely peeking over the mountains when they pulled out of the ranch's long drive and onto the county road. Cash could navigate the twists and turns with his eyes closed, and the looming darkness wouldn't slow him down. He just wanted to be in the air to catch most of the sunset with Nick. Cash signaled and turned off the main road onto a narrower, less traveled one.

"What the hell are you up to?" Nick asked.

"You're about to see in three minutes."

Nick sat up straighter when the sign for the county airport came into view. "Where are we going?"

"Not telling," Cash said when he turned into the drive.

A sleek black helicopter was waiting for them on the helipad. Cash pulled Nick's swanky sedan inside an empty hangar the airport reserved for VIP parking. He wanted nothing to happen to Nick's baby while they were away.

"Ready?" Cash asked when he turned off the car.

Nick grinned with unabashed excitement. "Is that chopper for us?"

"It is," Cash said.

"I won't ask where we're going again. I'm just going to enjoy the adventure."

Cash kissed him quickly. "That's my guy."

The whining whir of the helicopter's rotors was deafening as they approached the helipad. The pilot, Derrick, shouted his introductions before shaking both their hands. He reached inside the black beast and pulled out two sets of headphones for them and mimed putting them on. Cash and Nick climbed inside the aircraft and placed the headphones on their heads. They not only allowed them to communicate with the pilot but muted a lot of the noise from the engine and rotors. Derrick shut their door, climbed into the cockpit, and cycled through a series of equipment checks.

"You gentlemen ready?" he asked them.

"Yes, sir," they replied.

"We'll be just in time to see the sun disappear behind the Rockies," Derrick said as they lifted off the ground.

Nick reached over and took his hand. Cash lifted it to his mouth for a kiss before turning his full attention out the side window. The sun looked like it was melting into the mountain, making the snowy caps look like molten lava. The view was so breathtaking Cash couldn't speak.

"Incredible view, isn't it?" Derrick asked.

"Stunning," Cash replied.

"Indeed." Nick's voice sounded as thick as molasses. Cash turned his head and caught Nick looking at him instead of the sunset. Nick pointed at him and mouthed, "You are stunning."

Cash suddenly didn't care about Derrick's comfort level with two men kissing in his aircraft. He leaned forward and kissed Nick hard. Soft lips parted, inviting him in, but Cash kept it chaste. Mostly. He slid the tip of his tongue in just enough to make Nick tighten his grip. Their gazes and smiles held when they broke apart.

"You guys been together long?" Derrick asked.

"Twelve years," Nick replied. The answer rolled off his tongue too fast to be rehearsed.

Cash quirked his brow but didn't contradict him. He'd given his heart to Nick that first weekend together. Maybe Nick had done the same to him. They still had a lot to discuss, but this weekend would be perfect for it.

"About the same time I met my husband," Derrick replied. "We're incredibly lucky tonight because we'll have calm winds when flying into Denver."

Nick's right brow shot up, and his mouth curved into a wicked smile. He might know where they were going, but that didn't tell the full story. Cash winked and turned his attention back out the windows as the world around them grew darker. They flew in companionable silence until the city lights of Denver appeared on the horizon. At first, they looked like a million fireflies flickering in an inky black sky, but the cityscape took shape as they got closer. The helicopter's lights bounced off the buildings' glass as they weaved among them.

Derrick spoke with air traffic control to identify his aircraft, his flight plan, and landing destination. Cash watched Nick's face for his reaction and was glad he did. The twinkling in Nick's gaze threatened to outshine the dazzling lights around them. A few minutes later, Derrick smoothly landed the helicopter on top of Cash's apartment building.

Nick removed his headphones and hung them on the hook in front of his seat. Cash did the same, and they unlatched their seat belts. Derrick exited the cockpit and held open the back door for them. They thanked the pilot for the ride before ducking and jogging toward the door on top of the building. Cash entered a code into a keypad and the red light turned green. He pulled the door open and guided Nick inside with his hand on his lower back. Nick whirled on him as the lock reengaged.

"You paid to have a helipad added to the roof?" Nick asked. "I can't believe the owners allowed it." He tilted his head and said, "Wait. You bought the building, didn't you?"

"Yep," Cash said. "The previous owner hired the shittiest companies to manage the property. When I complained, the pompous asshole suggested I find a better company if I didn't like the way things were. So I did, but I bought the building from him first."

Nick whistled. "Bet that cost a small fortune."

"Not as much as it would have if he hadn't let the property managers run it into the ground. I made the necessary repairs, which meant a high retention of current tenants. Then I converted the empty apartments into weekly Airbnb rentals. I'm on my way to recouping my money faster than my projections."

Nick backed Cash toward the wall near an elevator bank. "As much as I find your financial prowess utterly sexy, I'd like to know what you plan to do to me."

"To you or with you?" Cash asked when his back hit the wall. He lost his ability to think when Nick pressed the full length of his body against him. "You're hard."

Nick's mouth spread into a wicked smile. "So fucking hard." He pushed the call button and said, "Is this your private elevator?"

Cash reached between their bodies and stroked the back of his fingers over Nick's erection. "Yes," he whispered huskily. "Opens up inside my apartment."

"Cameras?"

Cash swallowed hard, discovered he couldn't speak, and shook his head.

The elevator arrived with a *ding*. Nick fisted Cash's shirt and pulled him inside, then backed him against the wall. "Unzip me and take my cock out."

Cash fumbled with Nick's belt but deftly worked the button open and zipper down. He reached inside Nick's underwear and wrapped his fingers around his shaft. Nick punched his hips forward and bucked against his palm. Cash leaned forward and sucked at the sensitive spot on Nick's neck. "I'm going to have you just like I did the first time, Nicky."

Cash dropped to his knees and swirled his tongue around the head of Nick's leaking cock. Last time, he'd waited for the privacy of his apartment to go down on Nick, but privacy in his personal elevator wasn't an issue. Cash tugged the denim and cotton down farther to get better access. Nick placed his palms against the elevator wall and rocked his hips in shallow bursts, rubbing his dick against Cash's tongue. The elevator stopped, and the door opened to his apartment.

Nick took two quick steps back and tugged his pants up while Cash pouted and stood up. He picked up the weekender bag and stepped inside Cash's apartment. Nick stood in the living room, and Cash imagined he was cataloging what had changed over the years. They'd avoided the place after their wild weekend, choosing to meet in public places instead. They'd spent some time at Nick's condo because it didn't hold the same memories these rooms did. When Cash moved to the ranch full time, he'd taken his favorite furniture and art pieces with him. That was about the time he purchased and remodeled portions of the building. His city space had the same sleek modern feel but with a few minor differences. Cash was certain Nick's keen eye had clocked them all.

"The view is as stunning as I remember," Nick whispered. He gently set the bag on the black marble floors and crossed to the wall of windows. He reached out and ran his hand over the velvet replacement sofa Cash would fuck him on.

"Was just about to say the same thing."

Nick looked at Cash over his shoulder and smiled. The city lights reflected off the golden strands of Nick's hair. *Fucking beautiful.* Cash longed to see those same lights flickering all over Nick's skin as he moved in and out of him. Knowing they'd need the supplies he'd packed, Cash lifted the bag off the floor and followed Nick at a slower pace. He set it down on an ottoman as he passed. Nick turned his back on the city and faced Cash as he approached. His jeans hung open to give a peek at the underwear beneath. Nick was still hard, and a small wet spot made the green fabric look black.

Twelve years ago, they hadn't made it this far into the room before Cash fell to his knees and sucked Nick off. They'd stumbled through the door, which Cash had shut, locked, and shoved Nick against. It had been wet, sloppy, and oh-so fucking good.

"You made a man of me that weekend," Nick said.

Cash's breath hitched in his throat and his steps faltered. "You were hardly innocent, baby."

"True," Nick agreed. He'd been twenty-five after all. "But so much of my life up to that point was about following someone else's orders or wishes. My schooling, my friends, and even my career trajectory. I'd wanted to go into law enforcement after getting my criminal justice degree. The local academies weren't good enough. If I was to pursue a career in the field, it should be the most powerful agency in the country. But you…" He took the three steps remaining between himself and Cash. Nick cupped his face and stroked his thumb over Cash's beard. "Going home with you was something I did just for myself." Nick leaned in and kissed his lips softly. "I spent another twelve years toeing the line and working hard for one promotion after another. Nothing was ever good enough for the standards I set. Something was always missing." Nick nuzzled his nose against Cash's neck and inhaled deeply. "*You* were missing. I had you in my life," Nick said before Cash could protest, "but I didn't have you in my bed. I didn't get to lay claim to your heart. I didn't get to call you mine. The rest of the bullshit didn't matter. So I returned to you, Saint. You're my heart, my home." Nick took Cash's hand and placed it on his erection. "Please make me yours again."

Cash growled low in his throat as he stroked the length of Nick's cock. "You've always been mine, and it's time I prove it."

Cash had expected a hot, hard fuck like their first time, but Nick's heartfelt confession set a different tone for Cash's seduction plans. He'd brought them to the apartment more as a full-circle gesture than starting over, so it only felt right to touch, kiss, and love Nick as the man Cash was now. He took Nick's hand and led him into the master bedroom suite. The room dominated one corner of the building, and with two outer walls constructed of windows, they doubled the amount of city light filtering into the space. It reflected off the tiny silver flecks in the black marble, turning the floor into a sea of stars.

Cash released Nick's hand to remove his phone from his pocket. He accessed the app that controlled all the smart features in the space. He adjusted the bedroom lights to the softest setting and met Nick's gaze. "Drapes open or closed?" The windows had a special treatment that allowed occupants to feel like a part of the city without allowing the city to observe them. Nick had taken full advantage of the nifty feature their first weekend together, but Cash didn't want to make assumptions.

Nick's smile turned wicked as he carefully pulled the sweater he'd borrowed from Cash over his head. He stepped out of his casual loafers and shoved his jeans down his long, toned legs. Cash had his answer and responded in kind but worked backward from Nick. Shoes and socks first, jeans, then shirt. They stood in their underwear facing each other, close enough to touch but neither moving. Nick's hands might've been still, but his eyes weren't. Cash felt Nick's ardent gaze touch him everywhere. It amplified his arousal and made him question which of them was the seducer. Cash inhaled slowly, feeling his nostrils flare as he did. Nick's arousal teased his senses and made his dick throb. Cash began his own perusal, starting with the luscious mouth Cash wanted on his body. Nick had more chest hair than he'd had then, and it was several shades darker than his sandy brown. Cash let his gaze linger on Nick's hard nipples and recalled how sensitive they'd been. Sculpted abs, though slightly less defined now, and a tapered waist guided Cash's attention to the erection bulging under the dark-green fabric. The wet spot was bigger, and it made Cash's mouth water. The quick taste in the elevator wasn't enough.

"I'm going to come just from you eye-fucking me." Nick's husky voice made Cash snap his gaze back up to his handsome face. "I'm not sure when this"—Nick gestured to his crotch—"will happen again. So…"

Cash took two steps forward and dropped to his knees. Nick palmed the back of Cash's head and pressed his face to his crotch. The scent was intoxicating, and Cash nuzzled his lips and mouth against Nick's erection through his underwear. Cash slid his hands over Nick's trembling thighs until he reached the waistband. He took his time slipping the underwear over Nick's erection and down his legs. Cash had fantasized about having this opportunity again more times than he could count. The reality far surpassed both his memory and imagination. Nick's erection felt like velvet-covered steel when Cash licked a path from root to tip. The fingers in his hair were tighter, and Nick's moans were needier than he'd dreamed. And fuck. Nick tasted so damn good. Man and musk, made just for him. Cash swirled his tongue around the swollen head, lapping up the precum pearl at its slit.

"Saint," Nick groaned. "Please."

Cash eased back and looked from his submissive position. "Suck you? Fuck you?"

Nick's wicked mouth curved into a wry smile. "Anything. Put me out of my misery."

Wants and needs. Cash wanted to make them both come hard and fast, but that wasn't what they needed. He rose to his feet, took Nick's hand, and led him to the bed.

Nick stretched out in the center, and Cash couldn't help but look at him in mesmerized wonder. Nick trailed his fingers over his erection and gasped from the pleasure of touching himself. His Nick. Naked, erect, and stretched out like a carnal offering. Cash shoved his underwear down his legs and kicked it free. Nick bent his knees and planted his heels wide apart, then sucked two fingers into his mouth while watching Cash's reaction. He lowered those wet digits between his legs and began prepping his pucker, swirling them around his rim before pushing the tip of his middle finger in the center. Nick and Cash groaned simultaneously, the latter as he climbed on the bed and positioned himself on his stomach between those splayed thighs.

Drawing Nick's fingers away, Cash gripped Nick's thighs and said, "I've got you, baby."

Cash's tongue followed the same path Nick's fingers had taken. He swirled his tongue around and around the crinkled rim until Nick's pucker quivered in anticipation. He wiggled the tip of his tongue against the entrance to get it sopping wet, then curled his tongue and pushed inside. Nick shouted something unintelligible and reached down to stroke himself. Cash smacked his hand away and continued wiggling his tongue deeper inside Nick's entrance until his nose pressed into Nick's taint. He nuzzled that erogenous zone while prepping Nick's hole. Cash had forgotten to grab the bag with the lube from Hope's store, but he kept a stash in his nightstand with condoms.

"Saint. So good it hurts. Stroke me."

Cash growled and nuzzled his taint once more before easing his tongue free of the tight ring of pulsing muscles. He leaned toward the nightstand, but Nick grabbed his arm.

"No condoms. I haven't had a sexual partner in a long time, and I've been tested for everything at least twice while searching for a diagnosis. I don't want to have anything between us."

"I haven't been with anyone either but kept up with testing," Cash said. "I've never been bare inside anyone. Never wanted it until you." The only time he'd ever resented even the thinnest latex barrier was with Nick. Cash's dick throbbed in time with his heartbeat. "Are you sure?"

"Never been more certain of anyone or anything. You're it for me, Saint." It was the closest thing to a declaration of love either of them had made.

Cash altered course to lean over Nick and kissed him hungrily for several moments before easing back. "You're it for me too." He pried himself away from Nick's hot skin and sexy body long enough to grab the lube. "We'll retrieve the good stuff later."

Ignoring his body's urges and Nick's whimpered pleas against his lips, Cash took his time prepping Nick to receive him. Once he worked three fingers inside Nick, Cash eased from the quivering clench. He drizzled lube along his erection and slicked himself before lining the head up with Nick's pucker. Cash met and held Nick's gaze when he pushed past the first ring of muscle.

Nick's moan was low and needy as he pulled his knees back toward his chest. "Kiss me."

Cash leaned forward, loving the rasp of Nick's leg hair against his ribs, and kissed him. Nick slid his hand into Cash's hair, holding his head in place. Cash's entrance into the tight channel was tentative and slow, inching forward small increments at a time to let Nick adjust. Their kiss was a carnal, hot melding of lips, teeth, and tongues. The only sounds in the room were soft pants, shared breaths, and the occasional gasp or moan as Cash slowly slid home. The dichotomy was a bit of a mind fuck and threatened to overload Cash's circuits.

Nick yanked his hair, but Cash wouldn't speed up, partly out of concern for Nick's comfort but mostly because he was probably two pumps away from coming. Nick bit Cash's bottom lip hard enough to make him jerk back, but he only smiled down at his frustrated lover. Nick wrapped his legs around Cash's back and used the hold as leverage to rock his hips up until Cash was balls deep inside him. Black dots danced in Cash's vision as Nick released a victorious shout and undulated his hips. With Cash's weight pinning him to the mattress, Nick could only work up and down a few inches. But the head of Cash's dick pegged Nick's prostate again and again.

"Yes! Fuck yes!" Nick cried out.

Cash's control snapped and he took over—pulling back and slamming home. Nick's cries became incoherent pleas as Cash pummeled him without worrying about finesse. He felt the warning tingle in his spine and angled his dick to nail Nick's prostate with each forward thrust. Nick stiffened beneath him, and his muscles strained beneath his skin. His eyes, glistening with unshed tears, found Cash's and held. *I've got you.* Cash snapped his hips forward again, and Nick released his held breath on a guttural cry. Cash dropped his gaze in time to watch the first jet of cum splatter high on Nick's chest. Mindless of his own needs, he pistoned his hips faster to draw out Nick's pleasure. Joyous laughter bubbled out of Nick's gorgeous mouth, and his body relaxed. Cash fused their mouths together and spilled inside the hot, tight channel still spasming around his cock.

He collapsed on top of Nick, who wrapped his arms and legs around him to keep Cash close. Nick kissed his damp temple and trailed his hand up and down Cash's back. They were as close as two people could be, but Cash craved more. He turned his head, and they kissed lazily until their breathing and heart rates returned to normal. Cash carefully withdrew and invited Nick to join him in the shower, where the kissing and touching continued.

Afterward, Cash's phone pinged with a message as they redressed. "Our dinner has arrived. I'll go down to the lobby to get it."

"Wait." Nick reached out and zipped Cash's jeans. They hadn't bothered putting underwear back on, which would've been obvious to anyone in the lobby. "I don't share."

"Neither do I."

It didn't take him long to retrieve their dinner and return to the penthouse suite. Nick had stretched out on the sofa and was gazing at the bustling city below when the elevator opened. He noticed the restaurant's name printed on the bag and smiled. It was the same place that had hosted the benefit where they'd met.

"Porterhouse with peppercorn sauce, baked sweet potato, and broccoli," Cash said as he set the bag on the coffee table.

Nick quirked a brow. "You remember what I ate?"

"I remember everything about you, Nicky."

Nick sat up and met his gaze. "I remember everything about you. Seafood fettuccine alfredo."

Cash smiled and handed him his food. "We can eat at the kitchen island or in the dining room if you'd prefer."

Nick shook his head and folded his legs under him on the couch. "This is perfect." He didn't dig into his food right away, though his eagerness to do so was palpable.

Cash retrieved a bottle of red wine and poured them both a generous serving. Then he sat on the couch next to Nick, mirroring his position, and tapped his glass to Nick's. "To us."

"To us."

They both took a drink, then tucked into the food. Their only conversation was a limited exchange about how good it tasted. It reminded Cash of the meal they'd shared at the benefit. Then, his thoughts had primarily swirled around how sexy Nick looked in his tuxedo and how much he wanted to see it strewn all over his apartment floor. Maybe he'd manifested that dream into reality, or perhaps his gaze had betrayed his intense reaction to Nick. The how and why didn't matter when the result far exceeded the fantasy.

"Did you save room for dessert?" Cash asked when they finished their entrées.

"No, but I'll give it my best shot." Nick reached into the bag and pulled out two containers. "Let me guess. One is three layers of decadent chocolate cake and the other is white chocolate and raspberry cheesecake."

Cash winked, and Nick opened the containers. He chuckled when

Nick handed the cheesecake to Cash and kept the cake for himself. "That's not the way it happened," Cash said.

Nick sighed and swapped boxes with him. They each took a bite of their dessert before swapping back. Cash had practically salivated when he'd seen the chocolate layer cake on the menu but was immediately jealous of Nick's cheesecake when it arrived. Nick had eye-fucked his dessert enough to make Cash blush. After a bite, Cash had asked if he wanted to switch.

"Thought you'd never ask," Nick had said as he slid his plate toward Cash.

What had followed was foreplay with food. Cash hadn't been able to tear his gaze away from Nick's lips whenever he brought the fork to his mouth. He had hoped his throaty purrs called to something wild and primitive in Nick. And, Christ, had he answered.

Twelve years later, Nick's smug smile said he knew exactly where Cash's thoughts had gone.

Pointing his fork at Cash, Nick said, "That expression right there is what gave me the courage to proposition you."

Cash snorted and nearly sent his bite of cheesecake down the wrong pipe. "You got out 'Do you wanna' before I said, 'Thought you'd never ask.' Later, I realized how presumptuous I was. You could've been about to ask if I wanted to join you for an after-dinner drink."

Nick's lips twitched. "A fine bourbon was on my mind."

Cash narrowed his eyes as he tried to figure out if Nick was joking.

Nick set his box down to kiss Cash hard on the mouth. "Get out of here with your doubts. The only shot I wanted was a ride on your cock." He winked and picked up his dessert to resume eating. "Luckily, I got several."

"As did I." Cash canted his head. Nick was the most relaxed he'd seen him...since the beginning. "Want to hear a secret?"

Nick arched a brow but said nothing because his mouth was full of chocolate cake.

"I strained my hamstring that weekend. Had to ice that son of a bitch down for a solid week after you left."

Nick swallowed his bite and grinned. "I noticed an occasional minor hitch in your step and chalked it up to a different type of overuse."

"Yeah, that too," Cash agreed.

They only made it through half their dessert before putting the leftovers in the refrigerator and cleaning up the mess. Once they restored order, Cash turned on the sound system through his phone and dimmed the lights.

"There's something I've always wanted to do with you," Cash said. When "The Only Exception" by Paramore began to play, Cash extended his hand. Nick accepted it and stepped into the circle of Cash's arms. "I remember this song playing at the benefit, and I wanted to dance with you so badly. I didn't have the courage to ask." He offered Nick a wry smile. "But right now, I don't need to worry about keeping an appropriate distance so a room full of people won't know how much I want you."

Nick sighed and rested his forehead against Cash's shoulder. After a few rotations, he turned his head and nuzzled his nose against Cash's neck. "So this is what it's like to date you, Saint."

Cash's heart pounded in his chest as he debated a reply. A simple yes or the truth? He wasn't exactly sure which he'd decided until the words tumbled from his lips. "No, Nicky, this is what it's like to be loved by me."

chapter
TWELVE

NICK JERKED HIS HEAD UP SO FAST HE NEARLY CLIPPED CASH'S chin. His heart pumped at about three times its normal speed. He hadn't felt this winded since completing the Bureau's PFT. The FBI didn't just put someone through a background check before letting a person attend their academy. They put candidates through four hellish physical tests that left Nick sucking wind and fighting off the urge to puke. Nick's response to Cash's remark triggered a similar reaction, though for a vastly different reason. Could a man like Cash truly love him?

Sensing Nick's distress, Cash smiled and kissed him gently. "You don't need to say anything back. I just need you to know a few things before we stray any farther from the friendship path we agreed on."

Nick stopped suddenly, forcing Cash to do so too. "Saint, we've already waded too far into the weeds. I couldn't find that old trail if I wanted to, and I don't," he said emphatically. "And if you're going to spill secrets tonight, I will too." Nick took a deep breath and said, "I only attended the charity event the second year because I knew you were going to be there."

Cash tipped his head to the side and studied Nick through narrowed eyes. "How did you know?"

"I asked," Nick replied. "It took me the better part of a year to work up the courage to approach you again."

"You spent four months at Quantico," Cash reminded him.

"Where I jerked off to memories of us. I spent the following six trying to convince myself that we really weren't as great together as I remembered."

Cash traced the curve of Nick's scruffy jaw. He hadn't shaved since arriving at the ranch, and he liked the rasp of Cash's finger over his stubble. Maybe he'd try growing a beard. "And the last two months before the benefit?"

Nick turned his head and nipped Cash's finger as it neared his mouth. "I worked up the courage to seek you out. Spoiler alert: I didn't have friendship on my mind. I wanted a neutral location rather than showing up at your apartment or office and risking rejection."

"Did you finagle another invitation to the benefit to see me?" Cash asked.

"Shamelessly."

Cash's eyes widened. "You involved your billionaire stepfather in your schemes?"

Nick laughed. "I tried to play it off real cool. Mentioned we had some fun conversations and that I thought you were interesting." Heat crept up his neck at the memory.

"And?" Cash prompted.

"Let's just say we didn't play our sudden departure as coolly as we thought."

Cash growled and kissed Nick hungrily. He pulled back suddenly and smiled. "They're just lucky I didn't throw you down in the center of the table and ravish you like I wanted to."

"Which time?"

"Both! I didn't know you were interested in me when you showed up for the second year. Why didn't you say something?"

Nick had been asking himself that for quite some time too. They'd both arrived solo, and the spark was just as intense as it had been the previous year. "You intimidated me, I think."

"You think? I'm not flattered," Cash teased.

"Not in a bad way."

"I'm not convinced intimidation is ever a good thing. What about me was off-putting?"

Nick shook his head vigorously. "Nothing about you repelled me. I just suddenly felt like an inadequate kid."

"With me?" Cash asked. "You grew up with the wealthiest man in the state as your stepfather."

"It's not about the money." Nick worked his bottom lip as he searched for the right phrasing. "You were different."

"How so?"

"Everything. You stood taller, carried yourself with more confidence, and took up space in a way that said you belonged there." Nick blew out a breath of frustration because he was botching his explanation. "The prior year, I got the impression you felt like an outsider."

"I did," Cash admitted.

"And so did I," Nick told him. "People forget that I wasn't used to a lavish lifestyle until I was a preteen. I still felt like an uncouth country bumpkin fifteen years later when I attended the benefit at Charles's behest. Fast-forward a year, and I had graduated from the academy and boldly finagled an invitation to force another run-in with you. But you weren't the person I remembered. The attraction was still there. I saw it flare in your eyes before you hid it beneath a cool mask. And that was new too," Nick added quickly. "You'd telegraphed your every thought the first time we met."

Cash chuckled. "And that's how Charles knew what we got up to when we left so suddenly."

"And everyone else too," Nick added.

Cash groaned and scrubbed a hand over his face. He stepped back from Nick, linked their fingers together, and headed toward the couch. This time, Cash sat cross-legged sideways on the couch, and Nick mirrored his position so their knees and bare feet touched. Cash took Nick's hands in both of his. "You're not the only one changed by our first encounter. You're the reason I seemed so poised and comfortable when we reconnected."

Nick straightened and scowled at Cash. "How could that possibly be?"

"You might've noticed I had a chip on my shoulder at the first benefit," Cash replied wryly.

Nick thought back to the moment he'd first seen Cash in the sea of black suits in the restaurant's private dining room. Though he had dressed just as elegantly as everyone else, there was a stubborn tilt to Cash's chin and an air of defiance that made him stand out in the crowd. The latter drew Nick to him like a beacon. Their eyes met and held for a few heartbeats before Charles approached Nick with someone he just had to meet. The introduction was brief and unremarkable. Hell, Nick couldn't even remember who it was. He wanted to save all his attention for the stranger whose attire read business executive but whose eyes promised trouble. Nick couldn't have turned his head more than a minute, two tops, but the mystery man had moved on.

He'd been more than a little disappointed, which had unsettled him. Nick had never lacked for company when he wanted it and even when he didn't. He'd circulated through the room and chatted with those he knew and introduced himself to those he didn't. He might've been newer to the game, but he'd been a quick study. By the time he reached the bar in the back, Nick had accepted that he'd either imagined the man or he'd left the benefit. He kept his back to the room while he waited for the bartender to pour his whiskey. That's when the hair on the back of his neck stood up. Nick had known the sexy stranger was approaching before his woodsy scent tickled his senses. He was half-aroused when he turned around and raked an appraising gaze over the man who'd captured his attention so thoroughly. Nick half expected the guy to be less impressive up close. He'd been so wrong.

"There you are." Nick hadn't meant to speak the words out loud.

"Here I am." The stranger's voice was rough and low, better suited for a bedroom than a boardroom.

Unfortunately for Nick, he'd spoken that one out loud too. It had set the tone for the rest of the evening, and luckily for him, they'd been on the same page. If he didn't pull himself from his trip down memory lane, Nick wouldn't get to find out how he had inspired the changes in Cash he'd witnessed the following year.

"I recall a slight chip on your shoulder," Nick replied, picking up the thread of their current conversation. "Barely noticeable."

Cash snorted. "It could've powered the world's largest supercomputer."

"Is this where you get to the part where I saved you?" Nick teased.

"Yes." Cash leaned forward and kissed him. "Do you remember any of the conversations we had between rounds of sex?"

"Every single word." They'd talked almost as much as they'd fucked that weekend, so they'd said a lot of things. "Which of my pearls of wisdom resounded with you?"

Cash narrowed his eyes. "Don't be a smartass. Your intelligence really wowed me, Nicky, and you saw me. Not just the wealthy veneer but the bitter, angry guy beneath it. The benefit organizers didn't invite me because they wanted me there. I was the potential enemy they wanted to keep closer than their friends. Word had gotten out that I was looking to buy struggling companies so I could break them down and sell the pieces for a higher profit."

"And I asked why you wanted to pivot from developing technology to profiting off someone else's downfall. You'd started making a name for yourself as a tech innovator. Hell, you even impressed Charles, and I can't say that about many people."

"The feeling is mutual. Charles is a good man."

"So I couldn't imagine why you would want to take the millions you made from creating and use them as a weapon."

Cash nodded. "You reminded me of the innocent lives that could get ruined in my wake. The lost jobs, homes, and dreams." Cash smirked at him. "You compared me to Richard Gere's character, Edward, in *Pretty Woman*."

Nick shrugged his good shoulder. "I said what I said."

Cash squeezed his hands. "And you were right. I was tired of being a bitter asshole hell-bent on making others miserable. Durrell Padgett had given me a second chance when I left jail. He'd taken me in to his home, given me a job, and showed me what a man should be. I'd worked my ass off and scraped every penny together to pay for community college and then my bachelor's degree. I'd made something of myself because of the grace he showed me and the lessons he taught me. But after my first taste of success, I'd forgotten all about those things, Nicky. I just wanted more money, success, and respect. You can't buy people's regard. You earn it. Tearing things down only creates fear. So I took a virtual stranger's advice and chose to build, mend, and redeem. I brushed that chip off my shoulder and dug in right away. By the time we met again, I didn't feel like an unwanted outsider. People didn't just keep me close to know what I was up to. Powerful people sought me for advice. I felt like I finally belonged."

"I could tell," Nick told him. "And I thought you were out of my league, where before we'd felt like equals."

Cash leaned his forehead against Nick's. "And I wouldn't let myself imagine there could be more for us. I fixated on the age difference. Twelve years doesn't sound like much, but it might as well be fifty when you're at different stages in life."

Nick tilted his head and considered what Cash said. His knee-jerk reaction was to deny they'd been in different stages, but he realized he was only thinking about the sexual chemistry. That had been every bit as strong as the previous year—stronger if he were honest. But Nick hadn't been relationship material back then. He'd just launched a career in the FBI, working a ton of hours and traveling a lot. What could he have offered Cash but occasional scorching sex? Their friendship had felt more important and even more intimate than sex over the years, laying the foundation for the future they both wanted.

"I love you, Saint." Emotion rose so swift and hard, swelling Nick's chest and making his eyes sting. "I've always loved you, but I am so fucking in love with you. You're not just the most important person in my life; you've become my life. These past five months have solidified that I don't want to live apart."

"We don't have to," Cash said in a rush. "I've kept this apartment because I wanted to keep one foot in your world. I'll split my time between Denver and the ranch. It's not like Ivan needs me there."

Nick stopped him with a kiss. "They want you there, Saint, and it's where you belong. It's where *we* belong."

"But your career."

"I'm resigning from the FBI at the end of my leave," Nick said. "Though my career was a source of pride, I was never happy. Instead of figuring out why that was, I put all my energy into earning the next promotion or position. I expected satisfaction to come with each new title or raise. I ended up with more responsibility and dealt with more bureaucratic bullshit than a hundred people could stomach."

Cash watched him without commenting for a long time. "Is that why you lost weight and—"

"Couldn't get it up?" Nick ignored Cash's scowl and continued. "Yeah, that was a big part of it. My therapist helped me realize I'd never properly grieved my mom's death. I'd been too worried about my brother to process the loss for myself. Stressors at work the past eighteen months just set off a tidal wave of hell in my brain." He exhaled. "I need to confess something." Nick's words caused frown lines to form between Cash's brows. "This shouldn't affect our relationship, but I'm afraid if you hear it from someone else, you might assign ulterior motives to me showing up on the ranch." Cash stiffened ever so slightly, and Nick could tell he was bracing himself for something bad. So Nick kissed Cash until the tension eased in his body. When he drew back, Cash's lips were pink, slightly puffy, and wet. He didn't dare let his gaze linger too long or he'd lose his courage. "My trips to Washington and Quantico this year were punishment for the off-book operation I ran that ended up clearing Kieran's name."

Cash's tension returned. "Wait. I thought that bust is what led to your promotion to Special Agent in Charge."

"It did." Pulling those initial strings led to a bigger theft ring. Additional tugging led to busting a major organized crime outfit. It was the kind of case that made careers…if part of the information hadn't resulted from rogue behavior. "But there were things the federal prosecutors uncovered during trial prep that raised some doubts about the validity of evidence and witness testimony. When called to the hot seat, I couldn't lie. I came clean about everything without throwing any of my colleagues under the bus." Nick thought back to his conversation with Andi and winced.

"I'm guessing by your expression they didn't allow you to take one for the team," Cash said.

Nick shook his head. "Not even close. They investigated everyone on my team and anyone they closely associated with in the Bureau. It would've been one thing for me to lose my job or face charges, but they were coming for my team too. I got suspended without pay for a month while they investigated. In the end, none of my actions threatened the prosecution. There were multiple, overlapping investigations going on, so the trial evidence wasn't tied solely to my off-book operation."

"You must've been so relieved," Cash said.

"Yes. I'd accepted that my career was over during my suspension and started thinking about different avenues. But the Bureau extended a very thin olive branch. They sent me to Washington for additional training and then on to Quantico to fill in for the agent on paternity leave. I guess it was supposed to be demeaning, but I absolutely loved working with the recruits. But transferring there isn't an option because you're not there." Cash started to speak, but Nick cut him off with a kiss. "Not an option. Our home is on the ranch, and I have a solution that keeps us there."

"I'm listening."

Nick told Cash about Andi's brother without admitting the initial reason he'd called her. If his hunch turned into something actionable, Nick would come clean to Cash. There was no need to ruin their night with supposition. "I have an interview at the police academy in Colorado Springs soon. A thirty-minute drive to work is much better than a long-distance relationship or you splitting your time between the ranch and Denver. I want to wake up in your arms every morning." Nick expected Cash to respond to this news with a smile and maybe some kissing and petting. He just stared at Nick with an unreadable expression. "Saint?"

Cash lurched forward, pushing Nick backward. He hit the couch with a slight wince, but his discomfort vanished when Cash followed him down. Nick unfolded his legs and wrapped them around Cash's hips.

"Say it again." Cash trailed kisses from Nick's collarbone to his earlobe. Nick squirmed when Cash found a ticklish spot. "Forgot about that one," Cash said, then kissed it again.

Nick fought off an unmanly giggle. "What part do you want me to repeat? The whole thing or—" Nick lost his ability to speak when Cash brushed his beard over the ticklish spot. "Oh my God," Nick said before giving in to a fit of giggles. That led to a full body search for additional vulnerable spots, lingering touches, and languid kisses. "I love you so much," Nick whispered when they were both naked.

"My recovery time has changed drastically since our first weekend together," Cash said stoically.

"And I might not achieve an erection again for a while." Nick looped his good arm around Cash's neck. "I'd settle for a soak in that giant tub overlooking the city."

Cash eased off the couch and stood up. "You grab the wine and glasses, and I'll find candles."

Nick didn't move right away. He lay there and feasted his eyes on the sexiest man he'd ever seen. Mmm, that ass. "You know," Nick said casually, "I'm suddenly in the mood to eat cake."

Cash stopped and pivoted toward the refrigerator until the true meaning of Nick's words registered. "You've got all the time in the world to feast on my cake."

The bathtub was big enough for four people, but Nick wouldn't have wanted to share this man or view with anyone else. Cash climbed in first, and Nick settled between his legs. The water was perfect—hot enough to ease the body and mind but without turning them into lobsters.

Nick ran his hands up and down Cash's hairy thighs. "This is the first time in my life I've felt bone-deep happiness. If Hope could bottle this up and sell it, she'd be a millionaire."

"Your bathwater? Don't give her any ideas." Cash kissed the side of his neck but avoided the spot that had triggered the tickle war. "You honestly don't mind giving all this up?"

"Giving what up? The city? I told you, Saint. You're my home."

Cash caressed his chest, belly, and inner thighs. His fingertips briefly brushed against Nick's balls before he began his upward trek. "You're my home too."

They lingered in the tub, talking and touching until the water cooled. Then they dried off, got into bed, and finished watching season two of *Heartstopper*. He fell asleep after midnight with Cash spooned around him. When Nick woke on his back the next morning, a stunning sunrise greeted him. He also had one hell of an erection tenting the sheets but no Cash to appreciate it. A note by the bed said he'd gone to get bagels. Damn, the place still didn't deliver?

Nick grabbed his phone off the nightstand and took a picture of the tented sheet. He uploaded the photo to their text thread and typed, *Hurry back.*

chapter
THIRTEEN

CASH STEPPED INTO THE LOBBY OF THE APARTMENT building with a bag in one hand and a drink carrier in the other. His phone alerted him to a text, so he tucked the bagel bag in the crook of the other arm and fished the device from his pocket. Instinct told him not to open the message in the busy lobby, so he waited until he was alone in his elevator.

His elevator. He fought back a snort. Whose life was this? On most days, Cash was still the half-starved kid who'd only survived his childhood through the kindness of neighbors in the mobile home park. He'd created a global tech development company from nothing and sold it for fifty million dollars. He owned multiple pieces of real estate, including a ranch where he gave second chances to younger versions of himself. Cash had gone from racing cars on dirt tracks to becoming half-owner of a racing team. More recently, he'd gone from a lonely middle-aged man to someone whose soul mate waited in bed for him. *Seriously, whose life was this?* He would've pinched himself to ensure he wasn't dreaming if he had a free hand.

Cash pressed the penthouse button, raised his phone, and waited for the Face ID to recognize him. He tapped on the message icon and then Nick's name. A tidal wave of lust surged through him when he saw the picture. "Fuck me," he groaned, willing the elevator to go faster. If his hands weren't full, he would've started stripping out of his clothes. The elevator stopped on his floor, and Cash burst through the doors as if shot from a cannon. Two steps into the room, he jerked to a stop. Nick hadn't waited for him in bed; he sat in the center of the velvet couch, stroking his dick. The early morning light filtered into the room at an angle that mimicked a spotlight, and the rest of the room faded into obscurity. Cash couldn't tear his gaze away from Nick's fist lazily working his shaft. The drink carrier trembled in his hand, and Cash pulled himself together. He casually strolled across the expanse of the room instead of sprinting toward Nick's lurid display. Cash set their breakfast on the coffee table and dropped to his knees in front of the sofa. He knocked Nick's hand away and put his mouth there instead.

"Christ, yes," Nick hissed when Cash sucked him all the way down. Fisting his hand in Cash's hair, Nick guided his mouth up and down his leaking shaft. Nick watched him through hooded eyes as Cash worked him over, alternating the pace and suction to maximize arousal. Cash cataloged every moan, plea, and groan he elicited from the man who'd owned his soul for so long. When Nick's thighs quivered, he pulled Cash off him. "Get your clothes off. I'm going to eat your cake and fuck it too."

Cash stood up to strip down so fast it left him dizzy. He gave him-self a moment to regain his balance before turning his back to Nick. A hard smack landed on his ass cheek as Cash bent over. He held on to the table with a white-knuckled grip to keep from planting face-first on the wood. Nick placed his hands on Cash's cheeks and squeezed, pushing the globes together and pulling them apart.

"Mmmm." Nick moaned like Cash's ass was the tastiest treat he'd ever seen.

In response, Cash's dick was harder than it had ever been, even the first time Nick had rimmed him in the same room.

"I'm going to wreck you, Saint," Nick warned. His breath ghosted over Cash's pucker making it pulse with need.

"Please," Cash begged. Nick was the only one who made Cash feel safe enough to show vulnerability. He'd bare anything and everything to this man.

Nick lurched forward and buried his face between Cash's cheeks, attacking his pucker with hot, open-mouthed kisses. Black dots danced before Cash's eyes, and he stiffened his arms to keep himself upright. Nick rubbed his whiskered chin against Cash's taint and the underside of his balls while working his tongue into the tight ring of muscles. Cash's dick jerked, and he thought he might come from this stimulation alone. Risking life and limb, Cash tightly gripped the base of his dick with one hand and kept the other square on the coffee table.

Nick eased up and said, "Don't you dare come yet."

"Just staving it off." But the lure to pump his shaft just once was too much to resist. A loud *crack* sounded in the room as Nick's hand landed hard on Cash's backside. Heat radiated from the spot and spread throughout his body. "Fuck," Cash moaned.

Nick chuckled as much as one could with a mouth full of ass. He eased his tongue free and said, "That was supposed to be a deterrent." Nick returned to his carnal onslaught until Cash's entire body shook with the need to come. He'd never had pleasure hurt so much before.

"Please," he begged. "Want you inside me."

Nick eased free of his ass once more and sank his teeth into a taut globe. He pulled a tube of lube from somewhere and immediately started priming Cash's ass. "Can't wait to stretch you open on my cock."

"Hurry," Cash hissed. But Nick seemed to enjoy dragging out his torture.

Cash didn't give Nick enough time to slick his dick with more lube once he eased his digits free. "Now," Cash said as he reached between his legs to grip Nick's erection. Then he eased back, lined up, and took Nick down to the root in one thrust. They shouted together as their bodies merged. Cash just sat there, letting his body adjust to the penetration while Nick cursed and held him with a bruising grip.

"Don't move," Nick snarled. "Not a single inch. You're so fucking tight, and I'll blow."

Cash was barely hanging on himself, so he should've listened to Nick's command. But he didn't. Cash used his thigh muscles to lift up an inch or two.

"Fuck!" Nick roared as his fingers dug deeper into Cash's flesh. Instead of holding him still, Nick bounced him up and down on his dick.

Their skin slapped together loudly as they chased their orgasms. Nick's body tensed under Cash's as he slammed him down one last time and held Cash flush against his pelvis. Nick gasped, held his breath, and bathed Cash's channel with his hot release. Then he pulled Cash back to lie against his chest and reached around to jerk Cash off. The explosion was immediate, splattering against his chest and abdomen. They remained in that position for a few minutes while they wound down.

"I love you." Sleep and sex roughened Nick's voice, turning Cash inside out.

"I love you too."

Separating their bodies turned into a hilarious scene since their limbs were still limp noodles. They stumbled to the shower and clung to one another beneath the spray. They looked more like shipwreck survivors than lovers, but they seemed content to just hold one another. Eventually, they untangled their bodies, but the touching didn't stop. Cash shampooed Nick's hair since his shoulder ached. Nick thoroughly washed Cash's body, paying extra attention to his favorite nooks and crannies. Once they toweled off and dressed in lounge pants, they resettled on the couch and enjoyed breakfast.

Halfway into his everything bagel piled high with cream cheese, Nick released a moan that made Cash a little jealous. "Even better than twelve years ago."

Cash washed down his bite of cinnamon raisin with a sip of hot apple cider. "Are you talking about us or the bagels?"

"Both. Either everything has gotten better with age, or I just haven't lived these past twelve years."

"I think both can be true there too." Cash sure as hell hadn't experienced life to the fullest, at least not in the romance department. He hadn't lived like a monk by any standards, but his sexual encounters were few and far between. Nick had never mentioned his conquests, and Cash didn't either. He wasn't about to ask questions now. "Especially the not living part," Cash said. How could it be otherwise if they weren't together?

Nick kissed his temple. "Me too, Saint." Then he continued to mow through his bagel. "What's on tap for today?"

"I didn't plan that far ahead," Cash admitted. "I thought we'd play it by ear."

Nick tilted his head to the side. "You still keep a sleek crossover SUV here for city driving?"

"I do."

"How do you feel about going to my place with me so I can pack up the things I'd like to have at the ranch with me? I'll sell or donate the rest so I can put the condo on the market." When Cash only stared at him, Nick laughed nervously. "Too soon?"

Cash shook his head. "God no. I'm struggling to believe this is real. You and me."

"Us," Nick said.

Cash swallowed hard. "We're in love."

"Very much so."

"And moving in together," Cash said.

"We are...if you're—"

Cash launched off the couch before he finished. "I just need to grab the keys."

Laughing, Nick reached for his hand before Cash could walk away. "And shirts and shoes. We don't need to go off half-cocked and mostly nude." Nick raked his gaze over Cash's body and lingered at his crotch.

"And maybe underwear. Those pants drape over your cock and balls so nicely."

Cash looked down at himself, then at Nick's crotch. "Perhaps we take a few minutes to put on real clothes before we pack up your condo."

Nick tugged him back down. "Or," he said, "we do that tomorrow before heading back to Redemption Ridge."

Cash eased back into Nick's embrace. "I like the way you think. What would you like to do today?"

After discussing their options, they decided to see a movie followed by a trip to the store so they could cook dinner together. They settled on a simple pasta dish, salads, and French rolls. Cash and Nick moved so well together in the kitchen that it felt like they'd been doing it for a long time. Cash's mind started to wade into the weeds again, trying to figure out the why and how of things that didn't matter. Nick's kiss would always pull him back. They took another long soak in the tub on Saturday night. Their laughter and conversation echoed through the apartment, turning the space into a home for the first time since Cash had bought it.

"I think I'll keep the apartment for the times we want to get away," Cash told Nick the following morning when they headed to his condo.

Nick smiled at him. "Or when we get kicked off the ranch for making too much noise."

Cash laughed because that was a high probability. "Maybe we could soundproof the bedroom."

"There's always that too."

Nick packed surprisingly little at his condo. Then again, the place was pretty sparse. He didn't have artwork or knickknacks to give the space character. Bare walls and neutral furniture seemed to be the theme, but Cash knew Nick had more depth than that. He'd just never attempted to make the condo a real home. Nick concentrated his efforts on important documents and family photo albums while Cash started packing up his closet.

"I probably won't need any of the suits," Nick said.

Cash considered the clothes for a moment and said, "How about a few? You'll want one for your interview at the police academy."

"True," Nick agreed. "Go ahead and pick out a few you like."

Cash pulled out navy and dove gray suits, white and light blue dress shirts, and ties that complemented them. He located a garment bag in the closet and placed the items inside. There was plenty of room for a few more suits, so Cash grabbed two more he'd like to see Nick in. Afterward, he grabbed belts and dress shoes before turning his attention to the more casual wear. "Will I find more of my clothes in here?"

"Don't think so."

"Sex toys or anything embarrassing?" Cash prodded. When he didn't get an answer, he stepped out of the closet to find Nick thinking too hard about the question. "Nicky?"

He jerked his head up. "I have just one dildo in my nightstand, and I'm not ashamed of it."

"Then why did it look like you were thinking hard enough to start a wildfire in your brain?" Cash asked.

Nick rose from the bed and walked into his closet. Curious, Cash followed him. Nick reached to the top shelf and pulled down a brown wooden box. "My keepsakes are in here." He turned the box around and opened it so Cash could see inside. Then Nick removed the movie ticket stub and bagel-run note from his pocket and added them to the collection. "I've kept every card, note, and receipt from the time we shared together." He sorted toward the bottom and pulled out a book of matches from the hotel they'd stayed at in Cabo.

"That trip was heaven and hell," Cash said. "To be so close to you and…"

"Not be able to touch me like you wanted to?" Nick asked. "No one fills out a pair of swim trunks like you do. God, I wore the skin off my dick."

Cash flexed his right fist. "Probably why I've got arthritis starting in my wrist."

They shared a laugh and a kiss, then Nick pulled out a beer bottle cap. Cash didn't drink often, but he loved Mexican beers, and the cap had come from one of his bottles.

"This is from the time we beat those bro dudes in beach volleyball in Miami."

Cash smiled from the memories, then mimed jerking off again. "Why the hell did we go to destinations where we practically stayed naked the entire trip? Sometimes you wore those skimpy trunks that would slip down your hipbones. Christ, I just wanted to kiss along your tan lines."

Nick mimed jerking off too. "I'm willing to bet we jacked off together while in separate rooms."

"Every night before bed so I could sleep," Cash said.

Nick nodded. "And every morning before we met up for breakfast, so I wouldn't ruin our friendship with an inconvenient boner."

Cash captured Nick's lips in another kiss. "Our next vacation is going to be so different."

"We won't leave the hotel," Nick agreed. "Hell, let's save the money and just not leave the bedroom at the ranch."

Cash laughed. "That's pretty much what the other lovebirds do. Why not us?"

They alternated between packing for their future while exploring the mementos from their past, so the excursion lasted much longer than it should have. After they hauled Nick's stuff to the SUV, they stopped for a quick bite to eat before setting out for the ranch. They kept up steady conversation for most of the drive, but Nick nodded off about three-quarters into the trip. Cash used the quiet to embrace his joy instead of questioning his good fortune. There'd been a void in his life that Nick's friendship alone couldn't fill. He wasn't about to stuff the gap with doubts and negativity. He wasn't as spiritual as Hope, but he certainly believed people received from the universe what they put into it. Manifesting, or whatever she called it.

It was just past suppertime when they pulled up to the ranch house. Cash didn't know if the crew had gathered in the dining room or if they'd chosen to have low-key dinners in their private quarters. Not that it mattered if they saw them carting Nick's belongings into the house. Cash had no intention of keeping it a secret. He reached over and squeezed Nick's thigh.

"We're home, baby," he said softly.

Nick murmured something unintelligible and shifted in his seat. Cash reached up and stroked his fingers over Nick's scruffy chin. He'd have a beard in no time at the rate his hair grew. Cash had never seen him with a lot of facial hair. Nick would let it grow out during their vacations but had to shave before returning to work. Cash's fingers brushed over Nick's lips when he turned in his direction. His eyes snapped open, and Cash felt his mouth spread into a smile.

"There you are," Nick said when Cash dropped his hand.

"Hi, baby."

Cash unbuckled his seat belt and leaned toward him. Nick did the same, and their mouths met in the middle. Cash hadn't meant to linger with a potential house full of people and a car to unload, but Nick's warmth drew him in. He teased Nick's lower lip with his tongue and eased inside when Nick opened in invitation. Cash lost track of time and his intentions then. He slid his hand into Nick's hair, canted his head, and deepened the kiss. God, he would never tire of having this privilege. To kiss Nick whenever he wanted to—

A low, sharp whistle pulled the two men apart. That's when they noticed every single member of the ranch standing in front of the SUV, wearing various expressions on their faces. Ivan, Rory, Finley, and Kieran looked incredibly smug. Harry, Dylan, and Rue practically radiated happiness for them. Tyler looked like he was seconds away from giggling, and Owen looked envious. Not because he wanted Cash or Nick but because he was in love with his best friend. Cash really hoped the two figured it out soon. He wouldn't wish twelve years of pining on anyone.

Cash rolled down his window and said, "What the hell are you gawking at? Don't act like you've never seen two people in love. First, there was Fin and Kieran practically setting the ranch on fire with their smoldering looks until they scratched that itch." Several of the crew guffawed, which drew Cash's attention to them. "What are you chuckling about, big guy?" Cash asked Ivan. "I've heard the hushed giggling coming out of your office in the barn." Ivan had the good grace to look a little sheepish, but Rory looked like the cat who ate the canary. "And you," he pointed to Harry. She put her hands on her hips and notched her chin up in challenge. "Do you honestly think I didn't know Dylan was climbing in and out of your bedroom window?" Cash turned to his K-9 trainer. "Dude, you could've used the front door. You're consenting adults." Harry giggled and leaned into Dylan's side.

Cash waited for the teasing and laughing to die down. "This is my time now, damn it. I'm in love with my best friend and have been for a long time." Cash's heart sank when Owen's face turned pink and Tyler's gaze fell to his boots. "But we'll do our best not to make it weird for anyone."

"Like making out in the car in front of the house," Nick added.

"Weird is cool," Rue said. "And it means the sexy sheriff is nursing a bruised ego and needs nurturing." He rubbed his hands together and walked away. That was the second reference Rue had made about Burke in a week. His tone was teasing, but the frequency lent credence to the comment being real.

"Happy for you, boss," Ivan called out. He winked and led Rory off by the hand before Nick's brother could hit them with a barrage of questions.

"Ditto," Kieran said as Finley blew them a kiss. They also turned and caught up to Rueben before he managed to get too far.

"And now we have two daddies," Tyler said exuberantly.

Nick made a slight choking sound and whispered, "Do you think he knows what that term also implies?"

Cash bit back laughter when he noticed Owen's wide-eyed expression. "No, but Owen sure as hell does."

Owen gave Tyler a playful shove, leaned in close, and said something

Cash couldn't hear. Tyler's eyes bulged out of his head and his mouth practically hit the ground.

"Don't worry about it, Ty," Cash called out. "Have a good night."

Owen and Tyler turned and followed Rue, Finley, and Kieran back to the crew's cabins. That left Harry and Dylan as the last two standing.

"When did you get so dramatic?" Harry asked, rolling her eyes.

"Night, boss," Dylan called out as they headed to their vehicle.

"Night," Cash told them. He glanced over at Nick, who watched him with a smirk on his face. "What?"

"It's just good to be home."

chapter

FOURTEEN

Nick's first day of physical therapy was on Tuesday morning, and he deeply regretted not accepting Cash's kind offer to drive him. Sweet-faced Heather from their Zoom called turned out to be a sadist. She put Nick through the paces for over ninety minutes while maintaining a chipper voice and constant smile. He was a sweaty, quivering mess by the time she hooked him up to the icing machine. Nick spent the full twenty minutes whining to Cash via text about how mean she was. Of course, his boyfriend promised to kiss everything better, which nearly created another problem for Nick.

He hadn't yet reverted to the early teen days when he'd gotten a boner if the wind blew just right, but Spiffy Stiffy had become unpredictable during recovery. He and Cash hadn't made love since Sunday morning, but the cuddling, kissing, and caressing felt just as intimate. Maybe even more so, though an insistent surge of need said otherwise.

Behave, he typed. *Wearing sweatpants and there's no place to hide.*

Cash sent back three laughing face emojis, an eggplant, and a tongue. Nick responded with the purple devil thingy and Cash fired back an angel wearing a halo. Yeah, that Heather looked angelic too. Nick wasn't falling for that ploy twice in one day. He nearly dropped his phone when the timer on his icing machine beeped. At least those twenty minutes had gone by fast thanks to his sexy…boyfriend? Is that the term guys their age used? Nick bit back a snort. Since when did thirty-seven earn a guys-their-age tag? And Cash might be nearing fifty, but he had more stamina and drive than most men half his age. He was a marvel to behold in the weight room, or any room for that matter. So they'd use the boyfriend tag until other titles became available, say fiancé or husband. Not like he was going to introduce Cash to everyone as his soul mate.

"All set," Heather said cheerfully. She'd appeared out of nowhere and nearly scared the bejesus out of him.

Nick dropped his phone, and Heather picked it up. "Thanks," he said. "Mind handing me my skin too?" Some FBI agent he'd turned out to be. He could face down hardened criminals and deadly gun barrels, but a five-foot-nothing physical therapist caused him to jump out of his skin for fuck's sake. "You just materialized out of nowhere."

Heather giggled and shook her head when she should've thrown it back and released a villainous muahahahaha. "I have a light step," she said, "but I'm pretty sure you were too focused on your phone." She turned the device around to show the lock-screen image. "And I can understand why."

Nick accepted the phone and smiled when his gaze landed on the selfie he'd taken of them the previous evening. They'd visited the sunflower field again and made out on the blanket until Nick's lips hurt. He'd snapped the photo of them with the flowers and fading sun in the background. Cash's handsome face and joyous smile actually made Nick's chest twinge. "Maybe a little," he admitted.

Heather smiled at him, then unhooked him from the machine. "You make a beautiful couple."

"And you're forgiven for being mean to me."

Heather snorted and said, "Oh, come on. Your evaluation wasn't that bad." Then she lowered her voice an octave or two. "Just wait until the real work begins next week."

"Wait. What?" Nick asked.

That's when Heather released the evil cackle, causing the other therapists in the room to laugh at their interaction.

"A warning would've been nice, guys," he told them.

Heather patted his uninjured shoulder. "Come on. Let's get you on the books for the next month. We'll start out with twice a week and reassess as we go. You're in excellent physical shape, so I expect you to be back in fighting form in no time."

Nick groaned as he slid off the table. "Two times a week?"

"You'll need to do your at-home exercises on the days you don't come in."

"No rest for the wicked, and the righteous don't need it," Nick replied as he followed her to the front desk. It was one of his grandmother's favorite quotes, and his mother had repeated it often. Nick found it curious how the brain could unearth gems like that at the perfect time. Little pearls of wisdom shucked from his mind's oysters.

"Do Tuesdays and Thursdays work for you?" Heather asked, pulling Nick's attention back to her.

"I'm very flexible, so put me wherever works for your schedule." They settled for ten o'clock on Tuesday and Thursday mornings. Nick quirked a brow when she handed him a navy canvas bag with the center's logo on it. "Parting gifts? Wine and bath bombs?"

Heather snorted. "Stretchy bands, illustrated workout sheets depicting how to use them, a long ice pad with a strap to keep it in place, and Biofreeze."

"Well, that's almost as good as wine and bath bombs," Nick lied.

Heather laughed and shook her head. "I like you."

Nick placed a hand over his heart and feigned a swoon. "I wish I could say the same."

The room erupted in laughter over their banter, and Nick bowed playfully to his audience before leaving. He'd always been a bit of a joker, but he'd suppressed it beneath rigorous expectations and obligations—both real and imagined. Maybe therapy was doing more for Nick than he realized. If not for wanting a functioning penis again, he wouldn't have gone to the sessions. Nick might not have ever found the courage to make a move on Cash. He could have settled for a life full of what others wanted for him instead of what he needed for himself. That would've been a crime because his existence was so much richer with Cash by his side, and not because of the money.

Charles might not be his biological father, but he'd always treated Nick as a son. He'd never shown favoritism toward Rory and made it clear Nick was an equal heir to the Snyder fortune. Some might've taken the easy road knowing that, but it made Nick work harder. He never wanted Charles to regret the investments he'd made in Nick's future. But Rory had forged his own path, and their relationship was even stronger for it. Nick didn't owe Charles undying servitude for doing the right thing for his wife's firstborn. His stepfather deserved honesty and the benefit of the doubt. And even though Charles was in the middle of a hotly contested bid for governor, Nick planned to have the conversation with him sooner than later. He didn't want Charles to find out about his future plans from anyone besides him.

His phone rang through the Bluetooth connection, and Andi's name popped up on the screen. She was getting back to him much quicker than he expected. Either her workload had lightened considerably over the past four days, or—

Nick cut off the negative thoughts before they could take off and pushed the button on his steering wheel to accept the call. "Hey, Andi," he said. "I'm surprised to hear from you so soon."

"Hey, Nicky. How's recovery going?" There was a hint of tension in Andi's voice that churned up his negative thoughts.

"My physical therapist is a sadist. Other than that, I can't complain."

"Give me her address, and I'll send her flowers." Then Andi heaved a sigh. "Listen, there's no easy way to say this."

"Hang on a minute," Nick said. "I'm driving. Let me pull over." Nick signaled at the next entrance and pulled into a shopping center. "Okay," he said once he put the BMW in park. "Hit me with it."

"Samuel Jeremiah doesn't exist. I mean, the person in the videos presenting himself as Samuel Jeremiah is using a false identity. I took the information provided on the church's website and cross-referenced it with the little detail I pulled from our sources. The man didn't exist before he bought the property near Last Chance Creek."

Nick's heart sank, but the news didn't surprise him. "No bank would've made a loan to someone without credit or a work history. He must've used cash."

"And he got the property for a steal," Andi said. "The previous owner died, and his kids just wanted to unload it for cash as quickly as possible. The images on Google Earth showed a dilapidated house with a tarp on the roof and equally run-down outbuildings. Looked like a small shed and a decent-sized barn." She sighed again. "Do you have anything with his fingerprints on it? I could run them through the database to see if anything pops up."

"No," Nick said. "And I wouldn't want to risk your career more than I already have. Thank you for getting back to me so soon. You're a skilled agent and an even better friend."

"You're pretty okay yourself," Andi replied. "Javier told me you have an interview at the academy soon."

"Did Javier volunteer that information, or did you torture it out of him?"

Andi laughed. "A little of both. He asked my opinion of you, and I wouldn't give it until he told me why."

"He hasn't called to cancel the interview, so you must've said something nice about me." Nick considered it for a minute. "Or he just wants to see what a fuckup looks like in person."

Andi's annoyed tsk made him smile. "Fishing for compliments doesn't suit you, my friend. I'm going to miss working with you."

Even if Nick didn't land the job with the police academy, they both knew his tenure with the FBI was over. "I'll miss working with you too, but I expect you to stay in touch."

"You won't be able to shake me, Nicky."

"Counting on it."

They wrapped up their phone call, and Nick pulled back into traffic. He ran through all the possibilities, which didn't take long because every avenue led him to the same person. Nick would've rather cuddled up to a rattlesnake than approach Sheriff Burke for help, but that didn't stop him from pulling into the sheriff's department's parking lot. He didn't see Burke's truck but entered the station anyway. He learned the sheriff was at lunch and chose not to leave a message since he knew the man's favorite lunch spot. Sure enough, he located Burke's truck half a block from the diner. Nick nabbed a spot while deciding how to approach the man. He could continue to be a cocky asshole and hope Burke's friendship with Cash would entice him to do the right thing. Or he could apologize for his behavior and attempt to make peace with the man whose friendship Cash valued. There was no doubt about which option he preferred, but Nick chose door number two.

Burke was sitting in the back of the diner with a newspaper unfolded in front of him. Though his pose looked casual to the naked eye, Nick didn't miss his subtle shift in focus when he stepped into the diner. He figured Burke probably did that every time the door opened, but Nick also bet his shoulders didn't stiffen for everyone. Nick gave himself a mental pep talk and forced his feet to move. Burke didn't look up even after Nick slid into the booth opposite him.

"Do you always drop in unannounced?" Burke asked.

Nick knew he was talking about the previous weekend when his arrival had interrupted Burke's date with Cash. One snarky remark after another popped into his head, but Nick suppressed them all. "Look, I know you and I didn't get off to a wonderful start."

Burke raised his head and leveled a sardonic gray gaze at him. "And?"

Of course he wouldn't make this easy. "It was mostly my fault."

When Burke only quirked a raven brow, Nick added, "Fine. It's all my fault. I acted like a possessive alley cat that wanted to mark his territory."

Burke's lips curved into a genuine smile. "Damn it. I really didn't want to like you." The sheriff lifted his coffee cup to his full lips.

Nick couldn't resist returning the sheriff's grin. "Guess I just have that effect on people."

Burke nearly choked on his coffee. "There's the cocky bastard I met." He set his cup down and held Nick's gaze. "Do you love him?"

"More than anything."

Burke searched Nick's expression, and Nick bared his every emotion to the man. What did he gain by not being honest? After a moment, Burke relaxed and nodded. He'd accepted Cash's choice, though that didn't necessarily mean Burke approved. Nick didn't need his endorsement to gain his assistance.

He took a fortifying breath and said, "And that's why I need your help."

Burke folded the paper and set it aside. "I'm listening."

Nick kept his voice low as he filled Burke in on what was going on. He didn't delve too deeply into his recent troubles with the Bureau but touched on enough to explain why Nick wasn't tapping into his resources. The sheriff listened without interruption, though Nick paused while the server delivered a country fried steak platter.

"Is there anything I can get you?" she asked Nick.

He planned to make a sandwich from leftover meatloaf when he got back to the ranch but ordered a double helping of banana pudding to go. "Want me to wait until you're done eating?" Nick asked once they were alone again.

Burke dug his fork into the heap of mashed potatoes with country gravy. He paused halfway to his mouth and said, "Hell no. I'm enjoying you groveling for my help." Burke punctuated that with a good-natured grin before he shoved the bite into his mouth. By the time he finished, Nick had brought him up to speed. Burke set his fork down and wiped his mouth with a napkin. "I appreciate your candor, and I know it wasn't easy. You feds have a reputation for being stingy with information. I want to go the rest of my life without hearing that something is on a need-to-know basis."

Nick fought off a smile but didn't interrupt.

"We share a common goal," Burke continued. "Both of us want to protect Cash and his crew from harm. So far, Samuel Jeremiah and his followers have only attacked their reputation."

"My brother Rory would beg to differ," Nick said. Staying silent was impossible on that point. Even if Rory hadn't been the initial target, he'd taken a blow to the head when he lunged to protect a dog from getting kicked.

Burke acknowledged him with a nod. "Point taken. I want to do everything in my power to prevent more violence or frame jobs, so I will also share what little I know."

"Thank you."

"We retrieved the canvas bag the man in the video used to dump the stolen tools in the ranch's truck. I got good fingerprints, but I couldn't get a match from any database. However, we found those same prints at each of the thefts. That guy on the video is our prime suspect, but I'm no closer to learning his identity. As much as I don't want to, I might have to ask the public for help. I know I'm going to get a ton of bogus tips. Every angry girlfriend, wife, or boyfriend will turn their man in."

Nick smiled. "Happens every time."

"I've pulled additional security videos from other stores on side streets, but I can't get a good look at his face. I've shown the best pictures to locals who've been here their entire lives, and they didn't recognize him. If something doesn't break soon, I'll enlist the press and put out his pictures to ask for help."

"But aren't most of the Salvation Anew members outsiders?"

"Yes," Burke replied. "Some locals have joined, and I hope to plead to their consciences."

"I want to know who Samuel Jeremiah really is," Nick said. "I can't quell the feeling that he's targeting Cash, but I can't prove it either."

"If it helps, I've come to the same conclusion." Burke blew out a frustrated breath. "I have a friend who's developing game-changing facial recognition software for Homeland Security. They can do all kinds of different metrics and image altering to find people with similar features. It wouldn't stand up in court yet, but it can give us a direction to go in. Right now, we'd be searching a giant-ass haystack for the needle. My buddy owes me a favor or two, and this feels like a good time to call in a marker."

"Wow. That must be some favor."

"I saved his life in Iraq."

Of course he did. Dude already had the superhero chin. Why not the bravery to go with it? Nick figured his work at the diner was done and scooted out of the booth. "I'll get out of your hair in case you want dessert." That reminded him to grab Cash's to-go container of pudding.

"You going to tell Cash what we suspect?" Burke asked.

Nick almost asked his opinion on that but changed his mind at the last moment. "That information is on a need-to-know basis."

If looks could kill, Nick was a breath away from a chalk outline and a body bag. "There's the asshole no one loves or missed."

More snarky replies danced on the tip of his tongue, but Nick swallowed them down. No sense in ruining their truce, tenuous as it was. He gave Burke a two-finger salute and headed to the counter to pay for his pudding. Nick debated Burke's question during the short ride home. What did he tell Cash and when? Right now, all he had was supposition. What advice would he give to someone else in the situation? Forewarned is forearmed, but it also causes undue paranoia. That was the entire reason Cash hadn't originally told the crew about the tracking devices in their vehicles. He was still on the fence when he arrived back at the ranch.

"Hey, Nick," Harry said when he stepped into the kitchen.

"Afternoon, Pumpkin Spice." Nick opened the refrigerator and put Cash's dessert inside. He noticed the container of leftover meatloaf was gone and bit back a dejected groan. Cash warned him that a person needed to move fast around there. He'd been late for lunch and missed out on the goodies.

"Whatcha got there?" Harry asked.

"Pudding for Cash."

"Did you eat at the diner?" Harry sounded more curious than accusatory.

"No, just wanted to bring home something special for Cash."

"That's so sweet," she crooned. "Oh! A package arrived for you. Rory put it in your makeshift office in the library."

His appetite disappeared in an instant, and he closed the refrigerator door. "Thanks!" Nick called out on his way out of the kitchen.

It did funny things to his insides to see Cash's address under his name on the shipping label. He tore open one end of the package, held it to his nose, and breathed deeply. God, he loved the smell of fine leather. He'd love it even more when stretched around Cash. Nick tucked the box behind his back and headed to the office next door. Cash looked up from his computer when Nick knocked on the doorframe. "Busy?"

"Never too busy for you. Get in here."

Nick shut the door behind him and took two steps before Cash's no-nonsense voice halted him in his tracks.

"Lock it too."

Nick retreated to do his bidding, then continued to his desk.

"What's behind your back?" Cash asked.

"A gift for you."

Cash's eyes widened in surprise. He was a man who gave and gave, and Nick wanted him to be a man who received and received too. "What's the occasion?"

Nick rounded the desk and kissed his upturned lips. "Because I love you." He pulled the box from behind his back and handed it to him.

Cash just looked at it for several moments. He trailed his finger over the mailing label twice before meeting Nick's gaze again. "This is the nicest gift anyone has ever given me."

"You haven't opened it yet," Nick teased.

Cash tapped the label. "I'm talking about this. Seeing your name with my address…"

"Does funny things to your insides?" Nick palmed the back of Cash's neck and kissed him again, longer this time. "Me too. Open your gift."

Cash turned the box and saw the open flap. "Someone already did." Nick knew the moment Cash smelled the leather because he laughed. "You didn't."

"I did."

Cash pulled out a pair of black Italian leather driving gloves. "These smell so good."

"They'll smell even better on you." The spark of desire he'd felt earlier during their text exchange returned. Nick wasn't sure if he'd achieve arousal, but he wanted to try. "Put them on."

Cash held his gaze for a few moments before he pulled one of them on and secured it around his wrist. He flexed his fist and watched the movement beneath the leather. "Fits like a…"

"Glove?" Nick asked.

Cash smiled and lifted his face for another kiss. "Thank you. I love them, and I love you." He inhaled sharply and closed his eyes briefly.

Nick straddled his lap. "Not a dream. I'm still here." He kissed Cash, taking his time to tease his lips apart before sliding his tongue against Cash's. Nick forgot about dilemmas, food, or anything except for the way his man made him feel. When Cash grazed a gloved hand over Nick's semi erection, he realized he was feeling all kinds of ways. Cash tugged his pants and underwear down to midthigh and stroked him until Nick was hard enough to hurt.

Cash retrieved a bottle of lube from a desk drawer and smiled sheepishly. "I believe in being prepared for when situations arise." Cash licked a path along Nick's cock, swirled his tongue around his swollen head, and lapped up the precum beading there. "And, baby, you have risen." Cash scooted his chair back and reached for the second glove. "Time for a test drive." Nick couldn't tear his gaze away from the sexy way Cash pulled the second glove on. "Get my dick out, then turn around and prep yourself for me. I don't want to get lube all over my new gloves."

Nick freed Cash's erection from his pants and nearly tripped over his own two feet when complying with the second part of his orders. Cash stood so close Nick could feel his body heat rolling off him.

"Work it open for me, baby. Two fingers. Deep as you can go." Cash bent Nick deeper at the waist, then massaged his ass with both hands.

"I'm ready," Nick said between panted breaths.

"Fuck yourself a little harder. Add a third finger."

Once satisfied, Cash drizzled extra lube over Nick's ass, lined up, and pushed home. Nick whined loudly, and Cash covered his mouth with a gloved hand to muffle the sound as he brought them to a fast, hard release. Afterward, Cash pulled out some wet wipes from the same drawer so they could clean up.

"Don't suppose you hid a meatloaf sandwich in there?" Nick asked, not bothering to cover his nudity. Hell, he debated a nap on the office sofa while Cash worked.

"No." Cash turned around to reveal a hidden panel in his credenza, and behind it was a mini refrigerator. "But I have one in here for you."

Nick shamelessly ate the sandwich while sitting on Cash's desk with his pants half off and his heart in his eyes.

chapter
FIFTEEN

"I CAN'T BELIEVE HOW EXCITED I AM TO HELP YOU PULL OFF Nick's surprise," Finley told Cash. "He really doesn't know?"

"Nope. I didn't even acknowledge his comments when he mentioned goats twice in one week."

They'd been spending the warm, late-summer evenings on the ranch, which included a lot of time with the horses. Nick had told Cash his grandparents raised goats on their farm in Oklahoma. A few days later, Cash overheard Nick telling Dolly the horse that she could use an ornery goat to keep her on her toes.

"There's already a Dolly, Loretta, and Patsy on this ranch. We need goats named Reba and Martina—little but feisty," Nick had told her.

Cash pretended not to hear as he visited with Kieran's feisty girl, Nellie. He'd put the plan into motion but figured he'd have to wait until Nick was at physical therapy to sneak the goats onto the ranch. As luck would have it, Charles had a nearby campaign stop late Saturday morning and wanted to see his sons. It had been quite the feat to revamp the empty horse stalls into goat condos on short notice, but Finley was an excellent co-conspirator. He'd done a great job preparing a cozy space for the ranch's newest additions. Harry and Ivan were also in on the surprise, and the two of them started plotting new commercial ventures with the goats.

"Their milk is a lucrative business," Ivan had said.

Harry had nodded vigorously. "From cheese to skin care products."

Cash had left the room when they'd started guessing the names Hope would assign to a skincare line made from goat's milk. Maybe they'd expand to milking goats someday, but Cash had purchased four female Pygmy goats from a rescue organization for Nick to cuddle and love. Cash and Finley took advantage of Rory and Nick's absence to pick up the cuties and set up the surprise. Their first stop was the feed store in Last Chance Creek. Fin pulled the truck and trailer into the parking lot and drove to the rear of the building to a pickup bay. Since he'd phoned in the order, it didn't take them long to unload the goats' food and bedding. Fin drove back toward the front of the store and pulled over to the side.

"I want to spread out some of that bedding in the horse trailer so the goats will be comfortable and won't slip around on the metal floor," Fin said.

Cash exited the truck to help, but his attention got diverted when he heard raised voices near the store. There were several men talking at once, so he couldn't make out their individual words, but he heard the pleading, "Leave me alone" that followed. Cash recognized the voice but didn't immediately know from where until Fin swore.

"Keegan is in trouble," Fin said.

Cash rounded the side of the truck and saw that three men had backed Finley's ex-boyfriend against the front of the building. Fin had brought the guy to the ranch a few times when they dated because Keegan wasn't out to his family. The young guy had been confused about his sexual orientation and turned to his mother's spiritual adviser for guidance. Unfortunately for Keegan, that had turned out to be Samuel Jeremiah. Keegan had cut off things with Finley and joined Salvation

Anew. The young man wore the simple style of clothes their congregation chose, which made him stick out like a sore thumb and slapped a bullseye on his back.

Fin took a step toward the feed store, but Cash held up a hand to stop him. "I'll handle this. You take care of the bedding." Fin held his gaze for a moment before nodding.

With his back to the building, Keegan had nowhere to go as the other three crowded him. Cash didn't know the source of the altercation, but it didn't matter. Three on one wasn't freaking cool.

"Hey," Cash called out, "what's the problem?"

Four heads swiveled his way, and Keegan's relief was palpable. The other three wore various expressions of annoyance—mild, medium, and spicy. Cash leveled them with his most withering stare. The mild guy's eyes widened a little, and he took two steps back. The medium guy held his ground but looked slightly less mutinous. And the spicy guy looked, well, spicier. He was the only one who turned to confront Cash.

"Stay out of it, old man," Spicy said. "This doesn't concern you."

Old man? *Ouch.* "That's where you're wrong." On both counts. Cash had never felt better in his life, and to the guys he said, "I don't like bullies."

"Let's go, guys," Mild said.

"Shut up, Joe," Medium replied to his friend.

"We're not the bullies." Spicy pointed to Keegan. "He is, but I think you of all people already know that."

So Spicy recognized him. "If you know who I am, then you also know I don't condone violence. I promote redemption, not rejection. You'll never reach anyone through intimidation."

"You confronted us," Spicy argued.

Cash stopped a few feet away and kept his posture loose. It wouldn't matter what he said if he struck a combative stance. Spicy neither retreated nor advanced, but Mild and Medium eased backward. "Come here, Keegan." The kid kept a wary gaze on the combatants as he eased toward Cash. "I don't know what happened before I arrived on the scene, but it's over now. Move along."

Spicy narrowed his eyes at Cash before shifting his furious gaze toward Keegan. "Fine, but this isn't over. I meant what I said. This town doesn't want your kind."

Keegan stood so close Cash could feel the kid tremble. How many times had Keegan heard he didn't belong or a variation of the expression? Cash had certainly heard it more times than he could count, including recently from people in Keegan's congregation. But two wrongs never made a right, and everyone deserved to have a sense of belonging. Cash held Spicy's gaze and repositioned himself to keep his body in front of Keegan's as the trio of trouble walked into the store.

Cash turned and assessed Keegan. "Are you okay?"

The younger guy kept his gaze averted but nodded slightly. Keegan looked anything but okay. He'd lost a lot of weight since the last time he'd been at the ranch, and he didn't have extra to spare then. His clothes hung on his thin body. On closer inspection, Keegan's white shirt was dingy and his pants were worn thin, almost threadbare in places. Cash caught a whiff of body odor when the wind picked up, and he knew damn well that Keegan wasn't okay. He raised his arm, hoping to place a comforting hand on Keegan's shoulder, but the kid flinched as if Cash were about to hit him.

"Hey, it's okay." Cash used the same gentle tone Finley used on skittish horses. "I just want to help."

Keegan raised his head and met Cash's gaze. It took everything in his control not to reveal how alarmed he was by the young man's appearance. The weight loss was even more obvious in his face than anywhere else. His gaunt cheeks made his hazel eyes appear larger, almost cartoonish. Keegan's despair threatened to unravel Cash's control, but he held steady until the younger man spoke.

"Why?" The word came out on a choked whisper. Keegan swallowed hard and tried again. "Why would you help me?"

"I always want to help people who need it. I've always welcomed you to my ranch. That hasn't changed."

Keegan's gaze darted to the right and held. Cash knew he was looking at Finley. "But…"

"No buts," Cash said gently, pulling Keegan's attention back to him. He had to tread lightly. Commenting on his condition could induce shame and make him retreat further. "This isn't about Finley, and you know damn well he wouldn't want you to be in a rough spot."

Keegan nodded, slowly and lethargically, as if the motion really zapped his energy. "I do."

"Are you safe?" Cash asked.

Keegan lowered his gaze to his feet again. "I'm fine."

Cash's mind raced with how to proceed. That wasn't a yes, but what could he do? Keegan was an adult he didn't have any authority over. He could hand him a business card and tell him to call if he wanted help. But what if someone found it in his belongings? The likelihood Keegan had any autonomy on that compound was slim to none. In fact, Cash had never seen a Salvation Anew member out alone. They were always in groups of two or more. Cash scanned the surrounding area and through the store windows.

"Are you by yourself?"

Keegan shook his head. "Never. Brother Austin had to move the van because they're shutting down Main Street for the music festival tonight."

Last Chance Creek had something going on every weekend during the summer. There was a large empty field at the edge of town that the event planners turned into a parking lot. The walk into town was a short distance, and they provided shuttle service to those who needed help. The festivities were a huge draw for tourists and locals alike. Attendance had waned when Salvation Anew started protesting everything and everyone, but there'd been a resurgence since the group was off licking their wounds. Running into Keegan was disturbing in more ways than one. Cash not only worried about his safety; he wondered what the group planned to do next.

Keegan snapped his head up and did his own scan. "You should go. It wouldn't be good if someone saw us talking." It wouldn't be good for Keegan. That's what he'd meant.

Cash eased back and held up his hands. "I'm going. I meant what I said, though." Hollow, hazel eyes met his. "Do you remember Finley's number?" The younger man glanced over Cash's shoulder and nodded. "Call if you ever need me, and I will help you. No questions asked."

"Is he happy?"

Cash knew who Keegan meant. "Very much. You deserve happiness and acceptance too. I wish you believed it."

Keegan drew in a shaky breath and averted his gaze. "Goodbye, Cash."

"So long for now." Cash needed to keep that door open.

Finley was leaning against the side of the truck with his arms crossed. He didn't bother to disguise his interest in the conversation's outcome. When he saw Cash heading toward him, Fin opened the driver's side door and climbed in.

"I barely recognize him," Fin said once Cash joined him. He blew out a breath, shifted the truck into drive, and pulled forward. "What happened?"

Cash filled him in on what he knew, which was very little. "If his number ever comes up on your phone, let me know right away."

"I will, boss," Finley replied. "You have to know that not everyone wants to be saved."

"Oh, I do."

Finley chuckled. "You just don't accept it."

Damn straight. Especially not with someone as young and impressionable as Keegan. Cash reached over and ruffled Finley's hair. "You think you know me?"

Finley smiled over at him. "Yeah, I do."

"We'll do whatever we can whenever he's ready," Cash said. That would have to be enough for the moment.

They shifted the conversation to their new goats and Nick's very first poker night. They'd gone to Denver the previous weekend, and Harry had been hosting poker at her place the night Nick had shown up on the ranch. It was odd how Nick had only been on the ranch for two weeks, but Cash struggled to remember a time when he wasn't there. Nick's presence permeated every room. Cash had always loved his ranch, but it had truly become home once Nick moved in.

The farm animal rescue was only forty-five minutes away. They would've had plenty of time to get the goats and return before Nick and Rory if the rescue owner hadn't been so chatty. She'd heard of Redemption Ridge and was a big fan of their mission. That was great, but he really wanted to have the goats all settled in before Nick arrived home. And maybe he was part of the problem because he'd fallen in love with the goats' best friend—a donkey named Jake.

"We've got plenty of room in the trailer and in the barn for Jake," Finley said. He pointed at the way the goats bounced around the donkey and rubbed up against him. "Seems like a docile jackass."

"Sarah," Cash said, "how much for Jake?"

And so they headed back to the ranch with four goats, Jake, and no time to spare. Cash expected an alert from the security camera on the gate when Rory and Nick beat them home, but none came. He breathed a sigh of relief when Finley backed up to the barn and shut the truck off. By the time they opened the trailer door, everyone on the ranch had joined them.

Harry squealed over the goats and kissed Jake on top of his head. The donkey flicked his ears and continued chewing on some straw. Tyler and Owen squatted down and started debating names for them. They'd run through every female name in the Marvel and DC universes by the time Cash stopped them.

"These are Nick's goats, and he gets to name them."

The guys conceded with good grace. Ivan, who tried really hard to maintain his tough guy persona, watched the goats' shenanigans and tried not to smile. He finally met Cash's gaze and warned they'd be trouble.

"We wouldn't have it any other way." Cash patted the big guy on the shoulder and helped corral the newest critters into the barn. The horses were outside frolicking in the meadow, but unfamiliar smells still distracted the goats. They leaped and bounced and played like oversized kittens.

Kieran leaned over to pet one, and it headbutted his hand. "They are the cutest things I've ever seen, but no one tells Little Mama I said that."

"How have I lived my whole life without a goat?" Rueben asked.

Dylan watched over the animals with a smile on his face. "How are we going to get them into the pens?"

"They'll follow Jake," Finley replied.

Harry scratched behind the donkey's ear and clicked her tongue before walking away. Jake flicked his ears and followed her deeper into the barn.

"Hey now," Dylan called out. "That's my girl, Jake."

The donkey swished his tail in response and continued following Harry. Sure enough, the goats bounded after them too.

Nick texted him when they were a few minutes out. Cash told Finley to put the trailer away, then hustled everyone else out of the barn.

"Act natural," Cash said.

They must've failed the assignment because the brothers wore identical looks of suspicion when they got out of the car.

"What's going on?" Rory asked as he walked toward the gathering.

"Just hanging out," Ivan replied casually.

Nick hadn't budged from his spot by the car, so Cash headed his way. He knew Nick had planned to tell both Rory and Charles of his decision to leave the FBI, and Cash worried it hadn't gone well. Was Nick having second thoughts and worried about how Cash would take the news?

"I can hear your wheels turning from over here," Nick said when Cash neared. "Give that hamster a break. I'm fine. *We're* fine. Everything is fine."

Cash wrapped him in a big hug and kissed the side of his neck. "Just fine?"

Nick pulled back and kissed him softly on the mouth. "I would've said things are excellent before we pulled up to find the entire ranch waiting for us."

"Not the *entire* ranch," Cash replied.

Finley ran around the side of the barn and pulled up short next to Kieran.

"Okay, now everyone is here waiting for us," Nick said. "What's going on?"

"You first," Cash replied. "Did everything go okay with Charles?" Rory only wanted Nick to be happy and close by. Charles could be a different story.

Nick inhaled deeply, and Cash couldn't resist bracing himself. His boyfriend snorted and shook his head. "Stop." Nick kissed him hard. "Charles said he only wants me to be happy. He apologized for making me feel like I needed to act a certain way to please him. He told Rory and I both how proud he is to be our father."

"That's wonderful," Cash said.

"And he said it's about damn time we"—Nick gestured between Cash and himself—"got our heads out of our asses."

Cash shouldn't have been surprised. "I thought I was a better poker player than that."

Nick laughed and kissed him again. "Speaking of poker, what time do the festivities start?"

"Not long from now," Cash replied. "I want to show you something first." He took Nick's hand and led him toward the barn. The crew parted to let them pass, then filed in behind Cash and Nick. Their excited whispers made him smile. A gift for one person on the ranch always turned out to be a delight for everyone.

Nick stopped short when Jake brayed and the goats bleated. He looked at Cash with an expression of pure joy. "You didn't?"

Cash laughed and nodded. "Finley and I picked up four Pygmy

goats from a rescue today." Jake brayed again. "And a donkey. Turns out the goats love Jake, so we couldn't leave him behind." And Cash freaking loved him, so there was that too.

Nick kissed him hard before hustling toward the stalls where the noises were coming from. "Oh my God!" Nick pulled the enclosure door open and stepped inside the converted space. He dropped to his knees, and the goats rushed him. "Hey, guys," he said as they bounced all over him.

"Girls," Cash corrected.

"Hey, ladies." Nick looked over his shoulder at Cash. "What are their names?"

"Whatever you want them to be." Cash stepped inside to give Jake equal attention. He didn't jump around to show his enthusiasm, but he did lean his body into Cash.

"This one is Reba," Nick said, pointing to one. Then he picked up the smallest one in his arms. "This one is Martina." The crew outside the stall all made helpful suggestions, and Nick settled on Tammy and Kitty for the final two goats.

They played with their newest pets long after everyone else left the barn. Rueben returned a while later, looking frustrated.

"What's up?" Cash asked.

"It's my turn to pick up the pizza, and my truck won't start," Rue said.

"Again?" The dealership had replaced the starter twice in the past year. Good thing it was still under warranty. "I'll call the dealership on Monday and ask them to tow it in again." Cash reached into his pocket and pulled out his key chain. "Take mine. There's plenty of gas."

"Thanks, boss." He took a few steps back. "We're trying the new pizza joint in Last Chance Creek that Tyler and Owen won't shut up about."

"Be careful," Cash called out. Would he always feel nervous every time one of his men drove into town? "Oh, and there's a festival going on downtown. You'll have to park in the field and hoof it."

Rue flexed his right arm. "I'm fit. No worries."

"I can't wait for poker," Nick said when they were alone again. "Rory told me Fin is the one I have to look out for, but he looks so innocent."

Cash laughed as he dusted off his pants. "Let's just say it's a good thing we don't play for high stakes. Fin would own it all. Ready to get cleaned up?"

"Hell yeah. Cleaned up equals getting my man naked." Nick wrapped his arms around Cash's neck and kissed him. "Thank you for the girls."

"You're welcome."

They headed back to the house, hand in hand. Cash got a gate alert on his phone halfway there. He thought it might be Rueben leaving until he saw his truck still parked near the house. He pulled his phone out to check the camera when his phone rang.

"It's Burke," Cash told Nick. Was he at the gate? He answered the phone instead of checking the feed. "Hey, Seth."

"Cash. Sorry for dropping by unannounced. It worked so well for that other guy. Thought I'd try it too." There was something off in his voice. He'd tried to disguise his tension with a snarky comment, but it hadn't worked.

"Funny man. See you in a few," Cash said before disconnecting. He opened the gate with his app, and they waited for Burke to make the long drive down to the ranch.

"This can't be good, right?" Nick asked.

"He's never just shown up before, so I'm not optimistic."

Burke pulled up to them and stopped. He killed the engine and stepped out of his truck. "Gentlemen," he said with a tip of his white Stetson.

"Evening," Cash replied.

Nick nodded at the sheriff. "Burke."

The sheriff smirked at Nick's lukewarm welcome before meeting Cash's gaze. Burke's brow furrowed, and Cash suspected he had bad news to deliver. He knew where all his people were, so this must have something to do with the prior incident. When Burke glanced at Nick but still didn't speak, Cash figured out what made him uneasy.

"Nick already told me about his phone call to his friend at the FBI and the conversation you guys had at the diner on Tuesday," Cash told him.

Boots crunched on gravel, and Cash turned to find Rueben walking from his cabin. His steps faltered when his gaze landed on Burke. Rue's dark eyes widened, and his lips curved into a smile.

"Well, isn't this a surprise," Rue said as he veered in their direction. "Is the good sheriff joining us for poker night? If so, I'll need to put on something a little nicer."

"Poker?" Burke quirked a brow.

Cash rolled his eyes at his friend. "There's no money involved. Otherwise, Rueben wouldn't have said anything."

"I wouldn't count on that," Rue said. "I made an awful criminal."

Burke laughed and hooked a thumb toward Rueben. "I like him."

"I like you too, handsome," Rueben said. "I hope you're still here when I get back." Rue winked and headed toward Cash's truck.

Burke turned sideways and watched him go. Rue looked over his shoulder and caught the sheriff in the act. Cash had never seen Rue give such a lurid smile, and he felt kind of dirty for seeing it now. He glanced over at Nick, who was getting a kick out of the exchange.

"What just happened?" Burke asked when Rueben drove off with a little wave out the window.

Nick sighed and shook his head. "The good people elected this guy as their top law officer in the county?" He tsked a few times. "That's what the young kids call flirting, Burke."

"Flirting?" The sheriff looked over his shoulder at the truck. "With me?"

So Rueben hadn't been joking about the handcuffs and other things he mentioned. "Yeah, flirting," Cash said.

"Huh. Interesting." Burke glanced over his shoulder one last time, but the black truck had already disappeared into the pines. He shook his head as if to clear his thoughts and fixed his attention on Cash. "So Nick told you about my friend at DHS who is working on cutting-edge technology in facial recognition?"

"He did," Cash replied. As a software creator, the notion intrigued him. Cash was also someone who worked to exonerate people who had been wrongfully convicted by junk science. And these kinds of advances worried him a lot, especially since they were likely powered by AI. "I take it you have some images to show us?"

"I do," Burke replied.

"Let's all go inside so we can get comfortable."

Cash led them into the house, made introductions between Burke and Patsy, then led them into his office. Burke and Nick both declined something to drink, but Cash grabbed a bottle of Modelo. He took them over to the seating area next to the fireplace since it was more comfortable.

Burke pulled out his phone, tapped on the screen, and handed the device to Cash. "Swipe right to see the various photographs. It starts with a current photo of Samuel Jeremiah taken off the internet. There are several images of him younger with different hairstyles and different hair colors. Look to see if anything jumps out at you."

Cash's hand shook a little when he started, but he settled down when none of the images of Samuel Jeremiah looked familiar. He must've flipped through a dozen or more photos before the first warning bell went off. Cash stopped on the computer-generated image of Samuel in his midtwenties, clean-shaven with black hair. The features didn't match his memory one hundred percent, but it was close enough that Cash couldn't ignore it. Acid churned in his stomach, and he stared down at Burke's phone.

He was stuck in the past, in a situation he'd never asked to be in and didn't know how to get out of. Cash had done the right thing. He'd gone to the police and told them about his unplanned involvement. Cash had thought he was giving a buddy a ride to the convenience store to get milk for his toddler. He hadn't known Mike had a gun hidden in his coat or that he'd stick it in the clerk's face and rob him. Cash hadn't known until Mike pulled the money out of his coat pocket back at his apartment. He'd been too stunned to say much, but he'd refused the money Mike tried to give him. Cash had made an excuse to leave the house and avoided Mike for a few days while he figured out what to do. He'd decided to do the right thing, and it altered the course of his life. The cops arrested Mike, but they charged Cash too. They hadn't believed he was an unwitting accomplice, and nothing Cash said could convince them. The public defender worked out a deal where Cash only served a year. The aggravated robbery hadn't been Mike's first offense, so he got sent away for two decades. And for a long time, Cash had clung to the adage that no good deed goes unpunished. He had done the right thing and gone to the police, and they'd turned against him. Durrell Padgett and a life of good deeds had helped Cash gain a more positive outlook. But his past had risen from the dead to wreak havoc again.

Nick squatted down next to him. "What's wrong, Saint?"

Cash forced his gaze away from the image to look into the eyes he loved so much. "Mike Carson."

Nick settled his hand on the back of Cash's neck. "He died during a prison fight."

Cash nodded and showed him the phone. "This guy looks just like him. It can't be a coincidence."

"Fuck," Nick said.

"Who is Mike Carson?" Burke asked.

Cash was too rattled to talk, so Nick answered for him. He'd been honest with Burke about his past, but he'd never mentioned Mike by name. There'd been no reason to...until now.

Burke met Cash's gaze and echoed Nick's sentiment. "Fuck."

chapter SIXTEEN

CASH TURNED TO FACE HIM, BREAKING THEIR CONNECTION, but not before Nick felt the impact of Burke's curse ripple through Cash. The sky-blue eyes Nick adored so much were heavy with dismay, fear, and guilt. Needing to touch Cash, Nick took his hand and stroked his thumb over Cash's knuckles. "No." He didn't need Cash to say a word because he could read his thoughts loud and clear. Cash blamed himself for everything.

"This is all because of me." Cash's voice wasn't small or weak; it was calm and resolute.

Nothing Nick or Burke could say would change his mind in the heat of the moment. His brilliant boyfriend would roll everything around in his mind on repeat and would eventually land in the same place Nick stood. And he would happily give Cash the space to do that once they knew more about what they were dealing with. Right then, Cash needed Nick to be the investigator who could cut through the emotions and coax Cash's analytical brain to the surface. There would be time later for the soothing and comfort he longed to give Cash.

Nick squeezed his hand. "None of this is your fault, but we'll talk about that later. Right now, we need to learn as much as we can about this man and his relationship to Mike Carson."

"He's right," Burke said. "I'm going to call a buddy in corrections to see what they know about Carson's next of kin."

"On a Saturday?" Nick asked. Corrections officers and other personnel worked around the clock, but prison administration kept standard business hours. Not just anyone would have access to inmate records. When Burke only winked at him, Nick said, "Iraq?"

Burked tapped his nose as he stood up. "I'll step over here to make the call while you see what Cash remembers about Mike's family."

Freaking superhero. Once alone on the sofa, Nick turned his full attention to Cash. "Did Mike Carson talk much about his family?"

Cash shook his head, then looked at him with a vague expression. "Iraq?"

"Turns out Burke doesn't just have a superhero jaw. He's the real deal. Saved people in Iraq who are now in positions to help us. Burke's calling in some markers." Nick didn't like Cash's pallor or his unfocused eyes. Normally, he'd kiss his man until he had his full attention, but that seemed rude in front of Burke. Nick squeezed his hand and said, "Hey, I need you with me right now."

Cash closed his eyes and swallowed hard. He cycled through a few cleansing breaths that improved his color. When their gazes met again, Cash was present. "Mike didn't mention his family members by name, but he made vague references about his dad disowning him after getting in trouble with the law."

"How'd you meet Mike?"

"Dirt track racing circuit. He was part of my pit crew. I replaced a popular driver and struggled to make inroads with the team. Mike was nice to me."

Cash rarely talked about his amateur racing days. It was something he'd left behind when he went to jail. Nick had seen a spark of something when Cash had driven his BMW for the first time. He'd found joy in the way the car hugged the sharp curves and accelerated out of them.

Nick glanced over and saw that Burke was deep in conversation. He decided to see what he could find online about Mike Carson. Any story about his death would probably include a statement from a family member, but maybe not if Cash's memory was accurate. Nick released Cash's hand but pressed his leg up against Cash's so they stayed connected. He hadn't finished typing Mike's name into the browser search bar before Burke let out a victorious sound. Nick glanced up to find him returning to the sitting area.

"I've got a place to start," Burke said triumphantly.

"Your buddy happened to be at work or near his laptop?" Nick asked.

"Wasn't necessary," Burke replied. "Steve remembered the inmate well because his father brought a wrongful death suit against the facility."

"How'd he die?" Nick asked.

"Another inmate had serious beef with Carson. His name is Richard Rollins, but he goes by Dicky. Sounds kind of innocuous, but he's a heavy hitter. I guess Carson and Dicky had history. Both men were repeat offenders so it's hard to say when and where the trouble started. They'd gotten into a few fights and were supposed to be kept in separate blocks. They weren't allowed to eat, shower, or be out in the yard at the same time. Yet somehow, Dicky found Carson alone in the showers after he'd had a mishap while working in the kitchen. Steve said the incident was inexcusable. Their lawyers and insurance company wanted to work out a settlement with Carson's father rather than face a jury at trial."

So his son didn't have value to him while he was alive, but he didn't hesitate to cash in on his death. Typical. "What's daddy Carson's name?"

"Michael Carson Senior, but he goes by Mick," Burke said. "Steve told me the guy was a real piece of work. Quoted a lot of scripture and such. Steve had to bite his tongue during negotiations because the man hadn't visited or written to his son even once during his incarceration."

"The timing feels off." Cash's voice was quiet and distant.

Nick looked at him and caught him staring off into space. He set his phone down and reached for Cash's hand. As soon as their skin touched, Cash met his gaze. "How so?" Nick asked.

"Mike's been dead for a while," Cash replied.

"Ten years," Burke clarified.

"So why has Mick Carson waited all this time to exact his revenge for a son he didn't care about?"

"You've been building your wealth over time," Nick told him. "But you didn't become a media darling until the last few years. So far, your press has been all positive. I find it hard to believe that not even one investigative journalist didn't look for a darker story to cover."

"It wouldn't take much digging to uncover the details of your arrest, conviction, and sentence," Burke added. "They would've found out that you turned Mike Carson in for robbing the store at gunpoint. They could've tried to track him down to get his thoughts about your success after leaving jail."

"And they stumbled onto a bigger story when they learned Carson died in prison," Nick added. "They would've immediately reached out to his next of kin for comment. And maybe Mick didn't take the bait right away. If he refused to take part, it probably killed the story, but the reporter had unknowingly stirred up trouble."

Burke nodded. "More like they kicked a hornet's nest. Maybe Mick blew through the settlement money and got curious about what the reporter said."

Cash blew out a frustrated breath. "That's a lot of supposition."

"Agreed," Burke said. "But it rings true. It's my job to sort this out." He squatted down in front of Cash and met his gaze. "And I will. There's a lot of information I can learn now that I have a legitimate starting point. You all need to exercise extreme caution right now until I have a better understanding of what's going on at that compound."

"Nothing good," Cash said softly. Then he told us about running into Keegan. The guy was half-starved, jumpy, and never alone. "I told

Keegan to call me if he ever wants my help, but I worry he's in too deep already."

Nick could tell how much that bothered Cash. "My Saint wants to save everyone, but what's the number one rule you decided when establishing the ranch?"

Cash sighed deeply and offered a weak smile. "Everyone here had to want to save themselves. I would just provide a fresh start and the tools to help facilitate positive change."

"And that's served you well, Cash," Burke said. "You should be damn proud of this ranch."

Nick was ready for the square-jawed superhero to move along. Burke must've sensed his irritation because he shot Nick a smirk before rising to his feet.

"I'll keep you posted as best I can, but I need you both to promise you'll stay out of this," Burke said, pinning Nick with a dark look. "I know when to seek help if I'm outgunned."

"Noted," Nick replied. It was beyond difficult to trust Cash's safety to someone else's hands, but something about Burke evoked trust. And Nick could tell Cash needed his boyfriend right then, not the investigator.

Burke gave them a brisk nod. "I'll see myself out."

Nick wrapped his arm around Cash's shoulders and tugged him closer. Cash buried his face in Nick's chest and rested a hand on Nick's thigh. Those simple gestures sent a zing straight to his balls. *Not now.* Two words he never thought he'd say regarding his libido ever again. Cash jerked back, and Nick wondered if he'd spoken his thoughts out loud, but he scrunched up his face and waved a hand in front of his nose.

"You smell like goats and donkey," Cash said.

Nick chuckled despite their stressful situation and stood up. He held out his hand to Cash and assisted him to his feet. "Let's get cleaned up and discuss what we're going to tell the guys, if anything, and what plans to implement to keep everyone safe."

Cash laced his fingers through Nick's, and they headed to the bedroom. Once in the shower, Cash leaned his forehead against Nick's shoulder instead of washing off. Nick settled his hands on Cash's lower back and vowed not to move them farther south. Cash's hands roamed lazily up and down Nick's back, setting off sparks with just the barest rasp of fingertips over flesh. The touch felt more like a mindless motion than a seductive caress while Cash's brain spiraled through a million thoughts. Nick's dick struggled to get the memo, so he thought about his taxes to keep a boner at bay. It was the least sexy topic to keep him occupied until Cash was ready to talk. Nick reached for the shampoo and went to work lathering Cash's hair. That at least got him to raise his head so Nick could look into his eyes. The sadness he saw there doused the embers burning low in his belly that even fiduciary thoughts hadn't been able to quash. Cash appeared to have gone ten rounds with blame, guilt, and remorse. They hadn't knocked him out, but he was wobbly on his feet.

"Huh-uh," Nick said firmly. "Nope."

Cash's mouth quirked up a little on the end. "What?"

"None of this is your fault. You'll eventually get to the point yourself, so I'll save you the exhaustive mind wrestling and ruminating. Are you listening?"

Cash huffed out a frustrated breath because he knew Nick wouldn't let it go. "Yeah."

"Great." Nick leaned in for a quick kiss, then pressed his fingers deeper into Cash's scalp. Cash's sigh was nearly a whimper as he closed his eyes. Nick hated to ruin the blissful expression on Cash's face, but he had things to say. "You were not responsible for Mike Carson robbing that store at gunpoint. You said you didn't know he was holding the place up, and I believe you. You did the right thing by turning him in. He wouldn't have stopped and might've killed an innocent clerk or bystander someday. That would've weighed much heavier on your conscience."

Cash sighed but didn't open his eyes. "You're right."

"Hell yes, I am." Nick maneuvered Cash to stand beneath the

spray and tilted his head back to rinse the shampoo from his hair, then got distracted by the suds cascading over Cash's gorgeous body. A few bubbles clung to him before losing the battle with water and gravity. "Hold on tight because I'm just getting started with my truth bombing."

Cash shifted his hands down to grip Nick's ass with both hands. A surge of lust hit Nick so hard it stole his breath. *Not now.* Cash's knowing smirk was freaking cute, and Nick couldn't resist giving him one little kiss.

"The parole board denied Mike Carson parole no less than five times before he died."

Cash's eyes snapped open and met Nick's. "I remember."

"None of that is your fault either. You didn't make the man instigate fights with other inmates. Carson is the one who refused to accept responsibility for his actions during those parole hearings. If he'd shown contrition and applied himself to his rehabilitation with even an ounce of the enthusiasm as the men living on this ranch, Carson could've been paroled. You're responsible for a lot of things, but Mike Carson's poor decisions aren't one of them."

Cash quirked a brow. "And just what are you blaming me for?"

Nick brought Cash's hand to his throbbing dick. "This, but we don't have—"

Cash dropped to his knees and took Nick's dick into his mouth down to the root. He bobbed his hot mouth up and down with the perfect amount of suction to curl Nick's toes.

"Time for this," Nick finished. He tried to resist. Mostly. Nick fisted Cash's hair to pull his wicked mouth off his dick, but his resistance crumbled when Cash swallowed around his swollen cockhead. The grip on his hair became Nick's anchor as he fucked Cash's face. It didn't take long before he spilled his release. Cash looked mighty smug as he swallowed it all down before letting Nick's cock slide free from his mouth.

Getting to his feet, Cash reached for the bottle of lube made especially for water sex. "There will always be time for this." He smeared lube up and down his gorgeous dick, then twirled his finger in the air.

Nick's legs were still shaking from his powerful orgasm, but he turned around and braced his palms against the shower wall. "Don't go easy on me."

"Wouldn't dream of it."

Cash nibbled his neck and sank his teeth into Nick's uninjured shoulder as he stretched Nick open for him. They moaned together when Cash sank home in one hard thrust. "Fuck, you make me feel so good." Cash eased back slowly and slammed forward a few times before setting off at an ardent pace. Nick loved it when Cash used his spent body to get off. He bunched his glutes and tightened the clench around Cash's cock, ensuring he'd lose his mind.

"Damn you," Cash snarled as he rutted like a wild animal. He came hard, growling as he spilled inside Nick. He rested against Nick's back for a few moments before pulling free. "There's never a bad time to love you."

Nick turned in his embrace, and they clung to one another for a few moments. They reluctantly separated to wash up, and that's when reality intruded again. "Are you going to tell the guys what we know so far or wait for more information?"

"Waiting could put their lives in danger," Cash said. "Besides, I promised to be open with them. I won't do anything to risk their trust. I'll tell everyone when Rue gets back with the pizza."

Nick pulled Cash hard into him. "I'm so proud to call you mine."

They shared one last, long kiss before turning off the water and toweling off. They dressed with no more kissing or fooling around. Cash's phone was pinging with one notification after another. Under normal circumstances, Nick would've teased Cash about being a popular guy. Their situation was anything but normal, so Nick kept his mouth shut. Cash crossed to the bed and picked up his phone.

"I have a missed call and voicemail message from Burke." He

swiped up and sucked in a sharp breath. "And I have three notifications from the vehicle tracking software. It detected a collision from one of the units before it went offline."

The absolute look of terror on Cash's face was something Nick would never forget. But the crew's vehicles were all at the ranch. It took Nick a second for reality to kick in.

"Rue!" Nick and Cash yelled as they sprinted toward the front of the house.

SEVENTEEN

CASH'S POUNDING HEART DROWNED OUT THE SOUND OF everything but his thundering pulse. He acted on pure instinct and crashed into Nick when they both headed for the BMW's driver side.

Nick gripped his arm to steady him. Cash saw his lips move but couldn't hear what he said. He finally read Nick's lips. "Breathe, Saint." Cash sucked in a short, choppy breath that did nothing to ease the tension in his body. Nick took Cash's hand and placed it on his chest. "Breathe with me."

They cycled through two deep breaths before Cash's pulse settled enough to quiet the roaring river of blood in his ears.

"Better?" Nick asked.

Cash nodded, not trusting his voice yet.

"I'll drive while you call Burke back."

Nick climbed in behind the steering wheel and fired up the engine. Cash already had the phone to his ear by the time he settled into the passenger seat beside Nick.

"Damn it," Cash said. "My calls are going straight to voice mail." Frustration and fear made his voice sound even thicker. "This can't be good."

Nick put the car in reverse and started moving. "Put your seat belt on." He was calm and cool like you'd expect a federal agent to sound in an emergency. "Don't let your thoughts wander. What's the last location of your truck before the tracker lost its signal?"

Cash snapped his seat belt on and fumbled his phone for a second. His heavy emotions escaped in an angry snarl. Nick settled a hand on Cash's thigh and squeezed, but he didn't linger. His left shoulder wasn't anywhere close to one hundred percent, and Nick needed his right arm to get them where they needed to go. Automatic headlights kicked on when Nick drove them along the winding drive through the forest. The sun hadn't dipped below the mountains yet, but the dense canopy of trees swallowed the remaining sunlight.

"Breathe, Saint."

Cash exhaled long and slow, then pulled himself together. The tension in his body eased up a little, and his second attempt to access the app was successful. "It says he…" His words faded into an audible gulp. "Christ, Nick. Oh fuck."

Nick stopped to let the gate open and reached over to comfort him once more. "Which way am I going, Saint? I can't do this without you."

"Turn right." Cash wheezed. It sounded and felt like he was only taking in about half the amount of air he needed.

"Deep, full breaths. Then tell me what you saw that freaked you out."

Cash complied and didn't speak until his breathing evened out again. "Hairpin curve."

Nick banged his fist against the steering wheel because he knew exactly which curve Cash meant. It was sharp with zero ability to see oncoming traffic. The road was basically carved into a mountain, leaving a sharp incline on one side and a deadly drop-off on the other. Nick had remarked on the lack of a guardrail each time they drove through the stretch of road. Cash had quipped that Coloradan mountaineers don't use guardrails. Then he reminded Nick that there were only three ranches making up the tens of thousands of acres accessible on the road. If it were a major highway, it would have more safety measures. Cash just prayed Rue wasn't a casualty to mountaineer machismo. He wanted to believe he'd just broken down or hit something in the road that bounced up and damaged the tracker. But Rueben would've called him, not Burke.

"H-h-his location dot wasn't on the road," Cash said. "It's far off to the left side."

Where the road dropped off into a heavily wooded ravine. Cash wasn't sure how far the drop was, but he surmised the fall could be a couple hundred feet. Luckily, the curve wasn't far from the ranch, so they wouldn't have to wait long for answers.

"You know those things aren't always accurate," Nick said. "Remember the time I nearly blew my CI's cover as a rookie because I thought a suspect was taking them out on a deep lake to silence them for good?"

Cash grinned despite the turmoil pressing heavily against his chest. He could still hear Nick retelling how he learned the lake's parking lot was a hot spot to solicit sex late at night. Neither the CI nor his tracking device had gone into the lake. Nick had wanted to bleach his eyeballs after he stumbled upon a threesome involving his CI. His team had harassed him for weeks afterward.

Cash tried to reach Burke again but got the same result. "Damn it."

"We're almost there, Saint."

They could see the bright blue-and-red emergency lights from Burke's truck bouncing in the trees below them as they slowly wound their way toward the scene. The trees were too thick and the surrounding area was too dark to see what was going on. *Please let Rue be okay. Please let Rue be okay.*

It only took a few minutes to reach Burke's truck, but it felt like forever. Nick pulled over as far as he safely could before he killed the engine. He pulled a flashlight from the glove box and settled a hand on Cash's leg when he reached for the door handle.

"Easy, Saint," Nick said. "I don't know how stable the ground is over there."

Cash considered it for a second, then exited through Nick's side. They carefully walked toward Burke's truck. The emergency LEDs on the light bar were bright enough to burn their retinas. Cash put a hand up to shield his eyes so he could follow Nick's flashlight beam. Burke's abandoned vehicle was the only clue something was wrong until they got close enough for their cone of light to illuminate the horrific scene. Huge ruts cut into the grass and soil on the narrow shoulder where a vehicle had gone over the side. The saplings nearest to the road were all uprooted or mowed in half.

"Christ," Cash whispered hoarsely. He lurched forward, but Nick held him back with a firm hand on his arm.

"Easy, Saint. We aren't trained to scale down a ravine, and I can't lose you."

"Burke! Rueben!" Cash shouted.

"We're down here," Burke called back. His voice, though muffled by distance and dense woods, was a welcome sound. "Rueben's conscious and talking, but he's pinned in his truck. Help is on the way. Stay where you are. Don't come down here."

Cash closed his eyes and sent up a prayer of relief until he heard Nick curse. He'd aimed his flashlight down the slope and illuminated the terrifying path Cash's truck had taken. The trees closest to the road were young and no match for the heavy vehicle. Deeper into the woods, the tree trunks became thicker. Cash's heavy-duty black truck was almost on its side and propped up against a thick tree. They could see a good portion of the undercarriage and part of the driver's side of the truck. A huge limb had come through the front windshield and exited the rear. The driver's side window was busted out, but they couldn't see Rueben because Burke was there with his back to the light. It seemed like he was holding Rue's hand as he talked to him. Burke's voice drifted up the hillside, but Cash couldn't make out what he said.

Nick moved the light beam around the front and rear of the truck, and they instantly realized how precarious Rue's situation was. If that tree went down too, nothing would stop the truck from plummeting to the bottom of the ravine. With the big truck blocking their view, it was impossible for them to see what kind of distress the tree was in. Burke had said help was on the way, but Cash became paralyzed with fear that they wouldn't make it in time.

"Rue," he called out. "We're here, buddy. We'll get you out."

A soft chuckle drifted up the hill, and Burke shook his head. "He said he appreciates you showing up, but you're interfering with his marriage proposal."

"Only Rue," Cash whispered. A lump formed in his throat, and a sense of peace washed over him. Rue was going to be okay. He had to be. "I can't just stand here and do nothing." But his so-called brilliant brain failed him at the moment. "What can I do?"

"Call Ivan," Nick said. "They might've seen us tear out of there and are wondering what the hell happened."

Ivan would've called him if that were the case, but Cash needed to let them know what was going on. "Thanks," he said, reaching for his phone.

"Make sure you tell them to stay put. The last thing the rescue team needs is more people in their way."

"Okay," Cash said. "But I'm not leaving without Rueben."

Nick leaned in for a quick kiss. "Of course we're not. Just tell them enough detail to inform them without inducing panic."

Cash nodded as he pulled up Ivan's contact. His foreman knew something was wrong as soon as he heard Cash's voice. He kept the call succinct but softened the conversation by relaying Rueben's proposal attempts. As Nick predicted, the crew wanted to rush to the scene but reluctantly agreed it wouldn't be wise. "I'll keep you guys posted. Send Rue and his rescuers good thoughts."

After Cash disconnected, he detected sirens in the distance. As the heavy diesel engines drove closer, their emergency lights bounced in the trees and the noise became deafening. Three sheriff's vehicles, two fire trucks, an ambulance, a mountain rescue truck, and a massive tow rig arrived in the most beautiful parade Cash had ever seen. His relief deepened, and his conviction strengthened. Rue would be okay.

The envoy switched to lights only as they stopped in the middle of the road, but the earsplitting sirens echoed in the trees for what seemed like an eternity. One deputy continued up the hill toward the ranch and Cash overheard a firefighter say that they were blocking the road at both ends. Nick placed his hand at the small of Cash's back and led him over for introductions. Captain Hart with Hart's Creek Rescue was perfunctory and professional, which Cash found reassuring. Hart didn't have time to hold his hand and offer hollow promises. His crew had a job to do, and they needed Cash and Nick to stay clear so they could do it.

"Understood," Cash said. "I just want to be clear about something. I only care about Rueben's safety. The truck isn't important."

The chief nodded briskly before barking out orders. In a flurry of activity, the crew donned safety gear and lit up the forest with emergency lighting. Cash and Nick moved out of the way and observed from a safe distance. Nick wrapped his arm around Cash's waist, pulled him close, and pressed a kiss to his temple.

"Rueben's going to be okay," Nick said.

"I won't accept any other outcome."

Captain Hart motioned for everyone to settle for a second so he could communicate with Burke. The men shouted questions and answers back and forth for a few minutes before Hart signaled for them to continue. A crewman pulled metal hoist wire rope from a spool on the back of the Hart's Creek Rescue truck and hooked the end to a spinal board. Three additional crewmen, geared in backpacks and rescue harnesses, hooked their kernmantle ropes to the sides of the truck before positioning themselves at the edge of the road. One of them got handed an extra rescue harness and a rope, and the other two took possession of the spinal board. They used the system of pulleys on their gear to adjust the rope so they could disappear over the side. Cash instinctively took a few steps forward before Nick tightened his hold on his waist.

"And just what are you going to do that these guys can't?" Nick teased.

Cash sighed. "You're right. It's just killing me to stand here and do nothing."

Nick pressed another kiss to his temple and held Cash even tighter. The gesture was meant to comfort, not restrain. Cash practically melted into Nick's touch. The setup happened fast, but the journey down to Rue seemed to stretch on forever. Luckily, Cash could tell what was happening from the shouted communications between Captain Hart and the crew.

"How the hell did Burke make it down there without equipment?" Nick asked.

"We'll find out when they bring his ass back to the top, but I suspect fear overrode his common sense." If Cash had been first on the scene, he probably would've attempted it too.

"I can feel you tensing up like you're about to bolt for the edge of the road," Nick said. "Maybe text an update to Ivan. They have to be freaking out right now."

"Good call."

Cash pulled out his phone and opened the group chat thread he'd set up for emergencies. If this didn't qualify, he didn't know what did. It was the first time he'd had to use it, and hopefully it would be the last. Rue was part of the group of course, but Cash suspected his phone had been damaged beyond repair. He could read the thread after his rescue and Cash got Rue a replacement phone. He typed a quick text to inform them of the progress and immediately received a reply from everyone. Cash figured they were together at Ivan and Rory's house, where the crew gathered for poker every Saturday. Tears welled in his eyes when he read just how much everyone loved Rue. Cash looked forward to him reading their sentiments too.

Nick leaned closer to read the exchange. "You have a remarkable family, Saint."

"I really do."

The men called out when they reached the truck. An argument ensued, and Cash surmised Burke had refused to go back up the mountain without Rueben.

Nick snorted and said, "I think that sly little minx is about to get his way. Do you think life has prepared Burke for Rueben Sanchez?"

Cash laughed and laid his head on Nick's shoulder. "Not in the slightest."

Captain Hart stayed by the edge of the road and called instructions to the hillside crew and the guy working the hydraulic winch on the back of the rescue truck. It seemed like hours passed before the crew's bright helmets came into view. Cash took a few steps forward, but Nick pulled him back again.

"Wait until everyone is up safely," he urged.

Two members stood on either side of the spinal board with Rueben, and the third assisted Burke's ascent. As soon as everyone was on solid ground, Cash and Nick rushed over to the group. Two EMTs approached the spinal board at the same time.

"One minute, please," Cash asked them. He dropped to his knees on the pavement without waiting for them to respond. They'd draped Rueben with a shiny rescue blanket and strapped him to the board. He didn't seem to notice Cash's presence because he was too busy frantically searching for someone else. Cash had seen the wild-eyed expression on frightened animals before, and it killed him to see it in Rue's dark eyes. He knew the moment Rueben's gaze landed on his target because the straining muscles in his neck relaxed, and he released a heavy sigh.

Cash chuckled because he knew who Rueben had been looking for. The sound got Rue's attention, and he attempted a smile.

"Hey, boss." His teeth chattered, probably from shock.

Cash wished he could grip Rue's hand to calm him, but it was tucked under the blanket. He rubbed his hands up and down Rue's shoulders and arms, hoping to stimulate some warmth to comfort him instead. Cash could barely swallow around the lump in his throat, let alone speak, but he gave it his best try. "I've never been happier to see you."

"Back at ya. I'm really sorry about your—"

Cash shook his head to cut him off. "I don't care about material things. I just wanted you home safe and sound."

"Makes two of us. Burke said I need to get checked out at the hospital, but I didn't break anything. Can you just take me home?" He sounded so small, and it made Cash's heart ache.

"I think Burke is right, but I'll tell you what. I'll stay at the hospital with you, okay?"

Rueben glanced in Burke's direction once more and scowled. Cash turned to see what had put the thundercloud in his expression. Captain Hart had Burke wrapped in a bear hug and didn't seem interested in letting go. When Burke wrestled free, Hart kept a grip on the sheriff's biceps. Their interaction seemed intensely...jovial if that was a thing. Their conversation appeared heavy while their expressions displayed affection and respect.

Rue released a little growl, then shouted "Hey!" loud enough to get everyone's attention. Burke broke away from Captain Hart, who smiled as he watched the sheriff walk away.

"Just who the hell is manhandling my man?" Rueben asked when Burke dropped to one knee opposite Cash.

Burke's mouth quirked into a wry smile. "That's my cousin, Kerry Hart," he said. It was worth noting that Burke didn't rebuke Rue's possessive claim. "Kerry and his crew are responsible for getting us to safety."

Rue didn't look remotely relieved. "Kissing cousins?"

Cash suppressed a startled snort, but Nick didn't bother.

"Gross," Burke said. "I'm not presently kissing anybody."

Rue's irate expression morphed into full out flirtation. He batted his mile-long eyelashes and said, "Want to change that?"

"Okay," said the female EMT before Burke could respond. "It's time to take Mr. Sanchez to the hospital for evaluation." Her tone was serious, but her eyes twinkled with good humor. "That was quite a ride you took, and I fear you might've bumped your head too hard if you want to kiss this big oaf." She hooked her thumb in Burke's direction.

The sheriff groaned as he stood up. Burke hooked his arm around the EMT's shoulder and introduced her as his baby sister, Shawna.

"And, no," Shawna said to Rue. "We don't kiss." She elbowed Burke in the ribs and added, "I can barely tolerate him." The huge smile and adoring expression she aimed at her brother said otherwise.

"I can't believe my good fortune," Rue said as Shawna and her partner lowered the gurney down next to him.

"You careened down a ravine and knocked yourself silly," Shawna said. "How is this fortunate?" She and her partner lifted the spinal board and gently placed it on the gurney.

"Well, I got rescued by my very own knight, and now I get to pump you for information about him."

Shawna looked up from releasing the spinal board straps. "Oh, honey, I will tell you everything you want to know."

Burke groaned and rubbed his temples. "I must be dreaming."

Rue snorted, then let out a giggle. Cash thought maybe he had rattled something pretty good. "Sugar," Rue crooned, "you'll be saying that for sure once I get out of the hospital."

"Now we're definitely getting a little loose-lipped," Shawna teased. "But I have a caveat to feeding you information."

Rue's eyes widened. "What is it? I'll do anything."

"Happy to hear it," Shawna said. Once they removed the spinal board from under Rueben, they strapped him down to the gurney and raised it for transport. "I will answer all your questions if you refrain from telling me the wicked things you plan to do to my brother."

Rueben's blinding smile was immediate. "Deal. I'd shake your hand, but mine is pinned down."

"I'll take your word, sweetie," Shawna said. "Catch you later, big brother."

Cash followed the paramedics and placed a hand on Rue's shoulder when they reached the ambulance. "I'll be there as soon as I can. Do you want me to call your abuela?"

"God no," Rue replied. "I really believe I'm fine, boss. Let's not upset her unless it becomes necessary."

Cash leaned closer to Rue's ear. "You just don't want her showing up and ruining your seduction plans."

"Gross," Shawna said. "I heard that."

Rueben winked, and Cash stepped back. When he returned to Nick's side, he was deep in conversation with Burke, Hart, and the tow truck driver. They were discussing plans to haul the truck back up to the road.

"I need you to be as careful as you can," Burke said. "That truck is evidence in a criminal case."

The tow truck driver nodded. "Was the driver intoxicated?"

The assumption pissed Cash off. He was about to let the guy know it, but Burke spoke up first.

"No, Cal. The driver wasn't at fault for the accident."

Cal looked down the side of the hill and back at Burke. "How so?"

"Someone cut the brake lines on the truck."

chapter
EIGHTEEN

BURKE'S WORDS LANDED WITH THE SAME INTENSITY AS AN uppercut to Nick's jaw, and he staggered back a step or two. Cash grabbed his hand and squeezed tight. The touch settled him but not by much. It had been Cash's truck and Cash's brakes someone had cut. Anyone who'd paid attention would know who drove the only black Redemption Ridge truck. Cash had told Rue he'd have to park in the public lot and walk into town to get the pizzas. Had someone cut the lines there? Had they meant to kill Cash, or would they settle for anyone driving a truck from the ranch?

Cash wrapped his arms around Nick and backed him up a few more steps. He put his mouth to Nick's ear and said, "I'm right here. Rue is going to be okay. We're going to take these assholes down." Of course he knew exactly where Nick's mind had gone.

"No," Burke said firmly. "*we're* not doing anything. *I* am going to take these assholes down."

Seth Burke looked every bit the badass hero standing in the middle of the road with the emergency lights acting as a spotlight. The man's square jaw and chiseled cheekbones looked more pronounced in the harsh illumination. He seemed bigger, broader, and badder. As intimidating as all that was, the hard expression in the sheriff's gray eyes held Nick's attention. Seth Burke had taken this affront personally. Maybe because of his friendship with Cash or perhaps because he'd bonded with Rueben while waiting for help to arrive. Nick got his answer when the tow truck driver asked Burke if he was certain about the brake lines.

Seth forced his attention to the man he'd called Cal. "I saw the entire thing with my own eyes. The truck was out of control as it entered the curve. It was coming straight for me. I swerved to the left out of instinct to avoid it, and the truck continued on a trajectory that took it straight over the side of the road." Seth shivered hard before pulling himself together. "It happened in horrific slow motion. I recognized the truck and had just come from the ranch. I knew who was driving."

Nick wondered if Burke replayed Rue's flirty interaction with him as he helplessly watched Rueben go over the side of the hill.

Burke briefly closed his eyes and shook his head. "I slammed on my brakes and looked over the edge. I saw where a large tree limb had penetrated clear through the truck cab and…" Burke's words trailed off as if he couldn't bear to finish the thought.

He'd feared the worst.

Burke cleared his throat and said, "I carefully made my way down to the wreckage."

"Not too carefully," a male deputy added as he joined the small gathering. "Your pants are shredded in places, and you're bleeding."

"Fine," Burke said gruffly. "I mostly slid down the hill on my ass, but I'll worry about my injuries after I clear the scene. They're a minor annoyance, not life threatening."

"Yes, sir," the deputy replied.

They stepped to the side to discuss something about the accident before Burke returned.

"Where was I?" Burke asked. "I didn't even realize I was banged up until someone mentioned it. Now it hurts like a son of a bitch."

"Adrenaline," Nick said. He'd worked with an agent who'd gotten shot and didn't realize it until someone made him aware. It had been a flesh wound, but it still would've burned like hellfire.

"You were telling us how you scaled down the steep hillside in mostly one piece to check on Rueben," Cash said.

Burke's mouth quirked at one end. "Yeah, that was it. Rueben was conscious but shaken up. His life must've flashed before his eyes." Burke took a deep breath and placed a hand on his sternum. "What a short fucking slideshow it would've been." The man pulled himself together again by his figurative bootstraps and squared his shoulders. "Rueben told me the brakes had felt spongy when he left town. There aren't many stops after leaving Last Chance Creek, but he'd lost fluid each time he pressed the pedal. Rueben said they were completely gone by the time he entered the hairpin curve. That's when I knew to check the brake lines for signs of tampering."

"It's a miracle Rue is alive." Cash's voice trembled with fear, but his eyes shone with appreciation when he stepped forward and hugged Burke. "Thank you for staying with him. He must've been terrified."

Burke patted his back. "He didn't let it show. He proposed marriage and…other things. Pretty sure I'll have a permanent blush."

"Good thing Rue isn't here to see this," Nick said, gesturing to the lingering hug between friends.

"He'll get over his infatuation soon enough." It sounded like Burke was speaking from personal experience.

"I wouldn't bet on it." Cash laughed and stepped back. "You need to get your wounds cleaned up. You don't want them to get infected. There's no telling what's embedded in your skin right now."

Burke winced. "It feels like I slid down a giant cheese grater." He tilted his head toward Nick's BMW. "You guys head on to the hospital to be with Rueben. I'll keep you posted if there are developments, and I'll check in once I get there." Burke spoke into his radio and let the deputy stationed at the bottom of the road know they were coming down.

Nick extended his hand to Burke, who accepted it. Unlike their first handshake, Nick wanted to show appreciation and respect rather than dominance.

"I'm going to get this fucker," Burke assured them.

Nick and Cash said nothing when they walked to the car, maneuvered around the emergency vehicles, and carefully traversed the winding asphalt to lower ground. He reached for Cash's hand as soon as the deputy waved them through the roadblock.

"I think someone meant for you to have an accident." Nick's voice was thick with anger and trembled with fear.

"I know." In contrast, Cash's voice was soft with sadness and shredded with regret.

Nick immediately realized his mistake. Of course Cash blamed himself for Rueben's brush with death. If he hadn't snitched on Mike Carson, none of this would've happened, according to Cash at least. And just like he'd done in the shower, Nick fast-forwarded Cash's thoughts to a result he'd reach eventually. "Carson's reign of terror is over. He's just too stupid to realize it. He's got his eyes locked on one velociraptor while another is sneaking up on his blindside."

Cash snorted. "This is what I get for falling in love with a man whose comfort watch is the *Jurassic Park* franchise. Not sure I dig your comparison, though I feel as old as a dinosaur."

"Nonsense," Nick replied. "It was a metaphor for his vengeful plans." He glanced over at Cash and received his I-call-bullshit glare. "Maybe you should text the crew an update," Nick suggested. "They have to be scared out of their minds."

"Good call."

A few moments later, Nick's phone started pinging with one text after another. "What did you do?"

Cash's responding laughter sounded downright wicked. "I added you to the ranch's group chat. You're one of us now, baby." Cash changed his voice to sound ominous for the last part, but it infused Nick's heart with warmth, not fear.

He hated group chats with the intensity of a thousand hells, but belonging to those wonderful people would be worth any sacrifice. "I'm honored."

Cash cackled and Nick's phone pinged several more times. "The guys are upset they can't come to the hospital since the road is temporarily closed. I told them about Rue's shameless flirting to assure them he's okay. They're razzing him since they know Rue will read the messages eventually."

It seemed to help Cash too, so those notifications were a small price to pay, and there must've been dozens by the time they made the quick trip to Colorado Springs. Nick couldn't find an empty parking spot near the emergency room, so they parked in a visitor and outpatient lot farther away from the building. Shawna and her partner were just coming out of the hospital with Rue's vacated gurney when they reached the ER. She smiled warmly when she saw them.

"That Rueben is adorable," Shawna said. She had gray eyes just like Burke, and they shimmered with pure mischief. "If Seth knows what's good for him, he'll snatch that cutie up."

"Did you arm Rueben with helpful information?" Cash asked.

Shawna winked and said, "Maybe."

Nick peered through the sliding glass doors and saw the emergency room was packed. Shawna must've noticed his distraction because she asked her partner to load the gurney into the rig. She gestured for them to follow her inside, and they did so without asking any questions. Shawna took them through the EMT's entrance and led them through a maze of curtained triage rooms.

"Knock, knock," she said outside one. "You decent?"

"Depends on who you've brought to see me," Rue replied.

Cash sighed and shook his head. "Thanks for your help."

"My pleasure," she said to Cash. "See you at the family Thanksgiving, Rue. Make sure you bring your abuela."

Nick eased the curtain to the side and gestured for Cash to enter the tight space.

"Such a gentleman," Rue said. "Just like my Seth."

Cash rolled a stool next to the bed and sat down. "Seth, huh?"

"He told me I could call him that." Rue's voice and expression belonged to a lovesick teenager. "He held my hand and wouldn't let go until the rescue crew reached us. Seth said if I went over the cliff, he'd go too."

Rue closed his eyes and released a saccharine sweet sigh. Nick was positive he'd have a different set of memories and emotional reactions once his adrenaline and shock wore off. The failed brakes, careening down a steep hillside, and the near miss with the tree limb would catch up to him. Luckily, he'd have a host of people to help him through the trauma.

"Hey, Rue," Cash said. He gently squeezed the younger man's arm. Rue opened his eyes and turned to look at him. "I think you need to keep your eyes open until they can determine if you have a concussion."

"Probably," he agreed. "Shawna said I didn't present the classic symptoms, but she also stated head trauma could be tricky."

"Since your vision isn't blurry, I'll let you read all the warm wishes from the crew." Cash handed over his phone and smiled every time Rue did.

When he finished, Rue snapped a selfie and added it to the chat. He told everyone he loved them and would see them soon. A new barrage of messages arrived, and Rue returned the phone to Cash after he read them.

"I'm really sorry about your truck, boss," Rue said. "I wasn't driving recklessly."

Cash clasped Rue's hand between his. "I know, Rue. Seth told us the brakes went out."

Rueben nodded. "I worked in my uncle's garage to earn extra cash in high school. He'd have me pump the brakes to help bleed the lines sometimes. And that's what it felt like, but it didn't click at the time because you'd just had the truck serviced."

"The brakes didn't fail, Rue. Someone cut them." Nick had gentled his voice but didn't mince words. Cash sent him an uncertain look, but they couldn't afford to beat around the bush. "We think we know who set Tyler up and cut your brake lines."

"Those Salvation Anew jerks," Rue said.

"Yes," Cash agreed. "We're pretty sure we know who the leader really is and why he's targeted the ranch."

"Why?" Rue asked.

"We'll tell everyone together when we get home," Cash told him. "We'd planned to have this conversation over poker. I'm truly sorry we didn't figure this out sooner."

"Not your fault, boss."

"See?" Nick said.

A nurse whisked the curtain aside before Cash could respond. He wheeled a cart that resembled a toolbox into the already cramped triage room. "It's a full house in here."

"I'm the life of the party," Rueben told him.

"I bet." The nurse offered a cheeky grin before opening a laptop and reviewing the information they'd gathered. He cycled through a series of questions before removing equipment from the drawers and performing a cursory assessment. "I'm sure the doc will want to run some tests, but it appears you are one lucky guy."

Rueben smiled at the nurse. "In more ways than I can count."

The nurse patted his shoulder and told them a doctor would be by. "It's a packed house tonight, and she'll see patients in order of urgency. The good news is that you're low on that scale. The bad news is that you might have a long wait."

Nick had received a similar warning during his recent emergency room trip. His visit had taken five hours, so it was hard to tell how long they'd be there with Rue. Nick resettled in his chair and read through the group chat conversation. He snorted when he reached the part where everyone placed bets on how long it would take for Rue to win the sheriff's heart. Nick wanted in on the action. The shortest bet was two days, and the longest was two weeks. There was no doubt in Nick's mind Rueben's attraction flattered and intrigued the sheriff. He also knew Burke needed to make peace with his feelings for Cash, so Nick landed on six months. His fingers hovered over the keyboard as he studied Rueben. The kid was a charmer and seemed very determined that Burke would be his. *Two months*, he typed and hit Send.

Nick's entry sparked a flurry of activity, both welcoming him and debating his entry.

Rueben held out his hand for Cash's phone when he heard the notifications landing on both their devices. After reading the latest thread, Rue quirked a brow at Nick.

"Such little faith," he said.

"Hey, the bet is how long you take to win the man's heart, not to get him in bed."

Rue's devilish smile warmed Nick's heart in the cold, sterile space. When Burke showed up a few hours later, Nick wanted to amend his entry. The good sheriff wore a pair of scrubs he must've borrowed from the hospital. His skin looked a little gray, and his discomfort was clear with every step. But his face lit up when his gaze landed on Rueben. Cash vacated the seat by the bed and offered it to Seth.

"Thanks." Burke's grimace and slow descent were other clues to his pain level, but he seemed to stop caring when Rueben held out his hand. "This doesn't mean we're really engaged. I just wanted to find out what my sister said about me. I'm an elected official and need to be sure my secrets won't land in my opponent's hands."

Rue smiled slyly. "Guess you'll have to take me to dinner to find out. How does Friday work for you?"

"I'm free. How do you feel about steaks?" Burke asked.

"Love a good steak."

Nick's phone pinged with an alert when Cash messaged the group. *One month.*

The crew was outraged and accused them of having insider knowledge. Nick nodded his head toward the curtain, and Cash followed him out. It was doubtful the other occupants in the small space noticed. They stopped a nurse and asked where they could find the nearest vending machines, then followed her directions. Since there was no one else in the alcove, Nick cupped Cash's cheeks and kissed him hard. The emotions he'd suppressed during the heat of the moment surged upward. Someone hated Cash enough to want him dead. Nick had been the target of plenty of bad guys, but it came with the territory. Having that level of hatred aimed at Cash was a bitter pill to swallow. Nick embraced Cash and held on for a long time.

"I love you, Saint. I love you so damn much."

"Well, I was going to treat you to a candy bar, but now I'm going to buy you chips too," Cash said. He turned his head and kissed Nick's neck. "I love you too."

Someone cleared their throat, and the two men pulled apart. Burke stood there with his arms across his chest and a big smirk on his face. "A nurse just popped in and said it would be a little longer before the doctor would be by. I thought I'd buy Rueben a snack."

"That's what we were doing," Cash said.

"Uh-huh." Burke scoffed. "Looks like it."

Nick pulled his credit card from his wallet. "What'll it be, Burke? My treat."

They took a variety of sweet and salty snacks back to Rue's triage room. Burke made his excuses to leave after he ate a bag of Cheez-Its and a Payday candy bar.

Rueben reached out for his hand again, and Burke clasped it without hesitation. He batted his long eyelashes hard enough to stir the air. "Are you sure you have to go?"

Burke's grim expression softened. "I have to make somebody pay for what they did to you."

"Oh, wow." Rueben covered his heart with his free hand. "Friday?"

Burke nodded. "Cash has my personal number. Text me when you get your replacement phone." He again promised to inform them of any developments before he ducked out through the curtain.

Rue stared at the spot Burke had occupied with a wistful expression on his face. Nick figured he wore a sappy expression like that every time he'd pined for Cash during all those trips they'd taken as *friends*. An amazing idea struck him between the eyes. Cash had taken him to Denver to kind of relive their first weekend together. Nick wanted to reexperience their favorite vacation spots as a couple. But before that could happen, they needed to put Mick Carson behind bars. He promised not to interfere with Burke's investigation, but he couldn't sit idly by and wait for the next attack either.

When Rue got restless, he borrowed Cash's phone to play *Best Fiends*. Cash tipped his head back against the wall and shut his eyes. Nick dug through social media to see what he could learn about Mick Carson and associates. It was remarkable the things people put out for just anyone to see. He found an active Facebook account, but Mick hadn't updated it in over three years. Nick doubted he'd find a detailed manifesto in the man's posts, but he hoped to uncover something he could give Burke. Carson's posts were mostly scripture and updates about his personal life. Nothing Nick would call radical. He'd almost given up when he came upon a photo of a fishing trip. It looked like four men had ventured out on a boat and reeled in a great haul. He wasn't sure what about it had caught his attention until his third pass over the group. The young guy on the far right was looking away from the photographer, so only his profile was visible. Nick sat up straight as recognition dawned. The poorly healed nose gave him away. It was the guy from the security photos.

"What?" Rue asked.

His voice woke Cash, who'd dozed off in the chair. "What'd I miss?"

Nick stood up and walked over to Rue's bed. Cash pulled his chair up so they could all see what Nick had found. "Does the guy on the end look familiar to you?"

"That's the guy who framed Tyler with the stolen tools!" Cash exclaimed. "Who is he?"

"A guy in one of Mick Carson's Facebook photos," Nick replied. "It's from five years ago. A fishing trip." Mick had tagged first names only, but it didn't take long for Nick to click through the three guests. Each had the same last name, so he assumed they were related.

"Quinton Carson," Nick said, showing them the profile.

Before they could say more, the doctor finally appeared.

"Hello, I'm Dr. Rashid." The doctor barely stood five feet tall, but her confident aura made her appear taller. She tucked long, wavy hair behind one ear as she read over Rue's notes. Her kind, whiskey-colored eyes returned to Rue. "You're a very lucky man, Mr. Sanchez."

Nick held up his phone when she started asking him questions and tilted his head toward the hallway. Cash nodded, and he ducked out. Nick took a screenshot of both photos and sent them to Burke's cell phone with a message. *This is the guy who put the stolen tools in Tyler's truck. Possibly Mick's nephew or even great-nephew.*

Burke called him in under a minute. "I thought I told you to stay out of it."

"You're welcome," Nick replied.

Burke chuckled. "How's Rue?"

"Doctor is with him now. Hopefully, they'll run his tests and send him home. Hoping to be out of here in an hour."

"You just jinxed yourself. I'll see what I can find out about Quinton Carson. Do me a favor."

"Name it," Nick said.

"Text me when you hear what the doc has to say."

Nick really wished he could change his bet. "Absolutely." He disconnected the call just as a retching sound reached his ears.

Rue was leaning forward with a barf bag to his mouth when he stepped back inside the triage room. Nick hoped that wasn't a sign of a concussion.

"Let's order some scans to be on the safe side," Dr. Rashid said when Rue finished vomiting. She threw away the bag in the hazardous waste container and gave him a clean one. "Maybe it's a result of your adrenaline crashing, but you could have a concussion." She typed rapidly on the laptop and then gave Rue a gentle smile. "Orders are in. A nurse will come by when they're ready for you."

Rue groaned when she left. "Now I'm hungry again."

Cash ruffled his hair. "Maybe we can do saltines and ginger ale soon. Let's find out what the tests say first."

As Burke predicted, Nick had indeed jinxed them. Rue didn't get cleared to leave for another five hours. Nick volunteered to bring the car around while Cash waited for Rue's prescription muscle relaxers. He, amazingly, hadn't broken or severely injured anything. The doctor said he'd have bruises and discomfort, but that was it. Nick pulled his phone out of his pocket to text Burke when he stepped through the automatic sliding doors. The sound of a fast-approaching vehicle caught his attention. Nick turned his head and held his hand up to shield his eyes from the bright headlights.

An older, square body truck screeched to a stop in front of him. He recognized Tyler behind the wheel and Owen in the passenger seat. There was someone sitting hunkered over between them. Alarmed, Nick pulled on Owen's door handle.

"What the hell are you guys doing here?" Nick asked. "Cash told you to stay home where it's safe."

"We couldn't take it anymore. We needed to see Rueben," Owen said.

"We borrowed Finley's truck because no one would tie it to the ranch," Tyler added.

"Who's your friend?"

The guy sitting in the middle of the bench seat lifted his head. Hollow hazel eyes stared back at him, and Nick immediately knew who he was looking at. He was as forlorn as Cash had described, but he now sported early signs of severe bruising on his face. "Keegan, right?"

"I got away," Keegan rasped. He swayed forward like the words had drained the rest of his energy.

Nick knew from who, but he had to ask. "Who did you get away from?"

Keegan tried to speak but nothing came out but a dry sob. He swallowed hard and tried again. "Samuel, but that's not his real name." Keegan's voice sounded as fragile as he looked.

"I think we better get you checked out inside," Nick told him. "You don't look so good."

"Slashed their tires," Keegan replied, then shook his head. "Rueben was always so nice to me."

The guy wasn't making sense, so he turned to Tyler and Owen. "Tell me everything." Unfortunately, they started talking on top of one another. "One at a time," he said with patience he didn't feel.

Tyler and Owen had gotten restless, borrowed Finley's truck, and headed to the hospital. Along the way, they encountered Keegan, who resembled a ghost or zombie in the headlights. He was staggering around on the side of the road. They recognized him and stopped. Keegan was trying to walk to the ranch after escaping Salvation Anew's compound.

Keegan's head fell forward. "Tried to beat the gay out of me." His breathing didn't sound right. Nick thought he might have broken ribs.

"Fuckers," Tyler hissed.

Keegan tilted sideways, and his head landed on Owen.

"Did he say anything to you that made sense?" Nick asked.

"We got it in bits and pieces," Tyler told him. "We put them together, and Keegan confirmed our interpretation with a nod."

"They tried to kill Cash," Owen said. "Cheered when the emergency call came through the scanner. They forgot to secure the lock on Keegan's room in all their excitement. When they found out Rue got hurt, not Cash, they bragged about taking one of us out and vowed to go bolder and bigger the next time."

"Samuel Jeremiah did this? He cut the brake lines?" Nick asked.

Keegan lifted his head long enough to give a subtle nod.

"His name isn't Samuel," Owen said. "The guy who framed Rueben goes by Brother Quinton, and he slipped and referred to Samuel as Mick once."

Keegan swayed sideways into Owen again.

"Keegan stole a knife and slashed their tires so they couldn't follow him. Thinks they won't know he's gone until morning."

"We need to get you inside, Keegan," Nick said.

"I don't have money," the young man replied.

"I do," Cash said.

Nick turned and found Cash and Rueben behind him. He hadn't heard them approach.

"Rue!" Owen and Tyler called out.

They rushed to hug their friend while Cash and Nick helped Keegan out of the truck. He wobbled between them when his legs struggled to hold him upright.

"We've got you, Keegan," Cash soothed as he held the younger man close. "Everything will be okay now."

Rueben snagged a wheelchair out of the ER and wheeled it over.

"Sit down before you fall down, Kee," Rue said gently.

"I'm so glad you're okay," Keegan managed when Nick and Cash eased him down in the chair.

Rue kneeled down in front of Keegan and took both his hands. "I heard what you said. You were very brave."

Nick got out his phone again to call Burke when the man in question pulled up outside the ER.

"We called him on the way in," Tyler said. "Don't worry. We told the nice dispatch lady about Salvation Anew listening to the police scanner. She said she'd call his cell phone instead."

Burke jogged over and stopped when he saw Rueben and Keegan with clasped hands. "Replaced me already?"

Rueben smiled up at him. "Not a chance." He introduced Burke to Keegan as his future husband, and he introduce Keegan to Burke as the witness that will put Salvation Anew away.

Burke gently shook Keegan's hand. "You're very brave. Let's get you checked out first. Then we'll talk some more."

Cash sent Rueben home with Tyler and Owen and made them

promise to text when they got there. The rest went back inside the emergency room.

Nick looped an arm around Cash's neck. "You sure know how to show a guy a good time."

Cash wrapped his arm around Nick's waist. "This is almost over. I can feel it in my bones."

chapter
NINETEEN

CASH SAT DOWN BESIDE THE HOSPITAL BED AND TOOK Keegan's hand. "I don't want you to worry about anything. I'll make sure you get whatever medical treatment you need." Cash didn't just mean his physical injuries either. Those sadistic fucks had done a real number on Keegan's psyche, and Cash wouldn't stop until he was whole again.

Tears welled in Keegan's hazel eyes, and he shook his head. The young man opened his chapped lips to speak, but no words came out. Cash gently patted his shoulder but removed his hand when Keegan tensed under his touch. Mick and Quinton better hope Burke found them first. Cash didn't trust himself to keep a lid on his temper or his hands to himself.

"None of this is your fault, Keegan," he said. "I know it's impossible to think so right now, but I promise you will believe it one day."

Nick laid a hand on Cash's shoulder and squeezed. "This man always keeps his promises."

Keegan's tears slipped down his face, leaving clean paths through the dirt smudging his skin. Cash pulled a few tissues from a box and gently dabbed at the tears. Keegan didn't flinch away, but he kept weary eyes locked on Cash's face. His dire condition meant he got medical attention right away. Dr. Rashid entered the room before Cash could say anything more about Keegan's living arrangement after his discharge from the hospital.

She looked from Cash to Nick and Burke before shaking her head. "We don't offer friends and family discounts, fellas." Dr. Rashid's attempt at humor died suddenly when she examined Keegan closer. He wasn't coherent by that point, so Nick and Burke had to relay what they knew of his ordeal. Her kind eyes darkened with anger. She turned to Burke and said, "You are going to make his assailants pay, right?"

"Yes, ma'am," Burke said. "But I need to get more information from Keegan before I can bring them to justice."

Dr. Rashid shook her head. "Not in his condition, Sheriff. I don't have to run a bunch of tests to recognize that he's dehydrated, severely malnourished, and has suffered severe physical trauma. He's in no condition physically or mentally to answer questions. Statements given in his present state aren't admissible in court. A good defense attorney would have a field day over this."

Burke pinched the bridge of his nose and released a heavy sigh before he lowered his arm. "You're a lawyer too?" There was no heat in his voice, only frustration.

Dr. Rashid didn't take his question personally. She smiled gently and patted his arm. "No, but my father is one of the best defense attorneys in the state of Colorado. I'm pretty sure my first spoken words were the lawyer lingo I picked up at the dinner table. I'm also married to a prosecuting attorney. You never want to watch an episode of *Law and Order* or *Grey's Anatomy* with me. I'll ruin the magic for you."

"Defense versus prosecution, huh? Your family gatherings must be very interesting," Nick teased.

"Interesting is one word for it." She shooed everyone out of her way so she could examine Keegan. Dr. Rashid ordered several lab tests to determine the severity of his condition and determine his treatment.

Keegan looked wild-eyed and mumbled something Cash couldn't understand, and he looked downright terrified.

Cash returned to his bedside. "Are you afraid of needles?"

Keegan shook his head and beckoned for Cash to come closer. He attempted to speak again and this time Cash understood. Keegan was worried about money.

"I'm not," Cash told him. "And I'm not just doing this because you took an enormous risk to help me. I offered you my assistance when I saw you at the feed store. Remember?"

Keegan nodded.

"This is me helping anyway I can," Cash told him. "I just want you to relax and do whatever Dr. Rashid thinks is best for you."

Keegan inhaled deeply and nodded slowly. "Will you stay?" His voice rasped like dry leaves rasping against pavement.

"Of course."

"We both will," Nick told him. "Burke has a case to make against the people who hurt you. And when you're stable enough to answer questions, your statement will be the icing on the cake."

Keegan closed his eyes and surrendered to the blood tests. His severe dehydration made it difficult to find a good vein to draw from. It took two different nurses and a vein finder before they achieved success. That paved the way to hook Keegan to IVs to address the dehydration and malnourishment. The nurse also said they could give Keegan tiny sips of water but cautioned they needed to space them every ten minutes. Cash set a timer and encouraged Keegan to take a drink when he was awake.

Dr. Rashid returned with the test results faster than Cash expected. Her somber expression promised the news wouldn't be good. She attempted a gentle smile to soften the blow before speaking. "I'm going to admit you to the hospital for treatment, Keegan. You've barely avoided a crisis with critical organs." She looked up at Burke. "This is one of the worst cases of neglect and abuse I've ever witnessed. It kills me to say this, but you'll need to wait at least three days before you can interview him."

"Fair enough," Burke said, but it was obvious he hated the delay. He gentled his gaze when he looked at Keegan. "Nick's right. I'll work my ass off building a case until then. You just get better." Burke returned his attention to the doctor. "I need him in a private room because I'm putting security on him around the clock."

Dr. Rashid nodded her approval. "No problem."

Burke stepped out of the room, presumably to arrange Keegan's protection. Nick engaged the doctor in a quiet conversation about treatments. But Cash kept his attention on Keegan to see how he reacted to the news. The young man's chin quivered, and his eyes welled with tears again. For someone who'd just escaped a hellish prison, an extended stay in a sterile hospital room must've felt like jumping out of the frying pan and into the fire.

"Hey now," Cash whispered. "There will be plenty of time for tears, and you sure as hell deserve the time and space to shed as many as you want. But you heard the doc. You're severely dehydrated, so you should hold on to those tears for now."

Keegan released a noise that could've been a choked sob or an attempt to laugh, but it sounded like an animalistic, mournful whimper. Cash hoped to go the rest of his life without hearing it again. Keegan turned his head, and his expression was just as pitiful. Cash's heart ached, and he wanted to close his eyes against the pain, but he couldn't—wouldn't.

"You will not be alone," Cash promised. "One of us from the ranch will be by your side for the duration of your stay." He turned and interrupted Nick and Dr. Rashid. "I'll pay for a double room just so we'll have a spare bed to sleep in."

"I was just discussing that with Agent Scott," Dr. Rashid said. "We'll also make sure he's admitted under a false name. We have protocols for when patients arrive here under these circumstances." She smiled gently at Keegan. "We won't let you down."

Such a thoughtful remark would've normally warmed Cash, but his heart stalled when Dr. Rashid addressed Nick by his professional title. Why had he used his FBI credentials while he was on medical leave? Habit? Did he think they'd persuade Dr. Rashid somehow? Technically, he was still an FBI agent until he officially resigned. Had he changed his mind? Cash reined in his wild thoughts and put his attention where it helped most. He turned back to Keegan and noticed he'd fallen asleep again.

"I'll go upstairs with Keegan." Cash didn't know how comfortable he would be with someone else from the ranch in his present state. Keegan obviously cared a great deal for Rue, but he would need a good night's rest after his ordeal. "We'll sort the rest out later."

"I'm not leaving until Burke has a man outside Keegan's door," Nick said.

Dr. Rashid held up her hands in surrender. "I'll let you guys battle it out with the floor nurses. I'll try to get his admittance pushed so we can get you upstairs quickly."

"Thank you for everything," Cash told Dr. Rashid.

"You're welcome." She narrowed her eyes and pointed at him, then Nick. "I don't want to see either of you or anyone else you care about in my ER anytime soon."

"We couldn't agree more, Doc," Nick said.

Once she left, Nick crossed the small gap and placed both hands on Cash's shoulders. He leaned down and kissed Cash's cheek. "You're an idiot," he whispered.

Cash whirled around and stared up at Nick. "Squat down here so I don't have to strain my neck while we have our first argument as a couple." He also kept his voice low so as not to disturb Keegan.

Cash and Nick had argued plenty of times as friends, but he expected this battle to land differently. Nick snagged the doctor's stool instead and sat down so they were eye to eye.

Nick had instigated the first blow and didn't wait for Cash to counter. "How could you possibly think I'd changed my mind about us?"

Cash flinched as he took the verbal volley on the chin. "I didn't think you changed your mind about *us*." But wouldn't that have been the natural conclusion his brain would've drawn if he hadn't slammed on the brakes? "And stop trying to circumvent the way my brain processes information. You've done that three times in the last…" Cash tilted his head to the side. "I lost track of time. Day?"

Nick chuckled, leaned forward, and kissed Cash's lips. "I will never try to disrupt your brilliant brain for business stuff." He kissed him again and lingered a little longer. "But there's no room for doubt with us. I love you. I want to be with you, not just for now while I heal. I want forever with you, Saint."

Cash leaned his forehead against Nick's. "Hearing Dr. Rashid use your FBI credentials threw me. I'm sorry."

"Habit," Nick said. "Being an FBI agent has been my total identity for the past twelve years. I naturally slipped into that role when I discussed the logistics of Keegan's protection. I haven't changed my mind. I want more from life than my career provided me. But I need you."

"So touching."

They looked up to see Burke standing inside the curtain. Cash rolled his eyes, and Nick flipped him off.

"I'll head out as soon as Keegan's security detail arrives," Burke said.

Nick told him about the conversation he'd had with Dr. Rashid, and Burke thanked him.

"Why can't you get an arrest warrant based on Keegan's condition alone?" Cash asked. "You heard what Dr. Rashid said. It's one of the worst abuse cases she's seen. Why isn't Keegan's word enough?"

"Because Burke didn't get the allegations directly from Keegan," Nick replied. "He got them from me, who only heard bits and pieces from Keegan. Tyler and Owen did most of the talking. It's really murky, Saint. If the evidence couldn't hold up in court, and it wouldn't in this case, then you shouldn't arrest someone solely on the information."

"Arrest him now and make the case afterward," Cash growled.

"The longest I could hold them is forty-eight hours, and I can't corroborate Keegan's story for three days. Not only would they walk away with no charges filed against them, they would know we were on to them and would hide the evidence of their crimes. No judge in his right mind would give me a search warrant based on the circumstantial evidence we have now. Even if I could finagle one, even the most inexperienced defense attorney would get the evidence thrown out at trial. I will have only one shot to do this, and I need to do it right."

"I know it's frustrating, but we are forewarned, thanks to Keegan," Nick said. "We can take actions to protect our people until Burke can arrest the Carsons."

Cash huffed a sigh and ran a hand through his hair. He'd waited twelve years for Nick. Allowing Keegan to recover for three days would normally seem like an insignificant amount of time if his crew wasn't in danger because of him. Nick narrowed his eyes and shook his head as if he knew the trajectory his thoughts had taken. *Smug bastard.* "Okay. You do what you need to, Burke, and we'll do what we must to stay safe."

Federal law prohibited most of the ranch's residents from owning guns, so they'd have to protect themselves in other ways. Mainly by avoiding the threat altogether. Cash's problem-solving brain kicked into high gear. By the time they transported Keegan upstairs with his deputy detail, Cash had commandeered a notepad and a pen from the hospital staff and had started making a list. So far, everything he'd come up with restricted the crew's movements. The ranch was their refuge, so the last thing Cash wanted to do was make it a different prison. He dropped the notepad on his lap and emitted a soft growl of frustration.

Nick had wedged himself in to lie sideways beside Cash on the narrow spare hospital bed. "Gimme," he said.

Cash happily handed the notepad to him and they switched positions. He lay down on his side, and Nick sat up in the bed.

"I agree you need to limit your exposure, so having groceries and supplies delivered to the ranch accomplishes the exact opposite. You don't know how far Carson's reach extends and you don't want his min-ions sizing up the ranch from inside the fence." Or attacking. Nick hadn't said as much, but he wasn't the only one in the relationship who could read minds. "Burke doesn't have enough deputies to provide the level of security we'd need, but you could hire a private team to offer pro-tection on and off the ranch. They'd have a license to carry weapons. A lot of ex-military men go into that line of work, so Burke might have a recommendation."

Cash deflated in the bed. "Why the hell didn't I think of that? I've hired a security detail for overseas business trips."

Nick set the notepad aside and lay down to spoon behind Cash. "Because you're exhausted after several traumatic experiences. We've got a guard outside the door and each other. Let's try to rest so we can make smart decisions."

Cash knew Nick was right. He closed his eyes and clung to the hope that the ordeal would soon be over and the true healing could begin for everyone.

Two weeks later, and with no end in sight, Cash's optimism fizzled. It wasn't because Keegan hadn't provided actionable information. He'd not only warned of bigger, bolder plans for Redemption Ridge's resi-dents, but he'd revealed there were large storage buildings on the prop-erty that were only accessible to Mick and Quinton. As for Burke, he hadn't sat idly by while waiting for Keegan to recover. He'd set up sur-veillance near the compound to track movement coming in and out. He'd struck out there but had recovered viable fingerprints from the wrecked truck's bumper and undercarriage. They matched the prints on the stolen tools and the canvas bag seized from the trash after the frame job. Quinton Carson didn't have a record, so his prints wouldn't be on file until Burke arrested and booked him. A fingerprint match could convince Quinton to roll on Mick. But they'd need to arrest the duo of doom first, and to do that, they'd need to find them. Burke had conducted several interviews with the Carson family members, who either wouldn't or couldn't provide insightful information.

Keegan's bravery had provided Burke the evidence to secure warrants to arrest Mick and Quinton Carson and search the compound. Unfortunately, the men were long gone by then. Keegan may have slashed their tires to help himself get away, but they stole a truck from a neighboring farm and fled once they realized he was gone. The Salvation Anew compound was divided in a weird hierarchy that allowed the women to live in the house with Carson while the men and children lived in tents or campers on the property. The cowardly leader left his followers to their own fate, which hadn't been promising in the first place.

Someone had locked all the food and staples in one of the storage rooms. The refrigerator and cupboards in the home were completely bare. The only cold storage for fresh food was inside the shed. Instead of seeking help, Carson's brainwashed and browbeaten followers stayed put, existing on whatever they could forage from the land. The contents in the other storage shed revealed the kind of bigger and bolder plans the Carsons had wanted to carry out. Guns, ammunition, homemade pipe bombs, and various other deadly weapons filled the space. Some items were still in their original USPS shipping material. Since they'd crossed state lines, Burke brought the feds on board to assist. The decision wasn't a happy one, but the sheriff wasn't foolish enough to resist the personnel and additional tools at the FBI's disposal. And since Nick hadn't tendered his resignation, the agents assigned to the case kept an open line of communication with him as a courtesy.

Seeing Nick flourish in his element had made Cash queasy about Nick's decision to leave the FBI. Whenever those doubts arose, Nick would calm them—privately and usually in the nude. He proved the tufted ottoman in the walk-in closet really came in handy for more than putting on shoes. And Cash's ties made an excellent gag to muffle his screams of pleasure when Nick hammered his *point* home. Sex with Nick went beyond a consolation prize for the turmoil the Carsons had thrust upon Redemption Ridge. It was downright therapeutic, though they'd curtailed shenanigans in the hot tub with the security team on-site. Cash reminded himself frequently that the situation was temporary, and they'd return to their normal lives eventually.

The crew had responded well to the new challenges. Well, Rueben had pouted a little when Burke postponed their date until after he caught Mick and Quinton. Instead, Burke had joined them for dinner on the ranch a few times and even played a few rounds of poker. He blushed at Rueben's overt flirtations but didn't return them in front of the crew. No one missed how long it took for Rue to say goodbye when he walked Burke out to his truck nor did they miss the sappy smile on his well-kissed lips when he returned. Rueben deserved his date with Burke, and the crew should've been able to come and go as they pleased without their security shadow. They weren't in the wrong, yet they were the ones getting punished. There were moments when Cash felt stifled and just the brush of a shirt collar against his neck was suffocating. He worked out more and fucked harder, but those only provided temporary relief.

Cash's brain would start looking for trouble as soon as blood flowed back to it, and he'd start the process all over again. He worked through problems best on paper, so he'd started making lists of things they knew and things they didn't. Burke's team uncovered the items stolen from the local homes inside one of the storage buildings. He surmised that Salvation Anew only took them to cast a poor light on Cash and his crew. Mick Carson had meant to turn the community against Redemption Ridge with his allegations. When that didn't work, he tried to frame them. Since that failed, he'd stepped up his game again and cut the brake lines on Cash's truck. It didn't take Cash long to realize the list of things he knew eclipsed the things he didn't. It only increased his frustration, so he turned his attention to the positive things he could do. Keeping morale up on the ranch and making sure Keegan was comfortable were his top priorities.

Cash tried hard not to think about the descriptors Burke used to define the conditions Keegan had lived in prior to his escape, but Cash pictured them every time he closed his eyes. He relived Keegan's mournful whimpers in his dreams. Cash had witnessed the man's night terrors during those first few days at the hospital, and he'd seen the echoes of them in Keegan's eyes the next morning. Keegan had fluctuated between sadness and anger, but the underlying emotion was always fear. Cash did his best to assure Keegan he was safe. He would never forget the look of awe on Keegan's face when Cash had shown him to Harry's former suite on his first day at the ranch. His lips had trembled, and he'd scrubbed at his eyes to keep the tears at bay.

"Now is a good time to have a good cry, and this is a safe place to do it. I promise no one here will ever make fun of you."

Keegan collapsed onto the bed like his legs had given out and sobbed into a pillow. Cash offered comfort where he could, then retrieved a bottle of water for Keegan when it felt best to give him some privacy. Keegan had only tried to pick out one outfit when Cash took him to the general store on the ranch. Cash noticed he'd chosen the most subdued colors, but he remembered Keegan had had a flair for bolder hues before his time with Salvation Anew. Cash picked out a flannel shirt with navy blue and aqua plaid, and Keegan offered his first smile since arriving at the hospital. The smiles came easier, even if sadness shrouded him like a cloak. Witnessing Keegan's recovery over the past two weeks was a solace Cash clung to when hope eluded him or when he noticed how happy Nick seemed when interacting with his federal friends. Nick had completed two interviews at the police academy and was waiting for the final round. Would teaching cadets really satisfy Nick, or would he regret his decision and resent Cash?

"You're doing it again." Nick's voice snapped Cash out of his musings. They'd been enjoying a beautiful evening on the porch while Keegan played with Patsy in the yard.

Cash turned his head and gave Nick his most innocent smile. "Guess you know what that means."

Nick placed his hands on the arm of the chair and pushed up, but

Rory bustled up the steps before Nick's sweet ass moved more than a few inches.

"I think I have a solution to your problem, Cash," Rory said.

Nick leaned into Cash's personal space. "You're not getting rid of me so easily, Saint."

Cash chuckled and rolled his eyes. "Maybe you could be more specific about the problem you mean."

"The big baddies," Rory said.

Nick snorted. "Did he say something about Daddies?"

"No, *he* didn't," Rory replied snidely. "I'm afraid I'll accidentally summon the bad guys if I say their names out loud." He tilted his head. "On the other hand, that's what I want to talk about."

"Summoning demons?" Nick asked. "Exactly what are you watching at night?"

Rory quirked a brow and smiled wryly. "Who has time for television in the evening?" He fanned himself in case the older folks were too dumb to understand.

Nick gagged. "I don't need to imagine what you're getting up to over there."

"Then don't, you perv," Rory shot back. "Be serious. I can't believe they let you into the FBI."

Nick leaned forward, lowered his voice, and said, "Don't you know? Charles bought my way in."

Rory snorted. "Yeah, right. Is that really what some people think at the Bureau?"

"More people believe it than not," Nick said, then pinned Cash with a firm look. "Which is just one reason of many why I'm leaving the Bureau regardless of whether the police academy job comes through."

Cash ignored him and gestured for Rory to continue. "What did you want to talk about?"

"Remember how we used PR to subdue this Samuel Jeremiah Mick Carson guy? We need to do the same thing to smoke him out of hiding."

"No way," Nick said. "You're not dangling Cash out like he's a juicy carrot."

"Ignore him," Cash said. "Convince me, and I'll do the same with Burke."

Nick crossed his arms over his chest and pursed his lips. Cash nearly asked for a quick recess so he could kiss the pout off his face, but their intimate moments were never short. "I don't like this," Nick said.

"Noted," Cash said and waved at Rory. "You have the floor." He clasped his hand over Nick's mouth when he tried to interrupt. "Behave and I'll reward you later."

"Ew," Rory said. "Now it's my turn to be grossed out."

Nick licked his palm, and Cash jerked his hand back, deciding to use it on Nick's ass later.

"You were saying," Cash prompted.

"It's a two-pronged attack." He recommended they do a video for their website and YouTube channel about Cash's history with Mick Carson and the current troubles with him. "Expose everything you know about the guy. Then we continue with our plans for the Pups and Pumpkins event this weekend. Really push the pet adoption on our social media sites and maybe do some flyers in town."

"This is a bad idea," Nick said. "We can't involve the public."

"We will send federal agents, deputies, and our security team undercover to mingle with the crowd," Rory said.

"We're private citizens," Nick corrected. "We can't send deputies and agents anywhere. Our security team is too small to cover us in a crowd that size. And besides, if we are all in town hoping to draw Mick out, what's stopping him from setting fire to everything Cash holds dear? This ranch is surrounded by forest."

As much as Cash wanted to reject that idea outright, Nick spelled out a serious threat—one that would be Cash's worst nightmare. He could replace buildings and possessions, but he couldn't risk anything happening to their animals.

Rory frowned and bobbed his head back and forth. "Okay, that's a valid point I hadn't considered."

"And we just can't risk something happening to our community," Cash said. "It's not fair to invite our chaos into their streets."

Rory huffed a sigh. "Fine. You're right."

"I appreciate your input," Cash told him. "At least you're doing something. I've just twiddled my thumbs for two weeks."

"And moped," Nick added. "You're using your extra free time to imagine problems where there are none."

"Sounds like this is a good time for me to skedaddle," Rory said. "See you at breakfast."

Cash wanted to dispute the claim, but Nick was right. He needed to do something besides worry about things he couldn't control. "I have this niggling idea the solution is contained in a locked memory."

"Let's go see if we can shake it loose."

Nick had given everything he had, but Cash staggered out of the closet on limp legs, no closer to a solution than when they'd entered. He collapsed onto the bed and fell into a deep sleep that ended abruptly when he dreamed of panicked horses and a smoke-filled barn. Cash was simultaneously cold and hot, sweaty, shaking, and his chest had hurt so badly. He suspected a heart attack but cycled through some deep breaths before calling 911. The tension eased, and his pulse returned to normal, but he still trembled all over. Cash took a shower to wash away the cold sweat and ended up sitting in the middle of the tiled floor to let the water beat down on him.

He had to stop trying to shoulder the burdens of things he couldn't control. The ranch already had a contingency plan in place for wildfire evacuations. They'd have to adjust it slightly to include Jake and the goats, but he believed in his crew. Cash realized he also needed to have faith in a universe or higher power that would help good triumph over evil. He pulled himself together, turned off the shower, and dried off. He pulled on a pair of sweats and a long-sleeved T-shirt and went to his office to avoid waking Nick. Cash made a cup of herbal tea, curled into a corner of the sofa, and started scrolling through Mick and Quinton Carson's social media posts. When that triggered nothing, he started looking at their family members' posts. Quinton's brothers had their accounts locked down pretty tight, but his father, Mick's nephew, wasn't worried much about privacy. It looked like he put every thought out there for the world to see. Cash slowly scrolled through the posts, going back farther than he had with Mick's. He stopped on a Father's Day tribute from ten years ago. It was a screenshot of an old photo from what looked like the late seventies or early eighties. There were several generations of Carson males at what looked to be a family reunion or picnic at a lake. The caption was a tribute to all the fathers in his family, and he waxed poetic about the fun times at the family cabin. Several of the men posed with stringers of dead fish.

Cash sat up so fast he sloshed tea over the side of his mug. That niggling notion tickling his brain transformed into a solid memory. Mike had once told him how much he hated fishing. The subject of hobbies had come up while the crew worked on Cash's race car. Someone had said they fished in their spare time. Mike had piped in and said he loathed everything to do with fishing. His parents forced him to go to the family's cabin in Twin Lakes as a kid. He didn't start appreciating those outings until he was old enough to appreciate girls his age in bikinis. He'd started calling it "Twin Peaks" from there on. Bolting to his feet, Cash ran into his bedroom and woke Nick.

"Again, Saint?" He rolled onto his back and rubbed his eyes. "I just got Spiffy to fire on all cylinders again, and you're going to wear him out."

"I remembered something Mike told me years ago. I think I have a possible location for Mick and Quinton."

Nick sat up and was immediately alert. Cash showed him the photo he'd found and repeated the Twin Lakes story.

"It might be nothing," Cash said.

"Or it could mean everything." Nick kissed Cash firmly on the mouth before dialing someone on his phone. "Hey, Burke," he said. "Sorry to wake you. Cash remembered something Mike Carson told him."

Cash listened to Nick's side of the story, marveling that he'd called Burke first. "Twin Lakes is not his jurisdiction," Cash said once Nick disconnected.

"No, it's not, but Burke deserves the opportunity to take the lead and make the calls." Nick tugged Cash onto the bed and rolled so he was spooning up behind him again.

"What are you doing?" Cash asked.

"Trying to get you to go back to sleep. You've done what you can. There's no need for you to stay awake all night for something that could take hours or even days to develop. It's time to let the professionals handle it."

Cash suspected the last bit was for his benefit, but he fell for it anyway. *Please don't let it be days.*

He woke sometime later to a trail of kisses along the back of his neck. "Do you know what day it is?" Nick whispered.

Cash arched his back and pressed his ass into Nick's crotch. He hadn't stripped down when he returned to bed, so there were too many clothes between them. "Mmmm. I've lost track of the days." Cash reached behind him and stroked Nick's cock. "It's bound to be a great day if I start off with this beast inside me."

Nick canted his hips to press harder against Cash's palm. "Keep it up and you'll distract me from my mission."

Cash stilled and looked over his shoulder. "I thought I was the mission."

Nick nipped the back of his neck. "Always, but there's something I wanted to tell you first. Something exciting."

Cash's pulse leaped. "More exciting than sex with you?"

"Maybe just this once."

Cash rolled over and stared into Nick's smiling eyes. "I'll play. What day is it?"

"Justice day."

The air caught in Cash's lungs. Was he dreaming? "Did they arrest Mick and Quinton already?" Cash looked at the clock and saw it was barely seven. He'd only been asleep for four hours. He'd hoped for a swift ending, but he didn't dream it would happen that quick.

Nick's mouth curved into a wry smile. "Yes, they were captured, but not because of any action we took. Our guys were still combing through the weeds and putting together a strategy when an eighty-year-old couple with a double-barrel shotgun and .357 Magnum made a citizen's arrest around the time you figured out a possible location. The Carsons broke into their bait and carryout store in Twin Lakes, not knowing the rear of the building was their residence. Beavis and Butthead were so busy stuffing food into their bags they didn't know they'd tripped a silent alarm until they heard the unmistakable sound of Ernest pumping his shot gun. The alarm also rang to the sheriff's department, who arrived minutes later to apprehend Mick and Quinton without resistance. Rumors are swirling that Emma fired off a warning shot that landed inches from Mick's feet after he took a step toward the door. If that's true, he probably really pissed his pants too."

"Sounds like something a coward like him would do." Cash threw his arms around Nick and rolled him onto his back. "Is it really over?"

"Well, there's jurisdictional fighting over who gets to charge the asshats first, so Burke hasn't had the honor of transporting them back here. With the case Burke built against them, those assholes aren't going anywhere for a very long time."

"I'm so grateful."

Tears of relief welled behind Cash's closed eyelids. The extra security could leave, and the crew could get back to normal activities. Rueben could go on his date with Burke, and Keegan could heal.

"How grateful?" Nick asked.

Cash kissed him briefly and was going back for more when someone banged on the door.

"Cash! Nicky!" Rory yelled. "Wake up!"

Nick groaned. "Cockblocking brothers," he whispered to Cash.

"I heard that," Rory replied. "The Carsons got arrested in Lake County overnight. It's all over the news."

"We know," Nicky called out.

"Get up. It's time to celebrate."

Nick slid his thigh between Cash's legs. "I plan to do my celebrating right here. Scram!" Rory's laughter echoed down the hallway as he retreated. Nick shook his head and smiled at Cash. "Where were we?"

"A show of gratitude."

Then he took his time proving it with his hands, mouth, and dick.

epilogue

THE CELEBRATIONS ON THE RANCH CONTINUED FOR WEEKS. Nick wasn't sure if it was because the group was a joyful bunch or if they just looked for any excuse to barbecue. The first party happened after Burke officially charged Mick and Quinton with a multitude of offenses and brought them back to Last Chance Creek. The Carsons clung to their innocence, but Nick figured they'd change their tune when their attorneys saw the evidence against them. Since they weren't talking, Cash didn't get the closure he deserved, so Nick kept digging.

Mick's financial records revealed he'd blown through Mike's wrongful-death settlement money about a year before he'd shown up in Last Chance Creek. That was also the same time Cash's name started popping up in Mick's internet browser history. The FBI shared the results with him, and Nick had noticed most of the articles Carson read were by the same reporter. A quick phone conversation with her revealed she had contacted Mick for his reaction to recent articles published about Cash. She'd taken a defensive tone until Nick assured her she'd done nothing wrong. Good journalists sought multiple angles to paint a complete story. She had no way of knowing her phone call would trigger a diabolical revenge plot.

Cash was a linear thinker, and he struggled to connect the dots logically. To him, Mick didn't financially gain from Cash's demise. He didn't understand why Mick would involve innocent people in his schemes. Why form a church? Had that just been a cover? Had it been a power trip for Mick? Was it a way to get others to fund his miserable existence? Cash had questions Nick couldn't answer. He wasn't certain even Mick could answer them.

One night, they gathered in the library to relax after dinner, and Nick could practically smell the gears smoking in Cash's brain. He lowered the book on tantric sex he'd bought from Hope's shop. He'd only reached item number two of twenty on how to deepen orgasms when Cash's thinking interrupted him. "You're trying to rationalize an irrational mind."

Cash narrowed his eyes. "Stop doing that."

"No, you stop. Are you going to let that man live rent free in your head?"

"No."

"Good." Nick read items three and four out loud before they retired early to their bedroom to test them out.

The next celebration came when Rueben finally got his date with Burke. The little minx left with the sexy sheriff on Friday night and didn't return until Monday morning. They all took one look at his moonstruck face at the breakfast table and whipped out their money. Kieran, who'd placed the winning bet, wore a smug smile as he fanned himself with his earnings.

The next milestone they honored was when Keegan managed a week of sleep without nightmares. Cash had found a wonderful therapist for him, and the young man was putting in the work. His wounds were just too deep to heal as easily as his bruises had. He still withdrew to his room at times or limited his interactions to Cash, Rueben, or Owen. The latter took everyone by surprise, especially Tyler, whenever Owen shared huge chunks of time with Keegan. Nick could tell it bothered Ty, but he wasn't the kind of person to make a fuss. Rueben and Rory stepped up to keep Ty company, but he seemed like a ghost of himself unless Owen was around.

The ranch threw Nick a party when he officially resigned from the Bureau and joined the police academy. As sweet as he found the sentiment, Nick was just happy to see Cash relax.

"You're where you want to be," he told Nick as they slow danced in the great room.

"You're my home, Saint." He'd repeat the words as often as Cash needed to hear them.

The biggest celebration came at the end of October when Cash turned fifty. Dylan smoked pulled pork, brisket, and turkey legs while Harry and Rory made a dozen side dishes. The bash was fit for the king of Redemption Ridge and Nick's heart. The cold front and freshly fallen snow kept the party inside, but they laughed, danced, and basked in the joy they found in each other's company.

Nick went to the kitchen to get water and found Tyler doing dishes. He knew he should mind his business, but it pained him to see Ty hurting so badly. If Nick could spare someone else a dozen years of pining, he would. Tyler glanced up and offered a pitiful smile when he approached.

"Why are you hiding in here?" Nick asked. He picked up a towel and went to work drying dishes.

Tyler shrugged. "Just kind of feel like a third wheel sometimes, I guess. Then I feel like an awful person for thinking that way. Keegan has been through so much, and Owen brings him peace. I'd have to be a real jerk to make things harder for them to be together." There was a slight emphasis on the last word that struck to the heart of the problem.

Nick knew he needed to tread lightly. "They're not together romantically."

Tyler shrugged again and shoved his hands into the soapy water.

"That isn't what romantic love looks like, Ty." *If you could only see the way Owen looks at you.*

Tyler's hands stilled, and he met Nick's gaze. His eyes were wide and wet with unshed tears. "When did you know you were in love with your best friend?"

Nick set his towel down and crossed his arms over his chest. "I didn't have a big a-ha moment," he admitted. "It happened slowly. I noticed little things at first. Catching guys checking Cash out made me jealous. Thinking of him falling in love with someone else and being intimate with them drove me mad. Not being with him became a bone-deep ache."

Tyler emitted a feral little growl that caught them both by surprise. He rubbed a hand over his chest like that might make the hurt go away.

"You'll miss a hundred percent of the shots you don't take," Nick said. "I wasted so much time pining after something that was mine for the taking all along. Swing for the fences, Ty."

"What if he doesn't feel the same way?"

"But what if he does?" Nick patted him on the shoulder. "Don't wait too long." He grabbed two waters and headed back to the great room, where he celebrated the man he loved.

When everyone left, Nick grabbed drinks, towels, and Cash's hand. He'd saved his birthday gift for when they were alone. They moved to the hot tub much quicker when it was colder, but the contrast between the chilly air and bubbling hot water made it worth it.

"Ready for your birthday gift?" Nick asked.

Cash slid his hand up Nick's thigh. "Always."

"You know how you whisked me away to Denver to relive our first weekend together?"

"Vividly."

Nick smiled and kissed him. "I want a do-over of our first vacation, so I booked a trip to Cabo. We leave in two weeks."

"Baby, that's incredible. Thank you so much." Cash pulled him close for a long kiss that threatened to derail Nick's thoughts.

He had more he wanted to say, so he reluctantly pulled away. "This time I won't go to my lonely room and wish I was with you. I can tug your ridiculously small swimsuit off with my teeth and blow you behind a waterfall. I will hold your hand and show the world you're mine, and I'm yours. I am going to kiss you when the sun rises and sets and when the stars come out to play. One glorious week, just you and me."

Cash was almost breathless by the time Nick finished. "I want all those things too, but on one condition. I want to take this dream trip with my husband."

"Damn it, Saint. I was going to propose behind the waterfall."

"Mmmhmm. Before or after you blew me? What was the order supposed to be? Climb behind the waterfall, hit your knees to propose, rip my swim briefs down, and blow me? Or get me all sexed up and then ask me to marry you? And where the hell were you going to hide the ring? If my briefs were small, yours were downright micro."

Nick cut off his diatribe with a hard kiss. "I would absolutely love to marry you, Saint. But we can't pull off a wedding in two weeks."

Cash's grin was downright wicked. "Bet me."

The End!

The Redemption series continues with Owen and Tyler in *Friends Like Them* and Rue and Burke in *The Keeper*. You can preorder both now. I chose advanced release dates so I could get the links, but I anticipate earlier publication dates.

Friends Like Them: https://mybook.to/Friends_Like_Them

The Keeper: https://mybook.to/The_Keeper_RR5

Stay tuned, stay connected, and find me on all the socials at inktr.ee/AimeeNicoleWalker

Want to be the first to know about my book releases and have access to extra content? You can sign up for my newsletter here: http://eepurl.com/dlhPYj

My favorite place to hang out and chat with my readers is my Facebook group. Would you like to be a member of Aimee's Dye Hards? We'd love to have you! Go here: www.facebook.com/groups/AimeesDyeHards

AIMEE NICOLE WALKER

Curl Up and Dye Mysteries
Dyeing to be Loved
Something to Dye For
Dyed and Gone to Heaven
I Do, or Dye Trying
A Dye Hard Holiday
Ride or Dye
Curl Up and Dye Box Set

Road to Blissville Series
Unscripted Love
Someone to Call My Own
Nobody's Prince Charming
This Time Around
Smoke in the Mirror
Inside Out
Prescription for Love

Welcome to Blissville Collection (Both M/M Blissville series)
Volume One
Volume Two

The Lady is Mine Series
The Lady is a Thief
The Lady Stole My Heart

Queen City Rogue Series
Broken Halos
Wicked Games
Beautiful Trauma

Zero Hour Series
Ground Zero
Devil's Hour
Zero Divergence
Zero Hour Box Set

Sawyer and Royce: Matrimony and Mayhem
The Magnolia Murders
Marriage is Murder
Killer Honeymoon

Sinister in Savannah Series
Ride the Lightning
Mr. Perfect
Pretty Poison
Sinister in Savannah Box Set

Savannah Universe Standalone Books
Invisible Strings
Bad at Love
About Last Night
Just Say When

Standalone Novels
Second Wind

Fated Hearts Series
Chasing Mr. Wright
Rhythm of Us
Surrender Your Heart
Perfect Fit

Redemption Ridge Series
Guys Like Him
The Fortunate Son

Coauthored with Nicholas Bella
Undisputed
Circle of Darkness (Genesis Circle, Book 1)
Circle of Trust (Genesis Circle, Book 2)

acknowledgments

Many, many thanks to Susie Selva for her incredibly thorough edits and to Lori Parks for her keen eye during proofreading. These ladies are consummate professionals and are an absolute joy to work with. And much love to Jay Aheer and Wander Aguiar for this gorgeous cover and to Stacey Ryan Blake for her stunning interior designs. All of you make my books sparkle and shine so beautifully—inside and out. I thank my lucky stars that I get to work with such wonderfully talented people.

Sending much love to Melinda James Rueter and Racheal Yunk for bravely reading my rough drafts and providing priceless feedback. And I don't know where I'd be without CC Belle, my amazing personal assistant, who brings organization and so much joy into my life. Love you, ladies!

xoxo
Aimee

about

AIMEE NICOLE WALKER

Ever since she was a little girl, Aimee Nicole Walker en tertained herself with stories that popped into her head. Now she makes a living by telling stories to others. She wears many titles—wife, mom, and grandma are just a few. Love inspires everything she does, podcasts keeps her sane, and coffee is the magic elixir that fuels her day.

Want to connect? All her links are in one nifty location. Go here: linktr.ee/AimeeNicoleWalker

www.ingramcontent.com/pod-product-compliance
Lightning Source LLC
Chambersburg PA
CBHW051241250626
47155CB00009B/3115